Please return/renew this item by the last date
shown. Books may also be renewed by
telephoning, writing to or calling in at any of
our libraries or on the internet.

Northamptonshire Libraries and Information Service

Northamptonshire
County Council

www.library.northa

D1333963

EMILY DIAMAND

templar

First published in the UK in 2013 by Templar Publishing,

an imprint of The Templar Company Limited,

Deepdene Lodge, Deepdene Avenue,

Dorking, Surrey, RH5 4AT, UK

www.templarco.co.uk

MIX
Paper from
responsible sources
FSC® C020471

ISBN 978-1-84877-554-1

Printed and bound by CPI Group (UK) Ltd, Croydon, CR0 4YY

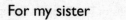
For my sister

Chapter One

Gray

I wasn't supposed to be there that night, you know?

It was Dad's weekend, and I should've been at his flat. Eating beans on toast, watching his box sets of Doctor Who. That's what he'd told Mum, anyway, but what he tells her and what we do are always different. It's why we weren't. In his flat, I mean. Why we were bumping along this dusty farm track instead, him parking the camper van at the end of it, us looking out over the valley.

It was a good spot. At the top of the slope, with a clear view across the fields. Lots of trees and well out of the way, not even a road going near.

August, it was. One of those on-off warm days, when the sun and clouds take turns in the sky. Dad spent the whole afternoon staring up or checking the weather forecast. Luckily, by the time we got parked the clouds had all drifted away. Everything glowed golden in the sunset. The wheat shushed and settled in the last bit of breeze, and swallows twittered high in the air, hunting flies.

Perfect conditions, my dad said.

He twisted in his seat.

"You ready to set up, son?"

I nodded, undid my seat belt and squeezed into the back. Started untying the ropes and bungees holding down all his heavy black boxes. There was all sorts in them: cameras, monitors, meters, leads, even a generator.

But then, there's always a lot of stuff, with my dad.

I did the untying, and Dad did the unloading. Putting the boxes down on the dry grass, opening them up and getting all the gear out. He was humming, happy.

"It's going to be a good night, Gray," he said, not looking up at me. "The weather's right, last week there were three genuines near Gloucester..." he trailed off, like he does when he's out there, and went back to his fiddling. I got my stuff last. Sleeping bag, coat, hat and gloves. It was still warm, but it gets really cold by three in the morning.

"Did you bring any food?" I asked, and Dad nodded.

"In the cupboard on the right-hand side. Have what you want."

I opened the cupboard door. Loads of little plastic packets, lined up neatly; whatever I wanted, so long as it was Super Noodles.

When Dad had everything ready, we sat in our camping chairs looking out over the valley. The sun had properly set by then, and the first bats were out, fluttering circles through the twilight. Dad pointed his fork, noodles squirling off it.

"Here they come." He meant the stars twinking into view in the sky. "It'll be tonight. I'm sure of it."

I just ate my noodles; I wasn't expecting much. Nothing, actually. And I bet Dad wasn't either, whatever he says now. The thing is, we'd done this stuff every fine summer night since I was eight and Dad had gone out by himself before that, which makes it years of waiting for something to happen. Years of watching and filming. Years of pushing through waist-high crops in the dark, me with my eyes out for an angry farmer, him with his dowsing rods, or one of his beeping meters. And in all that time...

Dad said he had loads of evidence, but most of it... Well, I wouldn't say this to him, but even his UFO mates didn't think much of it.

Until that night.

We ate our noodles. The sky inked into black, filling up with stars. Dad started tapping away at his tablet, doing his weird sums, and I reached in my pocket for my torch, so I could read my book. That's when I saw it.

A little flash, down in the field. Like a camera popping. Then another flash, and another. Not on the ground, like if someone was in the crops taking pictures. Up in the air.

"Dad," I said. "What's that?"

He hadn't even noticed, eyes down on the screen.

"What's what?"

Of course, by the time he looked up, they'd gone. Winked out. Dad eyed me, but he didn't say anything. Just pushed up from his chair, went and checked his laptop, playing back the readings.

"There's no change in the background fields," he said. "You joking, Gray? I won't be happy if you are."

"No. Honest." I wouldn't joke; he's got no sense of humour about this stuff.

Flash.

Flash, flash, flash, flash, flash.

They were back. Three, then five, then twenty. Hundreds of lights, flickering over the shadowy field.

"They can't be fireflies, they're too bright." My dad was whispering, like they might hear us.

The lights rose upwards, like sparks from a fire, and each one left a glowing trace, drawn on the dark. They zigged and zagged, up and towards each other, stretching a net of fire-lines above the field. And then they started drifting apart, stretching the glittering net, spreading it across the stars. Wider and wider, the lines getting fainter, until… snap! The net broke into a thousand fading whiplashes, the lights shooting back together into a single point. And out of that point: a burning streak. Straight up into the night. Like a flaming arrow, or a rocket going up, and so bright it etched in my eyes.

The next second it was gone.

We were both out of our chairs. Both staring.

"What…?" said Dad.

FLASH.

Light boomed silently over the field. A white-fire storm, a blazing whirlwind. Boiling up out of nothing, making a new sun overhead. It blued up the night, turning it back into day.

"Is it ball lightning?" I shouted.

A soundless wind flapped at our clothes, blowing my eyes to a squint.

"No! Much too big!" Dad's face was lit up, the happiest I've ever seen him. "It's them! They're coming!"

The swirling light-storm opened out, unravelling into streamers, coiling and twisting through the sky. The air shimmered, and wisps of steam blew in from nowhere. Wisps that grew into vapour trails, wrapping and turning around the light. Tighter and tighter, spinning the light inwards, pulling it into a single, glowing sphere. It hung over the valley. Every head of wheat was picked out clear, every leaf on the trees.

I mean, loads of people made reports that night, from Bristol even.

Everything went still; you could've heard a mouse squeak. I think I stopped breathing. Then the hairs on my arms stood up, just like they were being pulled, and the sun-ball started growing. Bulging and bloating, fading from blinding white, to yellow, to sunset orange.

"Here, take the camera!" Dad shoved his camcorder at me. He was holding a meter in each hand; they were beeping like crazy.

I bet you've seen the film. It's on loads of websites, it's even been on telly a couple of times. The ball of orange light suddenly booms outwards, blasting right past the camera.

There's nothing but colour for a few seconds, then the light starts sucking back, rolling like storm clouds, or water in a river. It rushes away from the lens, pulling together into a bright-glowing coil. The coil unfurls, slowly, like a snake made of light, or a huge tentacle. I wanted to run then, but I didn't. The light fills the sky above the valley, waving this way and that, and then starts moving. Up and up into the night, until it's just a faint streak, heading for the stars.

My dad yells out, "Look at that!" and the camera pans down. In the field, all the wheat's been flattened into this pattern. Circles inside circles, so many you can't tell how they all fit together.

You know.

After, I could hardly breathe, my heart was going so fast, and my legs were shaking right under me. All the hairs on my arms were singed off, and my skin looked sort of cooked.

An interesting story, Gray, and yes, I have seen that footage. Now, tell me. What has this got to do with the death of Isis Dunbar?

Chapter Two

Isis

"Jonathan, I had a brother called Jonathan."

A large, sad-faced woman was on her feet. Hands fluttering near her throat, mouth wobbling at the start of tears.

From her place at the back of the hall, hidden in darkness, Isis watched. Up on the makeshift stage, Cally had her head tilted, 'listening with her spirit ear'. She always started the show by telling the audience she'd be channelling the spirits, letting them speak through her. Isis hated her saying that; it made Cally sound like a mobile phone for ghosts.

A single spotlight picked Cally out. Pale and dark-eyed, with gleaming black hair and a shimmering purple dress. She looked exotic, out of place; Cleopatra in a community centre. Only Isis could see her mum, hiding beneath the sparkle.

"Jonathan…" said Cally softly, as if calling him back from some faraway land. She looked down at the woman. "He's recently departed?"

The large woman shook her head, just a little.

"Jonny died five and a half years ago…"

Cally nodded briskly. "That's right, he's saying five and a half years, which is very recent in the spirit world."

Isis kept one hand near the switches on the wall, just in case she had to bring the lights up suddenly. Other nights they'd had fainters, or people who couldn't stop crying. Her left hand was tight on the takings bag. It had £157 inside, which wouldn't leave much when the hall was paid for, and petrol, and the really cheap room they were staying in tonight. But the bag was still heavy, full of unsold tickets. Each one printed on black paper, with the words in glistening purple.

> **CALISTA DUNBAR**
> psychic clairvoyant
> Hill view community centre
> Tuesday, 10th December, 8 p.m.

Isis sulked and sighed in the dark.

I want to go home.

The woman in the audience started crying snotty tears.

"He died of cancer," she gasped.

Cally nodded again. "He says you shouldn't worry any more, the pain is over."

The woman smiled as she cried, gazing up at Cally.

From the corner of her eye, Isis saw a movement. The shape of a little girl, creeping up the side of the hall, barely visible in the coat-smelling dark.

Angel! She knew she wasn't supposed to do that.

Isis always told her, right before every performance, "Keep still and quiet when Mummy's doing her show." But there she was, toddling past the audience, wearing the princess dress she always insisted on. Heading for the stage, step by careful step.

She thinks if she goes slowly, it doesn't count.

In a few minutes Angel would be right up by Cally, and then she'd be running around, putting her off. It might even blow the whole gig!

"Come back here!" hissed Isis, but the curly-haired shape of Angel's head stayed stubbornly facing forwards, and she took another step. Isis couldn't even run and pull her back, because then everyone would turn to look and Cally's hold on the room would be broken. Isis had done it once, but never again; her mum had been "too angry to speak to you" for the whole evening after.

Up on stage, Cally was oblivious.

"It took Jonathan a long time to pass," she said, not quite a question.

The woman in the audience wiped her eyes with her palms.

"He used to complain about his cough, but we never thought it was much… Then he went for a check-up, and they said it was cancer…" She gargled a sob. "He was dead six weeks later."

Cally opened her hands to the woman, her face beautiful with sympathy.

"He says they felt like the longest weeks of his life, but now he's happy, and the pain is gone. You shouldn't blame yourself for anything."

The woman pulled a crumpled tissue from her sleeve, blew her nose in it. "Thank you, it's so good to hear from him…"

"WHAT ARE YOU ON ABOUT? He's not even HERE!"

Isis jumped, heart drumming in her chest.

"There's no Jonathan! You're leading her up the GARDEN PATH!"

Isis turned her head slowly, trying to look like she was stretching. At the back of the hall, behind the seated audience, was a small crowd of people. The standers, Isis called them to herself. Some young, some old, but always motley and slightly odd. Every performance they were there, huddled and yearning. Isis even recognised a couple of them.

But she didn't remember the old man in the middle of this lot, the one who'd just shouted. He was tall, and the tasselled fez perched on top of his almost-hairless scalp made him look even taller. His brightest features were his blue eyes, glaring at Cally. Otherwise he was crinkle-necked and tortoisey, fury fizzing out of him. Even from where she was, Isis caught the dusty smell of his frayed velvet jacket.

"I can feel my brother, sometimes," the large woman continued, as if there'd been no interruption. "When I walk past the betting office, I'm sure I can smell his aftershave."

Cally nodded. "He's with you often," she said kindly.

"He's not with you now!" called the old man.

The crowd of standers laughed; the audience stayed silent.

Breathe in, breathe out. Don't make a fuss. Everyone else is ignoring them, you can too.

"Well *I'm* here!" shouted a teenage girl, pushing out from the standing crowd into the seated area. She had long, straggling hair and her hippyish dress fell into rags around her. "*I* need to speak!" The people sitting on their plastic chairs shuffled a little, pulling their clothes tight, putting scarves and coats back on.

"I wouldn't bother," the old man said, as the girl waved and shouted. "No one here is listening."

Isis shuffled a few steps along the wall, to the large wooden door with 'Way Out' green-lit above it. She moved her hand to the soft steel of the handle. Sometimes the best thing was to leave; Cally would be fine.

But this door was heavy, the kind that really creaks when you push it. And then there was Angel, still creeping step by step to the stage.

The large woman sat down, and the hippy girl sloped back into the crowd. From the spotlight, Cally gazed around the darkened head-shapes of the audience.

"I'm getting someone else now. It's… a lady. I can't quite hear her name, but I think it starts with a B, or maybe an L. I'm hearing something like… Lin… Linda…?"

A flurry in the standers. A middle-aged woman pushed her way through them.

"Yes! Linda! Linda Belborough!" She waved her hands at Cally, dirty water sprinkling off them. But Cally kept her gaze on the people sitting down. A few shook their heads, then near the front of the audience a man raised his arm, uncertainly.

"I had a cousin..." he said. "Lindsey? She died a few years ago."

Cally cocked her head. "Oh yes, that's it, Lindsey." She spoke to the air, smiling. "I couldn't quite hear you, you need to speak up."

"I'm speaking perfectly clearly!" snapped the woman at the back of the hall. "And it's Linda, not Lindsey. I know my own name!" She pointed towards a middle row, a steady drip falling from the end of her finger. "I want to speak to my son over there. Him, with the beard."

The old man tutted, the tassel on his fez sparkling as he shook his head. "You're wasting your time, she's just another charlatan."

Isis leaned against the door. If it would just push quietly...

"Were you close to Lindsey?" Cally asked the man in

the audience. He stood up, looking awkward, and shook his head.

"I didn't see her very often. She lived over near Newcastle – it's a long way."

Cally pursed her lips. "Well I don't think she's here for herself. I think she's got a message for you from someone else. Is it…" She paused, finger in the air, eyebrows together. "Someone older? Who was very dear to you…?"

"Grampy John!" cried the man, beaming up into the stage light.

"Oh this is pathetic," said the old man at the back. He cupped his hands round his mouth and shouted. "There's NO Lindsey! And NO Grampy! Can't you HEAR ME?" Isis tried not to cough at the dust wafting out from him.

She pushed against the door. The hinge squeaked loudly and a few heads turned, including the old man's. His eyes gleamed blue, boring into her. She kept her face blank, glancing casually away.

And saw Angel, standing defiant by the edge of the stage. Her little hands gripping on, her dress crumpling as she raised herself up.

Isis gasped, reaching for Angel. She stopped herself, pulling in tight against the door, but it was too late.

The old man's finger was pointing, quivering at Isis.

"She can *see* us!"

Every head in the standers turned, their gazes tingling over her skin. Isis stared at her mum, eyes aching with concentration.

"Your Grampy says you shouldn't worry so much about little things," said Cally to the man in the audience. There was a tinkle of laughter in the room, and the man looked happy, teary.

Now the woman called Linda was walking around the edge of the hall. Sloshing past the chairs, leaving a trail of fading, watery footprints. Isis watched from the corner of her eye, holding herself completely still. Except for her heart, beating madly.

On stage, Cally was smiling, happily into the swing of her performance.

"Your Grampy says you should take time every day to relax."

Linda stopped right in front of Isis. Face-to-face, hazing the view of the stage. She smelled like seaweed.

Don't look, don't look, don't look.

The woman peered at her.

"BOO!"

Isis jumped, just the tiniest stutter in her body.

And Linda grinned, turning around.

"Mandeville's right!" she crowed, waving at the rest of the standers. "She *can* see us!"

Isis rammed her hand down on the door handle, pushing with all her weight. The door creak-slammed open, and she shot through the gap, tumbling into the lobby, shoving the door shut behind her. She stopped, heart hammering. In front of her were the main doors of the community centre, but they only led to cold winter rain in the car park, and an empty, night-time housing estate.

She ran to the far wall, pressing herself against it.

A damp stain appeared on the door into the hall, droplets of condensation forming on it. The stain darkened and spread, sliding down the grain, streaking into wet shadows. Limbs and a body, then a head. Water bubbled out through the varnish, collecting in vertical puddles and joining into the shape of a woman, who sucked herself out through the door, leaving it dry behind as she took a sloshing step forwards.

Following her, something like smoke puffed through the cracks around the door. It swirled vaguely in the air, then curled up and over Linda's sloshing shape, funnelling down in front of Isis. She pulled in against the wall as grey specks spun in the air. Not smoke, but a cloud of velvet fibres and dust, forming into the tall figure of an elderly, tortoisey, blue-eyed man.

Behind him, through him, Isis could see the other ghosts following. Fingers pushing through the breeze-block wall, a leg stepping out of nothing. Arms dripped out of the wall, bodies and heads squeezed from the wood of the door.

And the mouths. Open, clamouring.

"I want to talk to Jenny."

"It's really important — they aren't looking after my cats!"

"I left the house to *them* — they can't sell it!"

Bodies and limbs melted into almost-people. Rushing for Isis on wavery legs, crowding round her, pushing and slapping each other, shouting louder and louder. Wispy hands plucking at her clothes, cold fingers brushing her face.

Isis beat at nothing, the cold piercing into her.

"You can *see* us! You have to go on stage!" cried one.

"Chuck that fake woman off, go and do the seance properly!" screamed another.

They pressed in further, overlapping each other, pushing

themselves into a translucent wall of faces, bodies and reaching arms.

Isis swallowed dry nothing, trying to hold down her fear.

"No," she whispered, shaking her head.

There were astonished, outraged looks from the ghosts.

"But that woman's a liar!"

"She's just making stuff up!"

"There was no Jonny, and she got Linda's name wrong."

See-through heads and blurry, featureless faces pushed closer. Their words had no breath behind them, only a spreading cold.

Isis pressed her hands on the wall, holding herself up on trembling legs.

"I won't do it," she whispered.

"That woman gives them lies," said the ghost of the old man, his words piercing through the shouts, "while you could give them the truth." He was standing back from the mob, as if studying her.

Goosebumps shivered up her arms, even under her thick jumper. The clamouring phantoms had dragged the heat from her body, her breath was crystal-freezing in the air.

"Go away," she whispered. How long could she hold them off for? Would they be too strong this time?

"You're as bad as that phoney back in the hall!"

"Worse! Because you've got the gift, and you won't even use it!"

"Jenny!" "My son!" "The cats!" "They can't sell it!" The shouting went on, getting more and more desperate, starting to press against her thoughts.

Go away go away go away

A shadowy young man put his fingers to a tattooed neck, pulling open a wide gash and revealing the bright-white bones of his spine.

"Look what they did to me," he moaned. "You tell my brothers, they got to sort it out."

The spirits closed in. Smells of earth, ash and river water filled her nose.

"Go back in there!"

"You have to tell them!"

Shivers raked her body, chattering her teeth.

"N-no," she whispered "N-no."

Then, a jostling in the crowd. Cries of surprise, and a wavering in the mist.

Angel! Swatting with her fists, kicking her small feet.

Fury crumpling her little brow and scrunching up her mouth.

"You go-way!" Angel's voice squeaked loudly. "*My* sister! You go-way, you horrids!" Isis managed a smile, feeling her fight come back. She took a deep breath, then shoved her hands right into the ghost with the sliced neck. She gasped as a fierce, aching cold rushed up her arms, her fingers going white, then blue, then numb.

"Ow!" yelled the ghost, stumbling backwards, staring down at the hand-shaped holes in his shadow-body. "How did you *do* that?"

"Get away from me," whispered Isis. "All of you."

"Go!" shouted Angel, fists up. "Go-way!"

The ghost of the young man moaned, hugging the holes in his chest. They were closing, slowly, like ice refreezing.

Isis held her hands out, waving them at the other ghosts, praying she wouldn't have to do it again. Her fingers prickled and burned as the blood returned to them, but the ghosts backed away, fearful.

They faded and flopped into the walls, sliding and slipping through the woodgrain of the door. The old man with the fez was the last to leave.

"Do you even know what you can do?" he asked as he

swirled into plumes of dust, drifting into nothing. Isis didn't answer.

When he'd gone, Angel's small hands reached up.

"Carry," she ordered.

Isis leaned down and picked Angel up. Like holding the breeze from a butterfly's wingbeat.

"Thank you." Isis shivered, smiling. "You saved me."

Angel grinned at Isis from her round little face. "I do it."

Isis kissed her. Like kissing the mist rising from a river.

Her little sister. Three years old, five years dead.

Chapter Three

Gray

All right then. If you want to know, I met Isis the year after, in late March. The days were getting longer by then, there'd even been a few warmish ones, so Dad's round was picking up. He always gets busier in spring; lawns need cutting, stuff needs pruning. He started taking me out with him, on his weekends and the days he picked me up from school. That's another of Dad's things I didn't tell Mum, cos she would've got really mad about it, but I liked it actually. I liked being outside.

So, we were at this house. Mansion really. It had a massive garden, about the size of our school playing fields or something, with high yew hedges and big iron gates on the drive. Dad was doing the lawn that afternoon, driving round it on his mower. Green Garden Gil, that's what he calls himself – it's painted on his camper and on the trailer behind. Not that he's actually green, he just doesn't use any chemicals and tries to get people growing wildflowers and stuff.

Anyway, it was Mr Welkin's place. Norman. He was really rich – he'd made loads of money selling herbal remedies. You wouldn't think you could get to be a millionaire that way, but Dad said people will believe anything. And he was mad. I mean, completely fruit loop. He had long white hair, and he never wore shoes, even outside in the winter because he said they block 'earth energies'. He was into ghosts and UFOs. He told me Jesus was really an alien, and he was always quoting this Native American chief, who said it's only when all the trees are gone and the seas are empty of fish that we'll realise we can't eat money. He was into even weirder stuff than Dad, if you can believe it. I think that's why Dad got the job.

I suppose we'd been there about half an hour, so it was probably a bit after four, and Dad was mowing the lawns. He'd told me to stay in the camper, do my homework, but the cooler in that van hardly worked and the sun was shining in and turning it into an oven. And anyway, what's the point of going to a massive place like that and not even going round it? I mean, the garden has an actual stream running through it! And so many trees it's practically a forest, and all these yew bushes clipped into weird shapes. Dad said they were peacocks when they started, but over the years they'd grown out, so now you'd never know what they're meant to be. Norman Welkin asked Dad if he could prune them back to being peacocks, and he said he'd do his best, but when he'd finished they looked more like aliens than anything. I'm not sure if that's what he meant to do, but Mr Welkin really liked them.

Norman's garden is the best Dad goes to, so I didn't want to just sit in the van. Also, there were the biscuits. Old Norman always brought some out, along with coffee for him and Dad. Really good biscuits; he said they were organic. Whatever, they had big lumps of chocolate in, and that chunky sugar on top. Him and Dad would yak on about their latest theory, and I'd eat the biscuits.

Not that day. I waited twenty minutes, and Norman didn't show. In the end, I looked through the window into their living room, but there was only Sondra, his girlfriend. Not like that sounds, because she's really old, as old as him. They weren't married though, even though she lived there. She was as weird as him, sort of jittery, like she was expecting someone to creep up on her. She had grey hair down to her waist, and wore all these long, flowery dresses. She said she was an artist, but she showed me a couple of her pictures once, and they were all… swirly and mixed up. Rubbish, I thought. Anyway, she was in the living room with this other woman, one of her friends I guessed. And no sign of Mr Welkin, which meant no biscuits.

I trudged off, keeping out of Dad's sight, and I heard this sound over the noise of the mower. *Tatatatatata*, like someone drumming on the big horse chestnut tree. I knew it was a woodpecker because that's what they do in spring. It's hard to spot them without binoculars because they like to stay hidden, but I went looking anyway, staring up at the tree. It's why I didn't see her at first. Isis, I mean. She was sat against the tree trunk, on this bench that goes all the way round. Still as anything, feet together, hands in her lap. Like a statue or something, like she'd just appeared out of nowhere.

I thought she was a ghost for a minute.

"What are you *doing*?" I said.

She didn't move a muscle. "Sitting."

Little and thin, she was. She looked loads younger

than me, even though it turned out there's only two months between us.

"Who are *you*?" she asked, like she owned the place. Except I knew there was no way she was anything to do with old Norman or Sondra. For a start, she was wearing the same uniform as me, and rich kids don't go to our school.

"My name's Gray," I said. "My dad's the gardener here." I looked at her uniform, so it'd be obvious what I was thinking. "Who are you?"

She kept her same blank face, shivered a bit.

"Cally… my mum's in there." Her mouth pressed tight and she shut up, like she'd said too much or something.

"She a friend of Sondra?" I asked.

Isis wobbled her head a bit; not yes, not no.

Going out with Dad on his rounds, he'd told me how the rich types work. One time he turned up to do a garden and the husband had just run off with someone else. Other times, my dad has seen 'goings on'. That's what he calls it.

"Is your mum a private investigator?" I asked. We met one once – he was keeping watch on one of Dad's customers.

She didn't answer.

"Is Norman having an affair with your mum?" She could've been in there, having it out with Sondra. Which would've been pretty cool, actually.

"No!" Isis pulled back on the bench, like I'd spat at her or something.

"So what then?"

But Isis only shut her mouth up and glared. Wouldn't say another word.

The screaming started not long after that.

And what did you think of Isis, when you first met her?

I didn't want her to die, if that's what you're asking.

Chapter Four

Isis

Cally got the call from Sondra Borwan while Isis was walking home from school. When Isis opened the door of their flat, Cally was waiting for her. Coat on, car keys in hand.

"We're going out, I've got a job."

"Job?" For a hoping moment, Isis thought Cally had finally gone through with her promise to Grandma Janet. *Real work, bringing in regular wages, even if it's just at the supermarket.* She flash-dreamed that other life: Cally being awake at the same time as Isis; Cally making new friends, and being happy; no more dark days, no more seances. Back to how they used to be. Back to normal.

Angel's head drifted out from inside the sofa.

"A lady," she lisped. "She want Mummy to listen."

Isis tried not to blink as her dream ran into nothing.

"It's a reading," said Cally, blushing slightly, chin up.

"You said I wouldn't have to go to any more!" said Isis, challenging back. What had been the point of all their fights during the seance tour, if she still had to do this?

Cally jingled the keys in her hand.

"Don't be silly, Isis, I can't leave you here by yourself, can I?"

Isis dropped her school bag onto the floor.

"I don't want to go."

Cally picked up Isis's bag, and put it on the table. "Isis, this could be really important for me. The client's rich, I could tell from her address. She wants someone who can get there right away, and she called *me*! If I do well, and she recommends me, this could be my breakthrough!"

"I won't!" said Isis, even though she knew she would, that she'd already lost the argument. And going to individual readings was almost as bad as working the village halls. Cringing in the corner of someone's living room, while Cally told them what the spirits were saying. Worse still when the spirits were there too, angrily contradicting.

It took about twenty-five minutes to drive through the

traffic-clogged roads of Wycombe, and out the other side to the wealthy, tree-lined lanes. Sondra Borwan lived in one of those villages where the cottages all had hanging baskets and pretty gardens, and the pub on the green did expensive Sunday lunches. Isis huffed a circle of mist on her window as they drove, drawing an angry face in it. Then she wiped it off with her sleeve.

Cally, who'd been chatty and excited about her new client, had fallen into silence when they'd hit the country roads. Hands tight on the steering wheel, eyes narrowed, she stiffened every time they came to a tight bend. They were nowhere near where it had happened, but the hedges looked just the same, the way they stopped you from seeing what was coming around the corner. Isis winced at a shot of pain all down one side. It wasn't really there, only her body remembering the sudden shock of metal.

It was years ago, she wanted to say to Cally.

The car's indicator ticked as they turned off the road, pulling up in front of iron gates set between tall, black-green hedges. Through the gates Isis caught a glimpse of mellow brick and glinting windows.

"Wow," she breathed, "it's huge."

Cally came back from her thoughts, and smiled at Isis.

"What did I tell you?"

They had to buzz to get in, and the gates slowly swung open. Cally's rust-patch of a car crunched up the gravel drive, past the green swathes of lawn and tumbling shrubs. When they reached the semicircle steps in front of the house, Cally parked the car in front of them. Then she sighed, settling her shoulders back.

"I'm listening," she said quietly, but not to Isis.

Sondra Borwan was already out on the steps, anxiously clasping her silver-ringed hands. She started forwards before they were even out of the car.

"At last! I was beginning to think you wouldn't come!" And she burst into tears.

Cally hurried up the steps, putting her arm around the woman's shoulder as if they were friends. "How long has Norman been missing?" she asked quietly.

Sondra let out a sob. "Four and a half hours. He went for his morning walk at about eleven, and he hasn't come back. I was in my meditations until two o'clock, so I didn't realise at first, but then…" She gasped a breath, clearly trying to get control of herself. Fanning her face with her hands, bangles jingling.

"Would he normally come back?" asked Cally.

Sondra nodded, unable to speak.

"And have you called the police?"

Sondra nodded again, and let out a wail. "They said he wasn't missing if he'd only been gone a few hours, he could've just gone to the shops. But they don't understand, I know he's not all right! He wouldn't just go off, not when we had yoga planned." She lowered her voice. "I knew a psychic was my only hope."

Cally nodded. "I'll do my best to find him."

Sondra fluttered her hands. "Of course, I know the country's best psychics personally, but I can't ask *any* of them. Norman would never forgive me, not after what's happened recently. Then I remembered my cleaner telling me that she'd seen you in Aylesbury, last autumn."

Cally gave a stiff smile. "Oh," she said. "Well, you did the right thing. The spirits will tell me where your husband is, and what he's doing."

Sondra nodded, calmer now, caught by Cally's soothing tone. "I was desperate, I had to ring *someone*."

"The spirits will help us," said Cally. Isis could see she was offended, but trying not to show it.

Sondra's eyes filled with tears. "That's what Norman always says."

And the two women went into the house, leaving Isis standing there.

She held back, not following them inside. Instead, she carefully checked every window. Although the house looked modern, that didn't mean anything. New houses are built where old ones used to be, and people die all the time. But there were no faces at the glass, no figures on the rooftop. Isis turned, glancing casually at the garden, as if she were admiring it. There was nothing there either, just a gardener driving a ride-on lawn mower, and he was definitely alive.

Which only left their car. Isis watched two short legs misting out through the shut door, feet flapping, trying to reach the ground. The legs wriggled, and the bottom half of a little girl's dress flickered out through the side of the car, up to the waist. The legs kicked, and toes hit gravel.

She was wearing the sandals again.

White strapped, with a stitched design of pink and yellow flowers. The day they'd gone to the shoe shop Angel had refused to try on anything else, and after Cally bought them, Angel had worn her new sandals all the time, even to bed.

Isis shuddered. One of the sandals had been ripped

from Angel's foot, that last day. There'd been mud smeared across the flowers.

She shut her eyes, opened them again. It was only another memory.

Angel pulled the rest of herself out of the car, then turned and smiled at Isis. Her not-there curls bobbed above her not-there head as she trotted over, soundless on the gravel. Isis smiled back.

"Big garden!" said Angel, a whisper in the air. "Where the swings?"

When Isis found them, the swings were hidden in a forgotten corner of the rambling gardens. Old and wonky in their frames, their metal feet lost in long grass. Whatever children they'd been meant for must be long grown up, and Isis wasn't sure they were even safe to sit on. Of course, that didn't matter to Angel. Isis pushed the swing and it flew up on its rusting chains, unweighted. On the seat, Angel laughed and shrieked.

"Higher, higher!"

Angel could go higher than anyone – there nothing to hold her down. Isis tried to think what it had been like, pushing Angel when there'd been something to push, but her muscles couldn't remember.

She hit her palms against the swing's seat, batting it up into the air.

"Wheee!"

Angel was the only one in the family who'd stayed the same after she died, and Isis smiled as she watched her, pushing until her arms started to get tired.

"That's enough," Isis said.

"No!" cried Angel. "More, more!" She hung stubbornly onto the chains, but without Isis's help the swing quickly settled back to stillness.

Angel twisted round on the seat; eyes wide, face pleading. "Pease?"

Isis shook her head. "I've been pushing you for ages."

"No fair!" Angel kicked her legs, but the swing stayed motionless. "More!"

Isis shook her head again.

"No," she said. "Let's play another game."

"I not want to!" the little ghost shouted at her. "I want swing! You a meany!"

"And you're being a brat!" snapped Isis, before walking away.

The air was damp, and there was a cool breeze,

but Isis felt warm even without a coat, frowning as she walked. Really, Angel was eight. So why couldn't she act like it? Isis knew the answer, of course. Angel was frozen, halted at the age of her death.

Isis followed the path as it meandered between deep borders, marking time until Cally finished. Shrubs and plants poked woody stems out of the earth. Crocuses and snowdrops speckled their colours in the flower beds, yellow daffodils just unfurling their buds. The path went on, heading under the spreading canopy of an enormous twisting tree. She saw the bench, circled around its massively gnarled trunk, and sat down.

Her frown settled in as she stared back the way she'd come.

It hadn't mattered when she was younger, and if Angel hadn't been there she probably would've ended up like Cally. But now... Isis was getting older. She was in secondary school, she'd be choosing her options next year, then it'd be exams, and leaving home. She tried to imagine going to college, getting a job, having a boyfriend.

Isis leaned against the rough bark of the tree. How could she do any of those things, with Angel?

Lost in her uncertain future, she didn't notice the boy

until he was walking down the path straight for her. He was tall, a bit lanky even, with caramel-coloured skin. He'd come from the opposite direction she had, and he was looking up at the tree, his brown eyes deep set beneath heavy black eyebrows. The way his head was tilted made his chin look too big for his face, and he was scratching in the short black hair on his head.

Isis froze, only moving her eyes, watching him carefully. There. Wet footprints behind him on the paving stones. And there. His breath steaming into the air, his cheeks shiny with cold. Isis relaxed a little, but even so she kept still. It was a trick she'd learned over the years: people often only noticed her when she moved. It was the same for the living and the dead, whatever Cally told her audiences about the spirits seeing everything.

He almost walked by, and he probably would have if Angel hadn't shot out from inside the tree, leaping at Isis and laughing.

"Come, Isis, come!" she squealed. "Play hidey-seek!"

Isis jumped and the boy stopped dead in his tracks, noticing her.

"Jeez!" he startled back a step, "what are you *doing*?"

Now Angel was jumping around Isis, clambering

onto her lap, grabbing her arm with butterfly fingers.

"Come, Isis, *come!*"

Isis tried ignoring her, but it was hard. Hard to think, hard to follow even the simplest conversation.

"Sitting," Isis answered the living boy, not her dead sister.

"Don't sit! Come with me!" cried Angel.

The boy was wearing school uniform, the same one as hers. She recognised his face as well, but she couldn't remember his name, not with Angel pulling at her.

"Who are you?" she asked.

"My name's Gray..."

Angel climbed onto the bench, putting her cold little arms around Isis's neck, shouting into her ear.

"Hidey-seek, *please.*"

Isis missed the rest of what Gray said, but she could tell he'd asked a question by the look on his face.

"Cally... my mum's in there," she said, hoping that would sound all right.

Angel put her hands over Isis's eyes, like frost on her eyelashes.

"Hidey," she said. "Seek. Hidey-seek. *Hideyseek!*"

Gray was answering her, but she couldn't hear over

Angel, could hardly see him through her sister's hands. And she couldn't slap them away, not in plain view.

"Come!" shouted Angel. "Come now."

"No!" snapped Isis. Out loud, not just in her head.

She clapped a hand over her mouth. What had Gray been saying? What had she yelled at?

"So why then?" he asked, frowning.

She'd have to guess, which never worked. It was guessing that got her into all the trouble at school, especially in the old Victorian buildings. The ghost children in their old-fashioned pinafores and knee breeches were always standing in front of the whiteboards, blocking Isis's view while they traced the coloured lines with misty fingers.

Keep quiet, and don't say anything, she told herself. He'll get bored and wander off.

"Can't you speak?" he asked, starting to sound annoyed.

Angel drifted through the bench onto the path, went up to Gray and kicked him. He leaned down, rubbing at his leg without seeming to notice.

"He a smelly," Angel said, fading. "Isis, come."

SLAM. The sound of a door, up at the house.

Isis and Gray both turned to look. Cally was flinging herself down the front steps of the house, and Sondra

Borwan was behind her in the doorway, floaty and furious, one hand on the door frame.

Cally stopped when she reached the gravel, turning back.

"If you don't believe," she shouted, "why did you even ask me here?"

"I believe genuine psychics, and you are clearly a *fraud*!" screamed Sondra, her whole body swinging forwards, only her hand on the door holding her back. "I can't believe you'd even suggest he was seeing another woman! And there's *nothing* he hasn't told me!"

"I can't help what the spirits say!"

"*They'd* never say such a thing!"

Gray looked at Isis.

"What's going on?"

"I don't know," she mumbled, a hideous blush crawling onto her face. She'd have to go to school tomorrow, and he'd be there. Pointing her out, telling everyone about this.

"You should leave!" Sondra yelled at Cally.

Cally swung round and stormed to the car, stopping when she realised Isis wasn't in it. She glared around the garden, hand above her eyes, searching.

"You might have fooled my cleaner," shouted Sondra,

"but I know the psychic world, I know real ability! Get out of here!"

"I have to find my *daughter*!" Cally snapped back. Isis pulled further into the shadow of the tree. She was in trouble now. "Isis? Isis!"

"Is that your name?" asked Gray. Isis nodded, miserable. He had that as well now.

"Isis!"

"Looks like you better go," said Gray.

Isis stood up from the bench. The drone of the lawnmower stopped.

"*Isis!*"

Why had she given in to Cally, back in their flat? Why hadn't she just refused and stayed at home?

Sondra Borwan was still at her doorway. "I'm calling the police!"

"Sondra's pretty angry," said Gray, sounding impressed. "I've never seen her like that before."

Isis stared at him. "You know her?"

Gray nodded.

Which meant Sondra would tell him all about Cally, and he'd tell everyone at school!

A man came round the side of the house, took a few

steps towards the two women, then stopped, uncertain.

"Is everything all right?" he asked.

"No, Gil, it's not!" Sondra pointed at Cally. "I want you to show this *fake* off my property!"

"As soon as I find my *child*!" yelled Cally. "You know, the aura around this house is really dark. Suffocating even."

"Thirty seconds!" shrieked Sondra. "You've got thirty seconds!"

"Oh no," groaned Isis.

"That's the quickest way to the house," said Gray, pointing at a narrow, shadowy gap between tall, evergreen shrubs. Almost a tunnel, after a few metres it opened out onto the lawn below the house. "There's steps up."

"Thanks." Isis could hardly look at him. Tomorrow he'd ask his friends if they knew a girl called Isis, and they'd say, "That freak job?" Then he'd tell them all about this, and it'd get added to the other stories, the ones already going around.

She started for the gap in the hedge, heading to her mum, but she glanced back as she ran, trying to read Gray's face. Was he the type to join in with the others, with the taunts in the corridor?

Her left foot caught on something. She stumbled,

pitching down onto the muddy grass, her fingers dragging through the scratching leaves of the bushes. She lay for a moment, hands stinging, and felt wet grass against her cheek.

"You all right?" Gray called.

If only the ground were softer, if only it could swallow her away.

She pushed to her feet, muddy and crumpled. When was he going to start laughing?

"Stupid," she muttered, at herself, at whatever she'd tripped over. She looked down, and saw what had caught her. Not a stone, or a fallen branch, even though it felt as hard. A large, bare foot was sticking out from the bushes, dirty heel against the grass. An ankle, then a yellow-corduroy-covered leg headed off under the leaves. Further in, against the dark earth, Isis could see a man's hand. Still and unmoving, pale blue and glassy.

She gasped in a hiccup, staring.

A thump of running feet, and Gray was next to her.

"That's *Norman Welkin*," he whispered. "Is he… is he dead?"

Isis leaned down and pushed at the man's calloused foot. The leg didn't move, it was stiff and rigid. As unyielding as a lump of rock.

Chapter Five

Gray

It was really horrible. And it was sort of exciting, you know?

Sondra rushed down and started screaming. Dad tried to hold her back, shouting at me and Isis to get away from the body. Isis's mum rang the police, and they turned up in about five minutes, sirens on and blue lights flashing! Five cars and a police van. Then there were coppers everywhere, shooing us away, taking charge of Sondra. Some of them had those white disposable overalls on, and they started poking around and taking tons of pictures. An ambulance came too, not that there was much point.

Me and Isis got taken into Sondra's house, into her hallway, and this policewoman kept asking us if we were okay. Then this other one came and asked us loads of questions, I mean, really loads, and he wrote everything down.

I thought it was going to be like on the telly, a real mystery, but the police seemed sort of bored.

"He probably had a heart attack," one of them said to us. "I've seen it a few times with pensioners. They can go just like that." He clicked his fingers. "He probably didn't even have time to cry out."

Still, they put up one of those tents around the body, like you see on the news when there's been a murder.

Sondra carried on crying and screaming. You could hear her further inside the house. And I felt sort of shaky – I kept seeing Norman Welkin's foot all blue against the grass. I'd only seen him the week before, you know? Eaten his biscuits.

Then the police said we could go if we wanted, and me and Isis went back outside. Dad was on the steps, waiting for me, talking quietly to Cally. Isis's mum, I mean. As soon as she saw us, she rushed over and grabbed hold of Isis, hugging her. Even Dad put his hand on my shoulder, asked if I was okay.

And that's when Dad said his thing to Cally. I should've guessed it really, Dad'll try it on with anyone nearly.

"Um, maybe we could all go for a drink?" he said, staring at Cally. "You know, calm our nerves."

Cally looked surprised, and then she blushed.

"Yes. That's a good idea," she said, smiling at him like she couldn't help it, the way women do.

"Cally, no!" cried Isis. But it didn't make any difference.

Which is how me and Isis ended up sat on one side of a pub table, with Dad and Cally on the other. It was noisy and chip-smelling, a bit too warm from the fire, and all around us people were eating, talking and drinking.

It was really weird, when Norman was lying cold in his garden.

You'd have thought Dad and Cally would have been worried. After all, one of Dad's customers had just died on him, and me and Isis had found his dead body. But they completely ignored us, like they'd got stuck, staring at each other. Dad started telling Cally about his chasing trips, and she even sounded interested.

Actually, I'd never seen him like that with anyone, even Mum when they were still together. Mind you, I can hardly remember that, it was such a long time ago. Mostly I remember the after bits. Like, me sitting on Mum's lap and crying, "I want Daddy, I want Daddy!" I don't even know why I wanted him, but I can remember Mum crying too.

Anyway, Isis didn't say a thing for ages. She was drinking this bottle of juice, looking like the pub was the last place she wanted to be. I ate a packet of cheese and onion crisps, then a packet of smoky bacon. Because I was in shock – I needed the salt. I thought Isis was too, or maybe she was just stuck up. Some girls are, specially the ones who're really into clothes. But she didn't look the type – her uniform was a bit too big for her, her shoes were scuffed.

She picked up one of the empty crisp packets, smoothed it out and folded it over and over into this little wrapped-up triangle. When she'd finished, she put it down on the table, and looked at me.

"He was really cold," she said.

"What?"

"The man in the garden. Mr Welkin. He was really cold."

"He was *dead*," I said.

She twizzled the crisp packet triangle on the tabletop.

"Yes, but then why couldn't I…" she paused, then said, "I saw his hand." She turned hers over, palm up, palm down. "It was all glittery."

There isn't another girl in our whole school who

would've touched a dead body. Only a few boys, probably. I picked up the last packet of crisps. Barbecue chilli.

"I saw this thing on telly," I said, crunching. "All the blood sinks down, because your heart's not pumping any more, and your hands and feet go black. Then you start drying out, so you shrink a bit and it makes your hair and nails look like they're getting longer. That's why people used to think they keep growing after you're dead, but they don't really..."

Isis made a yuk-face at me, shaking her head. "Not like that. I couldn't work out what it was for a second, and there wasn't even any frost on the grass. But he wasn't just cold, he was covered in ice. It was starting to melt, but he was definitely frozen all over."

"He had been out there all day," I said, "and he was in a shady place."

She sort of rolled her eyes then. And she was right, because the days were getting warmer by then, like I said. Not cold enough to freeze in the daytime, definitely not cold enough to get coated in ice. She opened her mouth, but didn't say whatever it was...

"He was *that* Norman Welkin?" Cally cried, across the table. "Founder of the Welkin Society?" She clapped a hand to her mouth, looking horrified.

Dad nodded.

Cally's hand dropped to her lap.

"I had no idea," she breathed. "Oh my God! Why did Sondra call *me*?"

"You're not one of them?"

Cally shook her head. "I want to be." And you could hear it in her voice, the longing. "Now, I don't suppose it'll ever happen."

Dad shrugged. "You're probably better off anyway. That lot, they all sounded a bit…" he did a crazy little whistle.

Luckily, Cally wasn't really listening. "Sondra said she *couldn't* call any of the psychics she knew."

Dad shrugged again. "You know those types, always falling out over their chakras or whatever. Actually, Norman had been complaining about his lot, the last year or so. How they were always ganging up on him because he wasn't actually psychic, just the man with the money. About a month back he even told me he thought some of the group weren't genuine, and he was a man who believed in *everything*. He was proper cut up about it. I told him to stop wasting his money."

Now Cally was listening. She looked horrified at Dad. "No, no! Norman Welkin created something wonderful!

The Welkin Society is *so* well thought of. Membership is a real mark of respect, it gives you credibility."

"Oh, yes," said Dad, seeing the look on her face and backtracking like a pro. "I meant he should rest up a bit, at his age, since it was all going so well."

Cally groaned. "The things I said to Sondra, I'll never get in now."

"With what's just happened…" Dad's voice wobbled a bit. "I mean, Sondra probably won't even remember."

"Do you think so?" Cally asked, hopeful sounding.

"What's up with your mum?" I whispered to Isis.

She looked at me. "Haven't you heard of the Welkin Society?"

Well yes, because old Norman was always going on about 'his' society, that he'd started. But I was never interested, I just thought it was a club for nutters like him.

Dad reached out, put his hand over Cally's. "Don't worry, it'll work out. I can put a word in with Sondra, if you want. Explain things."

"You can?" asked Cally, gazing at him.

Dad smiled. "We can talk about it this weekend." He looked at me. "You'll be all right with that, won't you, Gray?"

"All right with what?"

"Cally and Isis coming over this Saturday."

Isis glared at her mum, and Cally blushed.

"We've got a computer," Dad said to Isis. "You and Gray can play games on it. While I take Cally for a walk in the garden, or something…" Cally blushed even harder.

"Oh! No!" cried Isis.

"No way!" I said.

But what could we do? It was love at first sight with those two…

… Where am I anyway? I thought I was supposed to be having blood taken for tests, but this is like a storeroom or something. What's going on? Are you even a doctor?

No, I'm not. But I don't think you would have come with me if I'd told you the truth. We're somewhere quiet and we won't be disturbed, which is all you need to know at the moment. Look at me, that's right. You feel calm and safe. You feel perfectly relaxed. You want to tell me everything that happened, everything you know.

Oh… yes, I do.

Chapter Six

Isis

She pushed with her feet, idly spinning on the roundabout. Grey-tarmac road whirled into green-grass park, then back to tarmac. She was on her own, rustling in her raincoat. Apart from Angel of course, who was sat on the seat in front, drizzle falling through her.

"Erewego round the mubberry bush."

Angel held on vaguely to the steel frame, happily singing one line over and over.

Isis kicked her feet faster, eyebrows pulled down. Every time she spun past the view of the park, she could see them. Cally and Gil, cuddling on the bench under an umbrella. Cally and Gil, kissing.

Her mum had been different these past three weeks.

Happy. When Isis got home from school the flat was clean and the windows open. There were cooking smells wafting from the kitchen. Cally sang while she did things, and when the phone rang she ran to answer it. If Isis scrambled across the sofa, getting there first, it was always Gil.

"Hello, Isis. Can I speak to your mum?"

No. Go away.

"Yes, she's just here." Handing the receiver to Cally.

"Gil!" A smile curving Cally's mouth, her voice softening and filling with laughter.

I should be happy for her, Isis thought every time.

But all the years of darkness, all that misery! And now Cally just threw it off, for *him*? The best Isis could manage was a sourish ache. She'd wanted things to change, but this wasn't what she'd imagined. Now everything was about Gil, even things that weren't. Like the letter. It had arrived this morning, and was waiting on the doormat when Isis got up. It stood out a mile from the bills and junk mail.

"Oh!" She ran across the living room, picking it up. A thick cream envelope, addressed to *Calista Dunbar* in careful, flowing handwriting. It looked special, and Isis held it up to the light, but the paper was too thick to see through, and the back was sealed shut, with no way to peek inside. Definitely special, and she couldn't wait until her mum woke. So she took the letter into Cally's still-dark bedroom, yanking open a curtain. Daylight blasted over Cally, messy-haired under the duvet. She groaned and held her hands out against the light.

"What? What time is it?" Her eyes opened in sleepy confusion.

"Look at this letter for you!" said Isis, holding out the envelope. "Who's it from?"

Cally reached out a hand over the scrunched bedding, heaving herself up. She stared at her name on the envelope, frowning as she ripped it open and pulled out a thick sheet of paper. It was neatly scrawled with the same flowing script, and Cally's pupils darted as she read. A slow, open smile formed on her lips, and she turned the letter over, searching for more.

"What does it say?" asked Isis, trying to read the back.

Cally's eyes were wide. She let out a laugh.

"I've been invited to join the Welkin Society!" She held the letter up, pointing to the signature. "Look! It's from Philip Syndal himself! He's really high up in the society — he's one of the best psychics in the world! His tours are always sold out." She read aloud from the letter. *"I have heard extremely exciting reports from your seances, and the committee has agreed to consider you for membership.*" Cally stood up, feet still in the folds of her duvet. "Isis! This is it!" She was dancing with the letter, bouncy and happy on the bed. Isis got on too, jumping about on the squeaky mattress, laughing and holding her mum's hand.

Then Cally cried, "I have to ring Gil!"

And Isis stopped bouncing.

"He must have spoken to Sondra, he must have sorted everything out!"

Isis got down off the bed and walked out of Cally's bedroom, even as her mum was tapping into her mobile phone. From the living room, she could still hear Cally's excited voice.

"I just had to thank you for sorting things with Sondra, for getting me invited into the Welkin Society… oh, didn't you? Well you'll never guess, a letter arrived from them this morning!"

They were going to be over at his place in a couple of hours, but Cally couldn't wait that long.

"Let's all go to the park!" Cally said when they'd got to Gil and Gray's house. Like Isis and Gray were five.

"The weather's really horrible," said Isis.

"It's only a bit damp." Cally was smiling at Gil like she couldn't stop.

"We could go to the cinema," suggested Gray, "then you two can snog in the back row."

"Gray!" snapped Gil. "When you start paying, you can choose where we go."

"I can pay," muttered Gray. "Mum gave me some money."

Which hadn't helped, not at all, and now they were here in the drizzle. Just about the only people in the whole park.

Isis spun round again. Gray had already given up on the playground. He'd found some bits of biscuit in his coat pocket, and he was busy throwing crumbs to some eager, soggy pigeons.

"This is so cringeworthy," he'd said, as they walked behind their giggling, hand-holding parents. "Dad could've waited. Next weekend I'm at Mum's anyway." He glared at their backs. "I don't know why we couldn't just stay at home and let them go off in the rain."

"Cally would never leave me," said Isis. She blushed — she'd made herself sound like a baby.

"What about when you go to your dad's?" asked Gray.

Isis shook her head. "I don't."

Gray looked at her. "You don't see him at all?"

Isis shook her head again. "He left after…" She paused. Did Gray know what had happened to Angel? Had Cally told Gil? "He travels a lot. But I do get presents from him, at Christmas and my birthday. And he sends me letters, he always knows exactly what I'm up to."

Her dad. His absence was like a heavy coat, one she couldn't take off. She'd never really stopped wishing for him to be there when she got home from school, or to remember he also had a daughter who was alive. After he'd left, she'd wished for him every night, two years solid. Every birthday she made the same wish, blowing out the candles on her cake. It hadn't done any good. She and Cally had moved to a flat, and their old house went up for sale.

"What does he do?" asked Gray.

Isis looked at her shoes, water-darkened. "He works on cruise ships," she mumbled. "He does shows for the passengers." She looked up, glaring. "Not rubbish or anything. He does proper magic, and hypnotism and stuff. He's really good." She held herself rigid, daring him to make fun.

Gray didn't, only nodding. Then he tilted his head a little. She was learning to read him, and a tilt meant a question. She jumped in with her own, blocking.

"Why are you called Gray? Is it short for something?"

Gray rolled his eyes. "I wish it was, cos then I could call myself something else." He nodded at Gil, holding hands with Cally. "It was Dad's choice. That's what Mum says anyway. It's cos he's such a UFO freak."

Isis looked at him.

"What've UFOs got to do with it?"

Gray sighed. "The greys. They're a type of alien. They go on about them all the time at his conferences. Anyway, he thinks aliens are super intelligent and all that, so he wanted to name me after them."

Isis felt a laugh, but managed to swallow it.

"Why didn't your mum stop him?"

Gray shrugged. "He has this effect on women, you know? He can make them do what he wants. Not Mum any more, not since she left him, but with all the rest..." He stopped. "I mean, he's different with Cally, but, you know, he's had a lot of girlfriends..."

In front of them, Gil put his arm around Cally's waist.

All the rest.

Isis desperately wanted to ask Gray about Gil's other girlfriends, and at the same time she wished he hadn't mentioned them.

They walked on, in awkward silence.

"Whee! Faster!" Angel squealed on the roundabout.

"Don't you care?" whispered Isis. "Look at them!"

Angel glanced back at Isis, the shapes of the playground showing softly through her.

"Mummy happy," she said, as if that answered.

They whirled on, the drizzle slicking over Isis's face and frilling her eyelashes with water. Gray was a nearby blur, hunched against the weather. The rain felt like a cold compress, calming her. It fell cool onto her cheeks, then cooler. The roundabout turned again, and the air grew colder still. In a sudden, unnatural change, her breath was a cloud of steam, and she was circling through drops of ice.

She slammed her feet down, scuffing a circle on the tarmac. The roundabout squeaked to a stop, and Angel would've been thrown off if there'd been anything to her.

"What you doing?" Angel cried.

Isis ignored her, standing up slowly, her head still spinning. She searched the air with her eyes.

"Who are you?" she whispered. Frozen rain skittered and tinkled on her coat. "I know you're there."

She closed her eyes a little, peering through her lashes as a sudden puff of wind blew the ice drops into a glittering dance. They instantly lost their sparkle, each one dulled by a coating of dust, and she could smell musty old clothes. She tried not to breathe, backing away.

Now a set of dirty grey fingers were feeling their way out of nothing. Lengthening and growing, stretching into a long wavering arm. The swirling grey fell upwards, into a dust-cloud head, then drifted to the ground and made the shape of legs. The ice-rain slowed as it passed through the hazy body, speeding up again as it came out into the air.

As Isis watched, a tall, elderly man built himself in front of her. Smelling like old, feathery-edged books, or the woolly dust balls under her bed. He was wearing the faded memory of a velvet jacket, and on his head was the neat shape of a fez, a long tassel hanging down from the top. Only his eyes glowed. Blue, like back-lit sapphires.

"You were at one of Mum's seances," whispered Isis. The ghost nodded.

"I was."

Angel hopped down from the roundabout.

"You a horrid!" she cried. "Goway!"

The old man turned his head, dust trailing from him like hair.

"I've always rather agreed with the saying that small children should be seen, but not heard," he said. "Especially dead ones." Angel squeaked and shot behind Isis.

"Go *away*," hissed Isis.

The dust grew thicker in the air.

"May I not even introduce myself?"

Isis shook her head.

"But, my dear, you have been my fascination for some months now."

Goosebumps rippled up Isis's arms.

"Why?" she whispered. "What do you want?"

The ghost drifted towards her, greeny-brown dust floating out in front of him.

"I could appear in front of most people and all they would do is shiver, or think there was a draft. Even if I met them somewhere *charged* with psychic resonance, such as a ruined castle at midnight, I would appear to them as little more than a floating ball of light, or a snatch of disembodied words." He looked at her, from blue eyes in the dust. "But you can see me clearly, hear me distinctly.

Even here, in this grotesquery of childhood." He winced at the surrounding playground.

"I don't want to," whispered Isis. "I don't want to see any of you."

The elderly ghost raised a hairless eyebrow. "Even the little one, there?"

"She's different," snapped Isis.

The ghost peered at Angel, who was still hiding behind Isis's legs. "She certainly is that." He sighed, dustily, and turned a questioning look to Isis. "Do you think that's her own doing, or because of you?"

"I don't know what you're talking about," whispered Isis. She didn't want a conversation with this ghost; she knew how it would end. He'd want her to give a message to someone, or take on some pointless or impossible task. The ghosts claimed it was to 'bring them peace', but they always needed her running around for them first.

She turned, walking away from the roundabout. A choking little cloud of dust passed around her, swirling into a tiny tornado of dirty raindrops. The ghost formed himself in front of Isis, blocking her way.

"I'm not passing on a message, if that's what you want," she whispered. "I don't do that."

He scratched the side of his nose with a grey-mist finger, curling a puff of dirt into the air.

"Ah, messages," he sighed. "The phantom's hope and curse." He shook his head. "Don't worry, my dear, I have no words of comfort for my descendants. I checked on a couple of them, and they were really quite ghastly."

"What do you want then?" Isis whispered. The old ghost grinned, yellow teeth dangling in his gums.

"What do I want? Perhaps merely the delightful back and forth of a real conversation!"

"Talk to the other ghosts then," said Isis, irritated now.

He flipped a hand through the raindrops, spinning them into snow.

"When I was alive, I was desperate to. I took laudanum, hoping to drug myself into just such a conversation. Bigger and bigger doses, until…" He laughed, dryly. "Once I'd died, of course I could talk to them as much as I wanted. Only then did I discover how dreary they are." His voice dropped into a whine. *"Look what they've done to my house! They gave my furniture to charity! Not enough people cried at my funeral!"* His voice returned to its normal rasp. "The same thing, over and over." The ghost shuddered, sending a shimmer of mould into the air. "There's nothing of substance to them, you see."

"They're ghosts," said Isis. "Like you!"

"I know. I looked back on my former self and laughed at my foolishness. I'd caught myself in this wretched limbo, thanks to my own false hopes."

"Why don't you leave then?" said Isis. "My mum says ghosts should head for a tunnel of light. She says it leads to the next world."

The old dead man pulled a skeletal look of scorn. "Of course, how stupid of me. And does your mother happen to have a map to help me find this wonderful tunnel?" He sighed. "I sometimes feel as if the best of me has already moved on, and I can't even remember what it was." He tilted his mouldy head, peering at Angel, who was hiding behind the roundabout. "May I ask, were you able to see ghosts before her?"

Isis ignored his question.

"Is this *for* anything?" she hissed. "Can't you go away now?"

The ghost shook his head.

"How can I?" he asked. "Do you know how rare a true psychic is? Especially one so strong, so… sane."

Isis folded her arms. "Leave me alone."

The ghost put his hands together in prayer or pleading, his fingernails withered and cracked.

"We need you, Isis Dunbar. We need a saviour."

Isis stayed still. "What does that mean?"

He put a finger to his mould-speckled lips, then whispered, "We ghosts haunt the darkening plains, my dear. But there are darker places still, into which even the spirits fear to go. The unwary few who drift in and manage to return, they speak of creatures lurking there. Devourers of souls. *Things*. Now one of these has left its dark existence, and is in our very midst."

Isis came a little closer to him, despite herself. "What's it doing?"

The elderly ghost's eyes were lines of blue. "It is feeding, my dear."

"Who are you talking to?"

She jumped, spinning around. Gray was a few metres away, head tilted. He must've seen her. Heard her!

Panic flapped through her mind.

"I… um write poetry," she said quickly. "I was just… trying it out loud." She looked straight at Gray, trying to hold her gaze steady. *Poetry?*

Gray pulled his hands inside the sleeves of his raincoat.

"Why is it so cold over here?"

Isis shrugged, heart galloping in her chest.

"Goodbye!" said the ghost, waggling his fingers as he dissolved into the tarmac. "When we meet again, you may call me Mandeville."

Isis didn't answer.

Chapter Seven

Isis

"Go on, you do it. I can't." Cally's voice was breathless, a whisper. She was standing by the door, eyes wide, hands white-knuckled on the letter.

Isis pressed her finger on the grey plastic circle of the doorbell, and a ding-dong tune played distantly. They waited.

Isis turned to Cally.

"Are you *sure* this is the right place?"

They were in front of a large, squarely built house, one of many on the long street. Each one was planted in a wide plot, surrounded by blank, featureless lawns and reached by red-brick driveways. Only small differences picked the houses apart: a newly planted tree, a rosebush under the window, a different-coloured door. This one had diamond-patterned windows, which gleamed in the late afternoon sunlight, reflecting away any view of the inside.

Cally scanned the thick cream paper, and nodded. "Definitely. This is twelve Worthington Avenue."

Isis pressed the doorbell again. The tune tinkled, and this time the handle crunched downwards, the door swinging open. A plump, soft-faced man regarded them from under mousey, thinning hair. He was dressed in pale jeans and a lemon yellow pullover.

"Oh, hello," stammered Cally. "We're early I think. I'm Calista, and this is my daughter…"

The man smiled, his face transformed by dimples and wrinkles. Not handsome exactly, but… something.

"Of course!" he said, reaching to shake Cally's hand. "I'm so pleased you could make it. I'm Philip Syndal." He opened the door wider. "Please, call me Phil."

"I've been to your performances!" said Cally, smiling and enthusiastic. "And read all your books. But I never dreamed that… I mean, this invitation means so much… I just wanted to thank you. Thank you."

He smiled at Cally, then turned the beam on Isis, before beckoning them inside.

"You've been attracting attention with your work,"

he said, as they walked into his house. "We believe you could be a very useful member of the Welkin Society, especially at this time." Philip Syndal turned to Isis, examining her from his plain grey eyes. "And your daughter is welcome too."

He closed the door behind them, shutting off suburbia.

The inside of the house was completely different from its bland exterior. Isis stared at the wide, double-height entrance hall and the dark-wood staircase leading to the upstairs. The walls were painted green above the skirting, the colour blending into sky blue further up and then rich, midnight blue over their heads. Pinprick lights spotted the high, night-sky ceiling, with paintings of wistful, shimmering men and women curling between them. They were packed together; their oversized butterfly wings fluttering awkwardly from their backs, their limbs jumbled and confusing in some places. As if the artist had struggled to fit them all in.

Isis tipped her head back, staring.

"I see you've noticed my guardians," said Philip, standing close beside her.

"Are they… fairies?" she asked.

"Spirits, or angels perhaps." He gazed at the figures. "The artist was recommended by Norman." There was the tiniest pause before he said the dead man's name, his grief clear but restrained. "The artist says she paints what she sees. These are portraits of the beings she saw circling this house, acting for my protection."

"Oh," said Isis. She hadn't seen anything circling his red-tiled roof, except for a couple of squawking jackdaws.

"How wonderful to have them watching over you," said Cally. "So many people only think of spirits as being frightening, when there are also these messengers of goodness."

"The angels are always with us," said Philip.

"Oh I've read it!" cried Cally. "It's wonderful." It was the title of one of his books; they were all lined up neatly on a shelf back at their flat.

Philip smiled, modestly accepting her praise.

"*I* Angel," said a small voice.

Isis went still.

"I Angel," said the voice again. Isis turned her head, as casually as she could, and saw Angel standing by the door. She was wearing a pink dress, and the flowery sandals. The little girl-ghost spoke again.

"I here. I Angel."

Isis glared at her.

Go away! She didn't even dare whisper it, not here. She glanced back at Philip and Cally, now deep in conversation.

"Of course," Philip was saying, "this is a very difficult time for the society. Our founder was so dedicated, I hardly feel worthy to continue his work."

"Oh yes, Norman Welkin was a very great man." Cally said his name awkwardly, with an undertone of embarrassment.

"You were there, I understand?" said Philip. "When he was…" He stopped, looking up as if to hold back tears. Cally blushed and nodded.

"Sondra… called me to try and find him." She almost whispered the words, and Isis held herself still, hoping Philip wouldn't ask anything else. Like, whether Cally had a screaming match with Norman Welkin's girlfriend, just before he turned up as a body.

But Philip only wiped his eyes, his soft face settling into a mournful expression. "I still don't know why she didn't call me. I would have done anything for him, anything."

Cally shrugged, looking even more awkward. "I… don't think there's anything you could have done," she said. "He had already passed."

Philip nodded. "Which makes me even more grateful

for my powers. Because I can still gain from his wisdom, when he speaks to me from the spirit world."

"Oh yes, of course. I'm sure he has so much to tell you!"

Behind their backs, Isis flapped her hands at Angel.

"Go home!" she mouthed, making a 'get lost' face at the little ghost.

Any moment, Philip Syndal would look round and see Angel. Cally said he was one of the best clairvoyants in the country, so surely he'd spot a ghost right inside his house? She was always talking about his sell-out tours, and quoting from his books. She'd recorded a chat show he'd been on, watching it over and over afterwards, so many times that Isis knew the ten-minute snippet by heart. The host's mocking scepticism at the start, then her increasing astonishment as Philip Syndal revealed a string of startling facts about her, as told to him by the spirits. By the end, the woman was on the edge of tears, and the audience applauding wildly.

It was why Isis had told Angel to stay at home.

"The Welkin Society is for psychics," she'd whispered, last night in bed with Angel resting cross-legged on her pillow. "They'll see you."

Angel had nodded her little head in the dark. "I do it."

But she always forgot her promises.

Any moment now Philip would notice the little ghost-girl, and he'd ask Cally about her. The old double-dread swept through Isis. Of Cally being exposed as talentless, and at the same time discovering she wasn't even able to sense the spirit of her own daughter.

"It boring at home," said Angel from by the door. "I not like it on my own."

"Go *away!*" mouthed Isis. She sidled towards the door. If she could get in front of Angel, maybe Philip wouldn't see her.

"I'm so excited to be meeting everyone," Cally continued, pushing her hair back from her face and smoothing it down with her hand. The way she always did when she was nervous.

Philip Syndal smiled, his face transforming once more from bland into charming.

"Well, our meeting may be a little more sombre than usual, but having you here is the boost we need in this difficult time."

Isis took another sideways step, and the movement caught Philip's eye. His eyes fixed on Isis, then flickered past her. Towards the door, towards Angel.

Isis held a breath in her throat.

But there was no frown on Philip's face, no puzzlement at the small, mop-top ghost by his front door.

"Would you like, um, something to drink?" he asked Isis. "I've got some orange squash. And some biscuits. You can wait in the kitchen while the meeting's going on. There's a TV in there."

Isis breathed out.

"That's so kind, isn't it, Isis?" Cally said. She turned back to Philip. "I couldn't get a babysitter, you see. And of course I couldn't leave her home alone."

Philip nodded. "Of course."

He hadn't noticed Angel!

Or, he was even better at keeping secrets than Isis.

The kitchen door wasn't quite shut. Through the crack, if she stood in the right place, Isis could see into the hallway. Philip was welcoming a large, middle-aged woman, dressed in a vast red-velvet dress, her hair a bowl shape of short, dark curls. So far there'd been three men and four women, and Philip had led them all into one of the rooms off the hall. A room Isis hadn't been allowed to see.

Behind her, on the breakfast bar, a glass of orange squash sat untouched and a plate of chocolate biscuits uneaten. A fast-paced cartoon was battering out of the TV on the wall. Isis had turned the sound up a little too loud, to convince the adults she was busy, and as a result Philip was apologising to the curly haired woman.

"That racket will disturb the harmony of the spirits," she was saying, her voice crisp.

"The spirits are fond of children, Andrea," Philip said soothingly. "And we won't be able to hear in the other room."

The woman didn't look convinced, but headed through the door. As he followed her, Philip turned his head towards the kitchen, and winked at Isis. She jumped a little, then smiled.

There was a hint of tugging at her jumper.

"What you doing? I want to see!" Angel pushed her way to the gap in the door, desperately trying to squeeze her head through.

"There's nothing," whispered Isis. "They've all gone in."

"What Mummy doing?" Angel wriggled a bit further. "I want to see Mummy."

"No!" Isis put her hand in front of her little ghost-sister, holding her back. Angel was a nothing-cool kiss on her skin. "Mummy's in an important meeting."

And it was important. Cally had been jittering about it for the last three weeks. No, it was ever since she'd decided to become a clairvoyant. Isis remembered Cally's handwritten career plan, the one she'd come up with in the bad old black days.

- Contact the spirits
- Start doing readings
- Do a tour
- Join the Welkin Society
- Write a book

It was their grief counsellor who'd suggested the list, and Isis hadn't known if he was trying to encourage Cally or put her off. He'd passed Cally a pen and paper, saying, "Writing things down can help you to focus."

Then he'd turned to Isis.

"You're very quiet. How do you feel about your mother's idea?"

She'd been struck dumb for a moment, panicking he'd somehow found her out. It didn't help that a see-through Angel was jumping up and down on the sofa, right next to him.

Maybe Isis was really the one who'd lost it, maybe she should've been writing lists.

"Whatever Cally wants," she'd said at last. "I don't mind."

Whatever it took to get her mum back, instead of the shell-woman who'd taken her place after Angel died and Dad left. The shell-woman stayed in her room, curtains shut, while Isis got herself ready for school. She was sitting on the sofa, staring, when Isis got home. The shell-woman let their house drift into dirty chaos, and their meals transform from healthy, to oven-ready, to random. Worst of all, the shell-woman had nothing behind her eyes, like she'd left as well. Isis stopped calling her 'Mum' around then, but the shell-woman hadn't noticed.

The funny thing was, the grief counsellor was right: working at being a psychic had given Cally focus. Isis's mum had returned. Slowly, and in bits and pieces, but Isis had hoarded up those precious flashes, hoping. Even the seances and the tours were a little less humiliating, when she thought about those moments. And now here they were: number four on Cally's list. At Philip Syndal's house, joining the Welkin Society.

"We in kitchen," said Angel, as if she'd only just realised. "Can we make cakes?"

Isis laughed. Being dead hadn't dampened Angel's enthusiasm for baking. As a living toddler, she'd been able to shove an entire cupcake in her mouth in one go. Now, she floated on the sweet steam as they came out of the oven, the way birds ride updrafts in the wind.

"I don't think Philip would like me cooking." Isis could just imagine his face. "You'll have to watch the cartoons."

"I want cake." Angel hurtled headlong for the oven, straight in through its door. Her head came back out of the glass window. "It not even hot," she said. "He *won't* mind."

"I think he will." Isis knelt down, next to Angel's head. "You can't just make food in someone's house, not without asking them."

Angel's tongue peeped out of her mouth as she thought. Her face brightened.

"I ask him then!" she said.

"No!" Isis leaped to grab at the little spirit, but Angel was a wisp in the air, then gone.

"*Angel!*" Isis whisper-shouted, slamming open the kitchen door, running into the hall.

Angel was at the far wall, her small hands splayed against the greeny-blue, her head and shoulders already faded into it. Isis threw herself after, fingernails scraping wallpaper, but she couldn't catch her ghost-sister.

Isis slid down to the floor, a sick feeling reaching up to her.

Angel was in a room full of psychics. Any one of them might see her. All of them might!

All except Cally, who'd never seen Angel, not once. Not in the darkest days, not even when Angel's little ghost had stepped from her own mangled body, in front of her horror-struck sister and screaming mother.

Isis got herself up to standing, heart thudding. There was nothing else to do.

She walked to the door of the meeting room, and took hold of the handle. She could hear a man speaking, and another answering.

She pushed the handle down, and walked into the room.

"Can we help you, dear?" asked an elderly woman with high cheekbones and a narrow, almost lipless mouth. She was staring at Isis from her heavily made up, deeply sunken eyes. As were the other eight people at the table.

"I... er..." Isis kept her hand on the door handle, looking in.

It was Philip Syndal's dining room, but it was decorated

like the interior of a castle, with bronze candle brackets on the walls and a dark wood table filling the room. A dragon mural coiled across all four walls.

The members of the Welkin Society were sitting around the table, like knights of old. Instead of swords and silver goblets they were surrounded by files, folders and sheets of paper, business-like. The only thing Cally had on the table in front of her was the letter, her hands flat on the paper as if she was scared it might blow away.

She was glaring at Isis.

Isis smiled, trying to act normal, while scanning the room for Angel.

There. The see-through shimmer of a little girl, sidling along the wall, working her way to Cally.

"Is everything all right?" asked Philip, starting to get up. "Do you need any more biscuits? I can get you some…"

"No, Philip. Please." Cally scraped her chair back, the letter fluttering onto the floor. "I can deal with this."

She walked quickly round the table and grabbed Isis's hand, pulling her back out into the hallway and shutting the door behind them before Isis could think of a way to stay in the room.

"Please, don't embarrass me," Cally hissed, pulling Isis

into the kitchen. "The society aren't going to let me come to meetings if you keep interrupting."

Isis yanked her hand out of Cally's. "Then you should have let me stay at home!"

"You know I couldn't find anyone to look after you."

"I don't *need* anyone!"

Cally stood by the kitchen door, and took a deep breath through her nose.

"We can discuss this later. Just tell me what you want and then I can get back to the meeting." She flicked a glance back at the dining room. "They'll be waiting."

Isis followed her gaze, and saw Angel slinking out through the wall. Little arms waved.

"Isis! I here!"

There'd been no shouting from inside the room, no cries or questions. Angel was out, and no one had noticed her. The knot in Isis's stomach untightened. She looked straight at Cally, and shrugged.

"I just wanted to know where the toilet is, that's all."

Cally laughed, and rolled her eyes.

"It's over there, you silly." She hugged Isis briefly, then hurried back to the meeting. "Nothing to worry about—" she said as she opened the door. Her words were cut off as it closed behind her.

Isis ran into the hallway, plunging her hands into Angel's smoky form, grasping hold of her and pulling her back to the kitchen.

"Oooow!" wailed Angel, kicking with weightless legs, trying to hit Isis. "You hurting me!"

Isis's hands were going numb, she let go with one of them.

"Don't go in there again!" she hissed. "That was very naughty!"

She pulled her other hand out of the little ghost, who sank onto the floor, her edges dissolving a little.

"I not naughty," she wailed.

"Don't start crying," snapped Isis. "It won't work. I told you not to go in there! One of them could have seen you."

Angel became a little more solid, and started fiddling with the flowers on her sandals. "No one see me," she mumbled.

Isis sighed, it was hard to stay angry with Angel. She crouched down and touched a finger to Angel's cool-whisper cheek. "They *might* have," she said. "They're psychics."

"Like Mummy?"

Isis shook her head, her throat tight.

"Not like Mummy. Proper ones." She sat down on the tiles next to Angel. "This is Mummy's big chance, you see? It's what she really wants. But if the others spot you, and find out she can't..." Cally would be crushed. Cut to pieces. "They won't let her join their club."

Angel scrunched up the cloth flower. When she let go it was still perfect. She looked up at Isis.

"They dint see me," she said.

"That's because they weren't looking," said Isis. "I distracted them."

Angel's eyes were round in her not-quite-there face. "After. When you and Mummy wented out." A smile sneaked onto her lips. "I runned on the table."

Isis groaned, dropping her head into her hands. Angel poked her face through Isis's fingers.

"They dint see me. Even when I show my tummy, like this."

Angel stood, pulling up her dress to reveal a stretch of ghostly belly above pink tights. Through Angel, Isis could see the fridge.

"None of them?" whispered Isis.

Angel shook her head.

"Why did you do that?" cried Isis. "You could have ruined everything!"

Angel dropped her dress.

"I want someone to see me," she said. "Someone not you."

For a moment Isis thought of that future she'd tried to imagine, back in the garden. The one where she had a normal life, and didn't have Angel trailing after her. She shook her head, scattering the thoughts, and held out her arms. Her dead sister climbed onto her lap, with the weight of a falling feather.

"You've got me," whispered Isis, "and I've got you." She kissed Angel, like kissing a breeze. "Always and forever."

"Always and forever," echoed Angel.

Chapter Eight

Gray

My dad had this theory. Actually, he has a theory about most things. Aliens, 9/11, how the government are using the Internet to control us, why the oil companies bumped off all these people who invented water-powered cars. You name it, my dad's got a theory. So he had to have one about Norman Welkin, and why he died.

He'd been following it up, you see. Ringing the police, checking the local paper for stories, doing Internet searches.

"What's the point, Dad?" I asked him. "The policeman said it was probably a heart attack."

"Well he would say that, they're trained to put people off the scent," muttered my dad, frowning at his computer while it brought up about twenty trillion hits on unusual deaths. "Norman's death was strange. You said so yourself."

"No I didn't," I said. "It was Isis. You know – your weird girlfriend's weird daughter."

Dad's fingers stopped on the keyboard.

"Why do you think they're weird?" He looked at me. "Do you think *I'm* weird?"

I shrugged. "Of course. Doesn't everyone?"

Thing is, I should never have told him what Isis said. How it was like the dead man had been frozen and coated in ice. I should have kept my mouth shut, because as soon as the words were out, Dad's ears pricked up, and there was no stopping him.

He spent ages on the Internet, and then he got onto the Network, which is basically this club for UFO freaks. I mean, they don't call it a club, but they send each other emails all the time, and they have these meetings at hotels, where they give each other lectures and slide shows, and try and flog stuff like spaceship detectors, or anti-bugging gizmos for your mobile.

"Those losers," is what Mum calls them.

The reason I know all about them is cos Dad took me along once. It was to ConspiriCon, which is just for conspiracy theories. Like, who blew up the Twin Towers? Or were the moon landings really faked in some desert in America? Actually, those are normal-sounding, compared to what was at ConspiriCon. There was this man who said the world's really controlled by aliens. And another who said the ancient Egyptians had predicted the end of the world, and it's going to happen in about five years. There was a guy who went on about the earth being hollow, and how the government are going to hide inside it when things get too bad. Dad made me sit through a talk about how UFOs are just a cover story for secret government weapons, and halfway through this other freak stood up and started shouting, saying it was really the exact opposite.

We went there because it was Dad's weekend and he didn't want to miss out. On seeing me, or on going to ConspiriCon. So he just booked another ticket and didn't tell Mum. He didn't tell me either, not until we were on the motorway.

"No way, Dad!" I said. "I'm not going!"

"You'll enjoy it," he said. "You always enjoy our chasing trips."

"I like *camping*. I like being outside. This is just some crappy hotel, and everyone will have their shirt tucked in their trousers. I'm not doing it, Dad! I'm going back home to Mum."

"And how will you do that?"

I yanked at my seat belt, undoing the clip.

"Just let me out, I'll hitch or something."

"You won't." Dad reached with one hand, grabbing the seat belt and trying to clip it back in. The camper wobbled in the lane, a lorry slow-honked us. I suppose I could've grabbed the wheel and spun us off the road, but that was probably the only way I would've stopped him.

Sometimes, I totally get why Mum left Dad.

Anyway, it was the Network that Dad used to work out his theory about Norman Welkin's death. He sent off all these emails to his UFO friends, and he was on the computer all the time. Then, he got to use 'The Database'.

Honestly, that's how he says it, like he's in MI6 or something.

One of the super-freaks, this bloke called Stu Bradley, looks after The Database. Not that Dad ever calls him Stu, he always says, "The Keeper". Stu wouldn't even come to our house until after dark, which meant it was eight at night before he turned up.

"A dark green Volvo, that's what we're looking for."

Dad stood at the side of the window, like someone was watching us, and twitched his head to look every time a car went by. In the end this boxy old Volvo pulled up outside, really knackered, and Stu peered out. When he'd checked up and down our street, he ran for the house clutching a bag, the hood on his coat pulled right up.

He was really old, fifty or something, with long grey hair and grey stubble all over his chin. He didn't look special; you'd never notice him on the street or anything. Except for his cigarette stink. He smelled like an ashtray, and his teeth were this nasty brown from all the fags. As soon as he got inside, he lit up a cigarette, and Dad never even stopped him. The house filled up with smoke, not that Dad cared.

"Is that it?" he asked, nodding at the bag.

'Stu the Keeper' didn't say anything, just frowned at me.

"Don't worry about Gray," said Dad. "He can hold his tongue."

Stu the Keeper glared at me even harder.

"You can't tell *anyone*," he rasped. "Not what you see on The Database. And nothing the government could use to identify me." I nodded, trying to keep a straight face.

A stinkometer, that's what they could use. Or a dog. A dog could smell him from miles off.

Stu the Keeper turned to Dad.

"Have you unplugged all phones and electrical appliances? Are you disconnected from the Internet?"

"Yes," said Dad. "And we can go in the bathroom – it doesn't have any windows."

Like I said, they're pretty far gone with all this stuff.

"Perfect," said Stu.

So we went in the bathroom. Stu sat on the toilet, me and Dad perched on the side of the bath. The extractor fan hummed away, which was lucky because we'd all have got lung cancer otherwise. I mean, who smokes in a bathroom?

Stu opened up the big bag, took out a laptop and set it carefully on his knees. While he was waiting for it to start up, he turned to my dad.

"How's your work going? Got any further with your MDLP?" That stands for mobile disambiguated luminescent phenomena. Seriously. He meant the massive light sphere I told you about.

Dad nodded. "Yes, I have as a matter of fact. I've been doing some calculations based on the readings, and I think I've worked out the base preconditions, which means I should be able to predict any reappearance with only a ten per cent margin of error. I can go and get my notes if you like…"

Stu held up his hand. "One thing at a time. I'm here with The Database tonight." He nodded at the screen, where a small search form was flashing. "There she is."

"All right," said my dad, rubbing his hands together. "I'm after unusual deaths. But not mutilations."

Stu put his fag out in the sink, held his fingers over the keypad, and started typing.

The Database is a big list of all the weird things any of the UFO freaks have ever heard of, put into different categories. They think it's really secret, but half the stuff's on YouTube. My film of the sky-sphere is in there.

It was pretty boring once they got going, and smoky, so I went out and made cups of tea for them, and a hot chocolate for me. When I got back, they had the laptop on the toilet seat, and they were both kneeling on the bath mat in front of it. Dad took the cups of tea, and put them down in the bath.

"Check this out, Gray!" he said, pointing at the laptop. "I told you it wasn't just a heart attack."

Stu shook his head at me.

"You should never believe the police, Gray. They work for the government, don't they?" He pointed at the screen, where a list of results was sitting on the page.

"There are seventeen other unusual deaths with a strong resemblance to the one you discovered." He lowered his voice. "Seventeen."

I looked over his shoulder, reading the list. I pointed at one of the entries.

> Death of elderly man in North Wales.
> Natural causes. Police report notes the
> weather had been unusually cold for
> the time of year.

"That's just some old man who died," I said.

Dad slapped the side of the bath. "Come *on*, Gray, you should know how to join the dots by now!" he pointed to the text. "He was cold. The police said it was natural causes."

"Natural causes," said Stu, "is their way of hiding the evidence, shutting up the families and putting people off the scent. Deaths by natural causes always go in The Database. They might as well say cover-up and be done with it."

"Norman knew the *truth* about this world," said Dad. "He was a target."

Stu the Keeper nodded, his face all pulled together. "They don't want people knowing the truth. They've got the resources to make it look like a heart attack, but they can't hide every trace."

"Trace of what?" I asked. "And who's *they*?

"You know," snapped Stu, but I didn't. I couldn't keep up with him and Dad. *They* could've been the government, or aliens, or the Americans, or big business, or one of the weird groups they think are controlling the world. And as for the truth 'they' don't want people to know, sometimes it's aliens, or secret government plans, or stuff being done by big business, or weird groups controlling the world. Any of that... maybe all of it.

"Norman was one of my best customers," said Dad. "I owe it to him to find out what really happened."

"But what you've got doesn't prove anything," I said. "People die all the time."

Stu blew out a blast of smoke.

"People don't just walk into their gardens and drop dead," he said. I tried to argue, but he held up his hand. "When you've seen as many suspicious deaths as I have, you'll be able to spot the cover-ups too."

I wanted to ask Stu how many of those suspicious deaths were on TV programs, but Dad got in first.

"Norman may have had a heart attack," he said darkly,

"but that doesn't mean he wasn't murdered."

I didn't argue; there wasn't any point with those two. But now it's obvious they were going at it all the wrong way round. I mean, Norman Welkin's death was really weird. But it was weird because it *wasn't* like any of the others in The Database. Nothing they found in there was the same, even if they made out it was. No one *ever* died like Norman had.

Until Isis.

Until Isis...

Which is why I'm here, to find out what happened to her, and I think you know, don't you? Because Stuart Bradley was right about one thing, the police will never work out something like this correctly. And I doubt he and your father will ever get to the truth either. Last time we hacked their precious database, it was full of gaps and contained nothing we didn't already know about. You're the key, Gray, because you're the one she talked to.

She never told me anything.

Chapter Nine

Isis

After an achingly slow hour and a half of waiting, Isis looked into the hallway, at the closed-off door leading to the room full of phoney psychics.

She sighed. "What are they still talking about in there?"

"I find out," said Angel, floating off Isis's lap.

"No!" whispered Isis, waving her hands. "You promised!"

Angel paused, a wisp by the door.

"I not going in, only looking. I stay in the wall."

"No," said Isis.

"You can hold my hand," said Angel, tilting her colourless head, widening her black-hole eyes. "You'll see too."

"No." said Isis. "We decided not to do that any more."

"You 'sided." said Angel. "I want to!"

"It's spying…" said Isis, but she could hear the resolve in her voice weakening.

Angel grinned, knowing she'd won, and ran to the far wall of the hallway, her feet a few centimetres from the floor. She pressed her fragile forehead against the solid mass of the wall and pushed. Her eyes and nose, forehead and ears disappeared into the plaster. Her curly hair, then her neck vanished next, and when her shoulders were against the paint, she stopped.

All Isis could see was the toddler's almost transparent, headless form leaning into the wall. A short arm swung backwards, pudgy fingers wriggling at the end of it.

"This is very bad," said Isis, but to herself, because Angel wasn't listening. She crossed the hallway, took the small, weightless hand in her own, shut her eyes… and she could see.

Chair legs, with a man's legs and feet between them. The red velvet pillow of a woman's bottom, overflowing from her seat. The black-clothed back of a man wearing a suit, his ginger-haired head distantly above. It was a low-down, foreshortened view of the room. The view from near the floor. Angel's view.

The scene shifted. Angel was turning her head.

Philip Syndal came into sight, his chin looking very round and babyish from this perspective. His mouth was opening and shutting, his hands waving in silence.

"You need to put your ears through as well," whispered Isis. "I can't hear anything." Angel shifted position; there was a muffled rushing in Isis's ears, then words.

"... vote unanimously agreed, which means, Calista, I am very happy to welcome you to the Welkin Society. I hope you find it as rewarding as our other members do."

"Thank you. I can't tell you how pleased I am."

There was a jolting, sickening lurch in Isis's vision, as Angel wriggled sideways along the wall. Now Isis had a view of Cally, sitting three places along the table from Philip Syndal. Her mum pushed her hair back from her face and smoothed it down, a flush of colour in her cheeks.

"Mummy happy." Angel's whisper drifted through the wall.

Their shared view lurched again, and Isis swallowed, clenching the muscles of her stomach.

Angel was looking at Philip Syndal now, his features sagging from charming to solemn. "And now we must turn to the great sadness our group has suffered. There is an empty seat at this table, the seat of a visionary, of our founder. He was our protector, a kindly father to us all."

"A terrible loss," said the curly haired woman, Andrea.

"But the question is what we should do without Norman leading us."

"I wonder if we should even continue as a society," said a man's softly spoken voice. Isis couldn't see who it was.

"You may wonder, Ian," said Andrea, loud and importantly. "But I *know* he wants us to carry on. I have felt his presence many times in these last weeks, telling me to continue his good work."

"You, particularly?" said the softly spoken man.

Andrea turned and nodded at whoever it was. "*Someone* will have to take on leadership of the society," she said.

Philip Syndal looked sharply at her. "Yes, well. We'll come to that later." He turned his gaze to the rest of the table. "Norman set up the society to be greater than any of us. He created a beacon of hope in this world, and the next. We are a meeting point for clairvoyants, clairaudients, channellers, psychics and any persons with an ability that extends beyond the everyday, into the supernatural. Of course, it's very important who our next leader is, and there will be elections in due course. But as treasurer of the society, I will take on temporary leadership for now."

"When will the elections be?" asked Andrea.

Irritation flashed across Philip's face, but it was quickly smoothed into a smile. "It may take a few weeks, Andrea. I have to write to our more far-flung members."

"I hope it's not too long," she muttered. "As I said, I have felt Norman's presence, I am sure he is calling me."

"Well I've felt him too!" snapped the posh, elderly woman.

"And me," said the man Isis couldn't see.

Philip Syndal picked up his papers, shuffling the top two sheets. "I'm sure Norman visits us all," he said. "Perhaps in our meditation today, we will hear him speak."

"I would be utterly amazed if they did," said a voice next to Isis, inside the wall. She gasped, letting go of Angel's hand and falling back into the hallway. Her stomach lurched at the sudden change, and she pressed her hand over her shut-tight mouth, holding back a retch.

Angel tumbled out of the wall after her.

"Isis poorly?" she asked, looking worried.

"I let go too quick," Isis whispered.

Part of the blue painted plaster of the wall dissolved into the powdery shape of a tall, thin man. A body pulled itself out, then a head, leaving the paint unmarked and perfect. It was the ghost from the park and the seance. Mandeville.

He nodded his head in greeting. Angel squeaked and huddled up to Isis.

"Very good to see you again," he said.

Isis swallowed and shivered, her stomach slowly untwisting.

"I must say," Mandeville continued, "your channelling powers are unique. You are a true adept."

"What are you doing here?" hissed Isis. "Are you waiting for a seance?"

"In there?" Mandeville laughed, dusty fibres coughing out of his mouth. "Those fantasists won't be summoning anyone. They might sleep a little during their so-called meditation." He slithered down to the floor, his limbs feathering outwards.

Isis shuffled away from him. The kitchen door was open behind her and noisy cartoon chatter was spilling out through the gap, but the bright voices sounded odd and out of place now.

"Are you following me or something?" she asked.

"Or something," said Mandeville, with one of his yellow-teeth smiles. He stretched out his long legs in their velvet trousers. The material was ancient and decaying; in places the pale glow of his bloodless flesh showed through them. "You aren't the only one with an interest in the Welkin Society."

"I don't have an interest," said Isis. "It's Cally who joined."

"Really?" Mandeville looked with his blue-star eyes at the wall, beyond which the Welkin Society were still in their meeting.

"You know," he said, "I was devoted to seances when I was alive. I personally knew several of the great psychics of my time. Mrs Pargetter, Arthur Wrioseley, Sebastian Blackstone. I was amazed and entranced by their performances, I even wrote an essay for the *Occult Review* on the nature of phantoms."

Angel crept around behind Isis, hiding from him.

"I believed the psychics without question," continued Mandeville. "That is, until I died. Immediately, I rushed to a seance, and what did I discover? My revered teachers were really fraudsters and fakes! Mrs Pargetter was deaf to my cries. Arthur Wrioseley couldn't see me. As for Sebastian Blackstone, the disembodied voices he so marvellously conjured turned out to be his wife shouting from inside a cleverly concealed cupboard. I had laboured so hard, sacrificed my *life* in the cause of spiritualism, only to find I could pass nothing on. That's when I made my vow to spend my ghost-hood searching for a true channel so I could speak to the living."

"You wanted to be famous," said Isis.

"No! I wanted to dispel fear, and help people accept their end." He tilted his head. "Perhaps a little famous. In any case, I went hunting for genuine psychics."

Isis caught her breath. She was suddenly desperate to find someone like herself.

"Did you find any?" she whispered.

Mandeville nodded, a grimy whirlwind, his head half inside the wall.

"But there was a problem."

Isis let her breath out. There were always problems.

Mandeville continued. "You see, my dear, I don't believe it's death alone that creates a ghost. It is the form of death. Most spirits, souls if you want, they pass quietly into whatever lies beyond. But those of us who die tragically, or unexpectedly, we are held back, caught in the mists, as it were. The murdered wife, the headless horseman – in my death I discovered the clichés turn out to be true. Of course, such phantoms are filled with longings, unhappiness and unfinished business. Anyone with real psychic powers is a burning flame, around which they circle like moths, endlessly, relentlessly." His eyes held Isis. "Eventually the psychic is driven insane by it." Sorrow flickered on his dusty features. "Every true psychic I ever found was mad before they reached adulthood. Locked in asylums, hearing voices. The poor things couldn't be cured, because the doctors never realised the voices were real."

The ghost examined her, as if checking for signs of insanity, and Isis shivered, not just from Angel behind her. Would she go mad too? Sometimes it felt all too possible. She wrapped her arms around herself.

"However, none of them were as strong as you. And you can do something I have never seen before." Mandeville's eyes were a distant blue, his gaze focused on her. "How did you do it? Putting your hands into that yobbish ghost?"

Isis squeezed her hands on her arms, locking herself together. She wasn't sure, but she could remember the first time. Angel had been clinging onto her all day, overwhelming in her neediness. Eventually, furiously, Isis had shoved at her, surprising them both when her hands connected with Angel's nothing-body. How had she done it? She couldn't explain, not even to a ghost.

"I just… focus," she said.

Mandeville was silent for a moment. Then he said quietly, "You could save us."

Angel squeaked again, and pressed close to Isis, sending a chill into her back. Isis didn't speak. She didn't want him to go on, she didn't want to get drawn in. He'd just admitted it himself: ghosts always wanted something.

Mandeville couldn't match her silence.

"Do you want to know what you can save us *from*?" She still didn't answer, so he carried on. "It has no name for itself, so I call it a Devourer because that is what it does."

He paused, obviously waiting for a question she had no intention of asking. After a moment he continued. "I only heard rumours of it, at first. Ghosts are always telling tales of things they've seen in the dark. Ghouls, demons and suchlike. Most of the time I ignore them, but there was one… she was little more than a wraith, barely a memory of herself, and so ancient she didn't even understand what a wheel was for. She haunted the long forgotten graves of prehistoric peoples, their remains mere shadows in the soil. And she told me of something in one of those graves, caught in the dusty circle of a primeval skull. It had attacked her, but she'd escaped. An eater of ghosts, she said, which intrigued me. It's hard to explain to the living, but to ghosts such ancient graves are like… a deep abyss in the ocean. And in the abyss was something wild, something left from a time before humans had language. I made the trek. From a safe distance, I spoke to it in simple words, as one might to a baby, and it learned them with a speed that amazed me. It has a natural cunning, where its own interests are concerned."

Angel was clinging to Isis, both of them caught in his story. Isis shivered, and not just from cold. When Mandeville had first mentioned the Devourer, he'd implied it had appeared on its own. Now it sounded like…

"You brought it out, didn't you?" asked Isis.

The ghost clasped his fingers into a bony basket. "The wraith who told me about it had managed to fend it off, and she was little more than a whisper. So I concluded it must be feeble, able to frighten but not to harm. I only wanted to help, my dear. I was going to protect the next psychic I found by giving them this creature. I thought it would huddle unnoticed in their head, as it had huddled in the ancient skull, and scare away the worst excesses of the ghost world. I imagined it behaving like the faithful dog that protects its owner," he sighed, a mouldy plume.

"My imaginings were nothing like the reality. It never occurred to me the Devourer would grow so quickly, or that it was small only because it had little to eat. I never realised it would be so… ambulatory."

Mandeville leaned his head against the wall, sinking in a little. "I should have left it down in the dark. It's too bright here, too close to the living. With every ghost it devours it gets stronger, only wanting more. I'm frightened of what will happen, to all of us."

Isis stared at him, horrified. And she knew exactly where this was heading; Mandeville was a ghost, after all.

"You want me to sort it out for you," she said, anger clipping her voice.

Mandeville nodded.

"No!" snapped Isis. "Why should I? Why can't you ghosts sort out your own problems?"

He waved his bony hand, passing it into the wall. "Because we are incorporeal," he said. "Lacking in substance."

"Well you didn't need substance to make this problem," said Isis, "so fix it yourself! I don't care about this Devourer thing."

Mandeville looked at her. "And yet your own sister is a phantom."

Angel squeaked.

"Shut up! You're scaring her!"

The old ghost shook his head slowly. "Young people have so little nobility of spirit these days." Now she could see the wall, the air, quite clearly through his body. "But you cannot avoid attention forever, Isis Dunbar. You're like a blazing fire, this side of the veil."

"Attention from who?" she asked. Mandeville put a finger to his lips, and disintegrated into sudden particles, which dropped lazily onto the wooden floor then vanished.

Angel crept out from around Isis.

"He horrid," she said. "I glad him *goway.*"

It was 7.30 p.m. by the time the meeting finally ended. Outside in the street, the last light was fading. Isis sat in the kitchen, eating her way through the biscuits while thinking furious thoughts about ghosts. She had to watch telly for very young children, because Angel cried out, "Too scary!" if she put on anything but the squeakiest, silliest cartoons.

"You're a ghost," muttered Isis, not that it made any difference.

Eventually, the door into the dining room opened and Isis heard the members of the Welkin Society leaving.

Thanking Philip Syndal, saying their goodbyes in the hallway.

Cally came into the kitchen, holding Isis's coat.

"Come on, darling," she said, "school tomorrow."

Philip Syndal followed after, his eyes flicking around the room, as if checking it was all right. His gaze ended on Isis.

"Were you okay in here?" he asked.

"Yes. Thank you," she said.

"Good," he said, nodding slowly. Then he turned away, walking with Cally back into the hallway, and leaving Isis to follow.

The front door was open, letting the evening in.

"I'm so pleased you've joined us," said Philip, taking Cally's jacket from the coat stand, handing it to her. She looked awkward, yet pleased, as she put her arm into one of the sleeves. He held onto the coat as she put it on, so they were almost embracing. When he let go, Cally was in full blush.

"I can't tell you what this means to me," she said. "I'm so grateful to you for nominating me."

Philip smiled, the dimples shifting in his face.

"A medium of your ability? How could we not want you?"

Cally beamed and wittered all the way up the street

as they walked back to their car, Angel skipping invisibly in front of them.

"Philip's so wonderful," Cally said, "he has such a calming, beautiful presence. And his spirit guide is so powerful, so wise, just how he described it in his autobiography. Did you know, when he was a teenager he wanted to kill himself, but then this wise, ancient spirit came to him and showed him his true purpose in life? And Philip told me his spirit guide had singled me out personally…"

Isis glanced back, and stopped. Philip Syndal was standing in his doorway, a dark silhouette. He lifted his hand, waving at them, and for a moment Isis thought she saw something else.

Flying above his house, a shadow on the sky. Glowing into the furthest blue, shaped like a figure swimming in the night or maybe some strange, giant bird. Circling over the street. Isis blinked, and it was gone.

Cally opened the car door. "What is it? Have you left something behind?"

"No," Isis said. "Nothing."

Chapter Ten

Gray

I did tell Isis about them. The other deaths on The Database, I mean. It was on one of Dad and Cally's dates, when me and Isis had to drag along after.

Actually, you should have seen Dad's face when Cally turned up at the door with Isis!

"I thought..." said Dad. "Aren't we going out for the day? A walk on the Downs, just the two of us?"

"I know." Cally wafted in, that way she does. "But I had to bring Isis. I couldn't get a babysitter."

"She's not actually a baby," muttered my dad, but not loud enough for Cally to hear. Isis came creeping in then, like she didn't want to be seen. She had on these really pale jeans and a fluffy pink jumper. Out of school uniform, she looked about eight.

"Isis doesn't mind coming with us, do you, darling?" said Cally. Isis wobbled her head, sort of shrugging, and Cally smiled at me. "And I'm sure Gray doesn't want to be left at home, all by himself."

"I'm fine."

I mean, Dad's been leaving me home alone for years. Not that I tell Mum, cos she'd be just the same as Cally. Like, Mum's *always* at home when I am, always gets me to places on time, always has food in. When she got together with Brian, I didn't even meet him for the first three months, because she said she wanted to wait until she was sure about him. They've been going out for years now; he's probably going to be my stepdad.

Anyway, Cally was doing her Mum thing. *I* knew she wasn't going to walk out the door and leave Isis, but Dad tried it on anyway. Gave her his pleading look.

"Couldn't Isis stay here with Gray?" he asked. "They'd be all right for a couple of hours."

Cally looked like he'd suggested killing us and stuffing us in the bin.

"We can't leave the children by themselves!" she cried. She took his hand. "After... what happened," she said quietly, "I thought you understood how I feel."

Then Dad went red, which he never does.

"Yes, of course," he mumbled.

Actually, it wasn't so bad, because I like the Downs. They're these hills, about ten miles away. Not mountains or anything, but everywhere else around here is really low down, so there's not many places you get a view. And the wind rushes in your ears, the way it does on high-up places, and sheep *baa* in the distance, making everything sound lonely. Along the top of the Downs is the Ridgeway, which is a track that's been used since the Stone Age, so you're walking where mammoth hunters used to, or King Arthur, or whoever.

Normally I like it up on there, especially in spring, and we used to go loads, me and Dad. But there's no way *anyone* could've enjoyed the walk that day. I mean, trailing after Dad and Cally while they held hands and face-sucked each other.

It was disgusting.

Dad wasn't happy either. He kept checking back on me and Isis, like he was hoping we'd disappear. And Isis was her usual chatty self, meaning she said about two words the whole time. I don't think she got outside much, because she walked round every puddle, like she was worried about getting her shoes muddy.

Anyway, when we reached Hinner Wood, Dad had his brilliant idea. It's only a little wood, and mostly beech trees. You know, with straight grey trunks, and bright green leaves above. But when you get in, it doesn't matter it's small. The trees all lift their branches way up, and the light flickers down through them. Every step is a crunch on last year's leaves, and there's something really... well just *something* about the trees. It makes you happy to be there.

Dad and Cally were waiting at the edge of the woodland for me and Isis to catch up. He had his hand around Cally's waist, her head was on his shoulder. She was gazing up at the trees, and going on.

"You can really sense the natural spirits in places like this," she gushed. "They're more powerful where the land is untouched by humans."

"Actually," I said, "people come and look after these woods." There's this conservation group, they come here loads. Tidy up rubbish, clear bracken or chop down trees they think are dangerous. I even joined a couple of years back, but they wouldn't let me hold anything with a sharp edge 'in case I hurt myself', so I only went once.

Of course, Cally ignored me.

"The Native Americans understand," she said, "and other

tribal peoples. The spirits of plants and animals, of places even, are very powerful and wise. But we've lost touch with them in our modern, artificial world."

"I'm in touch with *my* nature," said Dad in his smoochy voice, and she giggled and blushed. He turned to me. "And Gray is too. He's a bird expert, aren't you?"

"No," I said, because I knew what he was planning.

"Yes, he is," said Dad. "He's got his own binoculars and he's always reading birdwatching magazines. We used to come up here all the time. What was that bird you always wanted to see, but never could?"

"I can't remember."

I wasn't going to help him out, and I wasn't very happy about him saying all that anyway. Only a couple of my friends know I'm into wildlife, and I don't want it getting out at school. Fast track to loser-land.

Dad looked right at me.

"I bet you could tell Isis all about these woods, while Cally and me sit on that bench over there."

Cally pulled away from him a bit, opened her mouth to speak. But he shook his head to stop her.

"Don't worry, Cal, if they stay in the fenced area they won't ever be more than a few hundred metres from us."

He smiled at her. "I can get to them in a minute flat, whatever happens."

Cally soppy-smiled at him, then turned to Isis.

"Would you like that, Isis?" she said. "Go and look at nature with Gray, while Gil and I…"

Snog. Grope each other.

Isis looked at her mum, then at me.

"I'm going," I said to Dad. "If I have to watch you two much longer, I'll be sick."

I didn't do any bird spotting. Not because I didn't have my binoculars, but because it isn't worth it in those woods. Thing is, there's all these birds in the books, but you hardly see any of them normally. Around where we live they've all disappeared because of farmers using chemicals and getting rid of hedges and stuff. You have to go to nature reserves or other places like that to see anything decent. There was a big article about it in *Young Birdwatcher*.

Anyway, me and Isis were just walking. Mooching about, kicking leaves and waiting for Dad and Cally to finish.

That's when I told Isis. About Dad thinking Norman Welkin had been murdered. I thought I might as well, seeing as she was the one who found him. I told her how

Stu and Dad thought his death was strange, and had looked for other cases where people had got frozen in weird ways.

She stood as still as a statue, listening.

"How many did they find?" she asked.

"Thousands of people who died of cold or heart attacks, but they got it down to seventeen where they thought it could've been the same. I'm not sure though, none of them seemed exactly like him."

"How did your dad find out about these other people?" she asked.

"I can't tell you," I said. "Confidential sources, you know?"

Isis nodded, thoughtful, and didn't even ask what I meant.

"So does your dad know what killed Mr Welkin?"

I paused, then shook my head. Thing is, Dad had loads of ideas, and so did Stu. They even came up with a name for what happened to him: spontaneous refrigeration.

"Like spontaneous combustion," said Stu, all excited, "but the other way round!"

They spent half the night in the bathroom, going through The Database and coming up with theories.

"We narrowed it to eight possibilities," Dad said the

next day. But if you've got eight possibilities, it really means you haven't got a clue.

"Maybe… aliens." I said to Isis, because that was what Dad went on about most. He always went on about aliens.

"Aliens?" said Isis, eyes going wide, and she started laughing. "Why does your dad think it was *aliens?*"

"Why does your mum think ghosts talk to her?" I snapped.

She stopped laughing, and her face went all closed up. I felt a bit bad, but it was her own fault.

"I'm just telling you what he found out," I said. "Think what you want."

Like I said, we didn't get on very well, back then.

Spontaneous refrigeration, now there's an idea we might be able to use. It could make a convenient cover story for certain activities.

But your father was wrong, of course. I can tell you from experience, Norman Welkin's death was nothing like the ones caused by aliens. Nothing at all.

Chapter Eleven

Isis

"Cally!" pleaded Isis. "Don't."

But Cally wasn't listening. Instead she was pushing past the queue of people waiting to get their tickets, causing a tutting wave of annoyance. When she reached the theatre's box office, she barged past the man at the front of the queue and said, "Excuse me, I'm on the guest list."

Isis shuffled backwards, getting further away from her.

The woman behind the counter sighed, and pulled out a sheet of paper from under her till.

"Name?"

"Calista Dunbar. I'm a professional colleague of Philip Syndal." Cally went on to loudly tell the woman how well she knew Philip, and about her own psychic performances.

Isis turned round, staring at the revolving door at the entrance, trying to pretend she was waiting for someone. As people circled into the theatre, Isis glimpsed purple reflections in the glass; Cally was wearing the same shimmering dress she'd worn on her seance tour. It had looked exotic then, but now, among the summer blouses, T-shirts and jeans of the people waiting in the foyer, she looked like she'd got lost on her way to a nightclub.

"Don't you think it's a bit much?" Isis had asked, back at their flat. Cally had carried on blow-drying her hair.

"If I want to get on," she'd shouted, pulling a brush through, "I need to make an impression. An invitation to one of Phil's performances is an opportunity to do that."

"But we'll only be in the audience, watching him like everyone else."

Cally switched off the hairdryer.

"The people around us could be *my* audience soon," she said. "I need them to notice me."

And they definitely had.

Isis caught a flash of blonde and pink. She turned round to see Angel, slipping through the crowd towards her.

"He got hair now!" cried the little ghost, waving her short, transparent arms. "He coming."

"Who is?" whispered Isis, barely moving her lips.

Cries of excitement rang through the foyer.

"Philip! Philip!"

"It's him, he's over there!"

"Please! Can I have your autograph?"

Philip Syndal charmed his way into the crowd. His hair had been styled to hide his baldness, and the yellow pullover swapped for a sleek black suit with a deep blue shirt. He looked sophisticated, if not exactly handsome.

A worried-looking usher was standing behind him, holding open a small door near the theatre's grand staircase. The usher kept glancing at his watch, but Philip ignored the time, moving slowly through his fans, speaking to everyone and signing autographs for anyone who asked. From her place near the door, Isis could see he was working through the crowd with a direction. He was heading towards Cally.

She was waiting for him by the box office. Hands together, head tilted, her dark hair flowing down her back. The purple dress shimmered. Silver bracelets cut graceful lines across her bare arms. She was the eye in the storm of clamouring, pushing fans.

She was in her stage pose.

Isis saw people glance at Cally, then fall back and form a pathway between her and Philip.

"Mummy beautiful," said Angel. And she was right, Cally had transformed herself, just the way Philip was able to. She didn't look ridiculous now, she looked...

"Like a princess," Isis whispered.

"Calista," called Philip. She smiled, still waiting.

Whispered questions and answers scurried through the crowd.

"Who's that?"

"Calista Dunbar, she's a new psychic."

"She any good?"

"Must be."

Cally held her place until Philip reached her. But he was different too. Glamorous, surrounded by the adulation of his fans.

"I'm so glad you could make it, Calista," said Philip, taking hold of one of Cally's hands, lifting it to his mouth. Sighs rose from the crowd, like they were watching a fairy tale. Philip held his gaze steady as he gently let go of Cally's hand. A flush rose at her throat, and her poise shattered.

"It was so kind of you to invite us," she said, too quickly, her voice squeaking. "I can't tell you how excited I am."

Her own glamour was broken, crushed by Philip's. No longer a princess, just another of his fans. An over-dressed one.

Philip held his arms out to the crowd.

"I'd like to introduce you to Calista Dunbar, a new talent who shows potential to become a true psychic, in the future." He smiled at the people surrounding them. "She's here to see how it's done."

There was a ripple of laughter, and the crowd stared at Cally, inspecting her.

Isis kept her place by the wall, hot with borrowed shame. He'd made Cally sound like she wasn't any good, but she didn't seem to have noticed.

"Have you got your tickets?" Philip asked her, and she nodded enthusiastically.

"Thank you." Cally held up two grey ticket stubs. "It's so kind of you."

Philip smiled, and turned to sign an autograph.

The tickets turned out to be for seats almost at the back of the theatre. As they walked to their row, the stage looked tiny and far away.

"It was still very generous of him to give us free seats," said Cally, her disappointment only just hidden by her bright tone. She peered and fidgeted, trying to get a better view, and when she saw an empty place five rows forwards, she hurried down to find out if it was free. Cally's excitement was plain as she headed back.

"One of their friends has a stomach bug and couldn't make it. No one's going to be sitting in that seat…"

Isis sighed, knowing what was coming.

"You go and sit there," she said to her mum.

"Are you sure?" asked Cally, worrying now. "Will you be all right back here?"

Isis nodded.

Cally turned to the middle-aged woman sitting next to Isis. Plump and pale, dressed in a white blouse and black skirt, like she'd come straight from work.

"Would you keep an eye on my daughter?"

"I'll be *fine*!" hissed Isis.

The woman smiled. "Of course," she said. "Don't you worry."

As Cally squeezed her way past people to get to her new seat, the theatre lights went down. A flute played a lilting, eerie tune into the red-glowing darkness. Dry ice hissed onto the stage, as coloured lights flame-flickered over the auditorium. There was a scatter of exclamations in the audience, and Isis realised Philip Syndal was on stage. From nowhere, as if by magic. He stood with his head lowered until the flute spiralled to the end of its lament, then a single spot brought him into bright, white light, and every other stage light went out.

Philip lifted his head.

"Welcome," he said, "to an evening of wonder. Tonight, I will take you to the border between this world and the next." The single light dimmed, fading into dull yellow. Philip was candlelit, a small flame against the dark. "Together, we will cross the border, we will go beyond... And those who have gone before us will turn back, and speak."

He opened his arms, walking to the front of the stage. The light followed him, brightening again.

"Spirits and friends, I am here. Speak. I am listening."

Isis felt a tingle on the back of her neck, her hair lifting at its roots. She could see Cally was entranced.

"Why he got a stick on his face?" A little voice peeped up to Isis. Angel bobbed up in front of her, trying to get a better view.

"It's his microphone," whispered Isis, peering through

the foggy blur of Angel's head. "So we can hear him."

"Are you all right?" asked the woman next to her.

Isis jumped in the dark.

"I'm fine," she said quickly, sitting still in her seat. She stared straight at the stage, watching Philip Syndal, ignoring the ghost freezing her lap.

Philip was really good, once he got going, and everything he said was spot on. No one shook their heads when he said something the spirits had told him about them, no one looked confused, or contradicted him apologetically. He never struggled to draw names from the air, the way Cally sometimes did. They were called out confidently, and hands went up straight away. The people who stood up from their seats gasped and laughed as he told intimate and accurate details about their loved ones, and the messages from beyond were loving and profound. The audience clapped long and loud after every reading.

Isis sat and watched, becoming more and more astonished.

How did he do it?

Because, for all his accuracy, for all the amazement he brought to the theatre, there was one thing missing.

The ghosts.

There were none up on stage with him. Isis peered hard, wondering if she just wasn't looking properly, but she could easily see Angel, who was soundlessly kicking her feet against the chair in front. Isis glanced to the back of the theatre, and she saw three ghostly forms, unnaturally bright against the black painted walls. But none of them had responded to Philip Syndal's called-out names, none of them had floated for the stage. They were looking around, anxiously, but not at Philip Syndal. As if they knew there was little chance of being noticed.

But if he wasn't actually communicating with ghosts, how could he know so much about everyone?

"Good, isn't he?"

Isis startled in surprise. She turned, and the middle-aged woman in the next seat was staring at her, fixing Isis with a piercing blue gaze.

"Don't you think he's good?" she asked again.

"Um, yes," Isis answered.

"It's especially impressive," whispered the woman, "given that the spirits are almost absent. How does he hear what isn't there, I wonder?" Her bright blue eyes dropped; she was looking straight at Angel.

Angel stopped mid-kick, turned and stared at

the woman. She squeaked and shot down under Isis's seat, cold-shivering straight through her legs.

Isis sat still, breathing shallow and fast.

"Um, I'm not sure what you mean..." she said.

"Please," whispered the woman, "there's no need for evasion with me. Not when we're already friends." She smiled, her teeth dangling yellow from her gums, her eyes glinting like backlit sapphires.

Isis gasped, pulling as far away as she could. The eyes weren't the woman's own! Someone else was looking out through her sockets.

"Surely you've heard of possession?" whispered the woman, lifting her hands from the seat. They dangled at her wrists, jerky and puppet-like. "It's quite fun, once you learn how."

"Mandeville?" Isis mouthed the name, not wanting to speak it aloud.

The woman dipped her head.

Now, Isis could make out the wrinkled features of an old man, sitting like memory inside the woman's face. And deeply hidden behind Mandeville's blue eyes, Isis could just see the woman's closed eyelids. As if she were sleeping.

"You shouldn't do that!" hissed Isis. "Get out of her, right now!"

"No. She's my protection." The ghost sniffed through the woman's nose. "In any case, I'm not hurting her. She'll think she fell asleep during the performance; she'll be disappointed, but that's all."

"Why do you need protection?"

He didn't answer, but his expression gave Isis a touch of fear. Mandeville seemed to bring fear with him.

She watched the performance in silence for a few minutes, then she turned to Mandeville.

"Why are there so few ghosts here?" she asked. "There were loads at Cally's performances."

The ghost/woman looked back at the few lonely spirits haunting the rear of the theatre. There was something like pity on his/her face.

"All but the fools know not to," he said quietly.

Isis nodded. What would be the point, if Philip Syndal was known to be a phoney? Cally's tour had been her first – maybe all those ghosts had been checking her out?

"But how does he do it?" she asked. "How does he get all this stuff right, when there aren't any ghosts telling him?"

The middle-aged woman regarded her with centuries-old eyes, and Mandeville's next words were loud enough for everyone around them to hear. "A lot of it is done using the techniques of magicians and illusionists; essentially he has learned how to guess well. The really precise, accurate titbits are garnered from letters." The woman lifted a plump, wedding-ringed finger to her nose. "Someone writes to him, telling him all about their dear departed, who they're desperate to contact. And he writes back saying he's too busy to do individual readings, 'but here's a free ticket to one of my forthcoming shows, do come along'." Mandeville sighed from inside the woman. "The poor supplicant is so grateful, and once they're here, they quite forget they've already told him everything he needs to know."

"Shut up will you?" said a man in the row behind, leaning forwards. "You don't know what you're talking about!"

The ghost twisted the woman's head, fixing the man with frightening eyes.

"Oh but I do." The possessed woman's hand landed heavily on Isis's shoulder. "And so does she."

Chapter Twelve

Isis

Philip put his fingers to his forehead. On a large video screen at the side of the stage, his fingernails gleamed in close-up. Next to him, a young woman was visibly shaking, her hands clutching a photograph.

The screen showed Philip's face. His eyes were tight shut. He was sweating, the collar of his shirt darkened and damp.

"Your brother is far away." Philip's voice sounded strained. "He's travelled a great distance into the realm beyond… He must have had a very troubled life, to go so far, and so quickly."

The young woman choked a sob, tears slipping from her eyes.

Further down the rows, Isis could see Cally leaning forwards in her seat, hands over her mouth.

Philip kept his fingers at his brow for a moment longer, then he dropped his hands, panting, and shook his head.

"I'm sorry," he said, the words trembling, "I couldn't reach him." He breathed deeply through his nose, and took a gentle hold of the young woman's hands, looking directly into her eyes. The camera zoomed in on them. "He doesn't want to turn, not yet," Philip said quietly, "and I can't force him."

"*Owowoo...*" The young woman's grief wailed out of her. Philip held her as she cried on his shoulder until an usher appeared from the wings, holding a box of tissues, and Philip carefully extracted himself from the girl's arms, passing her across. The audience applauded uncertainly, some calling out sympathetic comments to the girl as she was helped away. Philip Syndal left the spotlight, walking with sharp steps to the back of the stage, where someone rushed out with a glass of water and a towel. He took them with angry movements, scrubbing at his neck with the towel while the video screen showed empty blue.

Worried murmurs threaded through the audience.

"Is he all right?"

"Well he can't get them all, can he?"

"He must be feeling terrible."

Isis was nudged, hard, by the woman in the next seat.

"A very clever deception, don't you think?" Mandeville whispered through the woman's mouth. "He's very practised at this."

Isis wanted to ignore him, but…

"How is that lying?" she hissed back. "He said he couldn't reach her brother."

The possessed woman made a gasping noise, which might have been laughter.

"He's using the truth as a lie. He does that a lot. Of course, the girl's dead brother isn't here, I expect it was a random strike on the name he called out. But a young girl, with a suicide sibling… all that pent-up feeling, just effervescing inside her. Phil must have been quaking in his boots. Think how it would have looked if he'd got *those* details wrong! Not good for his performance, I think you'd agree. Whereas now…" The ghost flapped the woman's hand, gesturing at the conversations continuing around them.

People were worrying about Philip, and whether the performance might end early. Isis couldn't hear anyone doubting his ability.

"But he failed. Shouldn't that prove he's not a real clairvoyant?" she whispered.

The ghost/woman's hand lifted awkwardly, slapping heavily onto Isis's arm.

"It doesn't prove anything of the sort." The woman's features pulled into a sharp frown. "Phil didn't say he *couldn't* contact the brother, only that the boy's spirit *wouldn't* speak to him." Blue eyes sparkled icily. "Your mother could learn some tricks from him."

Isis turned away, furious.

On stage, Philip Syndal had returned to the spotlight. His shoulders were drooping a little now, and he looked tired.

"I'd like to apologise for what just happened," he said quietly. "Especially to Amy, who so bravely came up here. Sometimes journeys to the beyond are not…" he sighed, glancing briefly to the side of the stage "… straightforward. Sometimes those gone before us don't want to be reached. They don't want to come back to this world." He lifted his head, pulling back his shoulders. "So I'm not sure it would be right to continue tonight. I feel it would be better to call an early end to this seance and, of course, I will refund anyone who feels unhappy about this. I will also be signing books afterwards in the foyer."

"No!"

"Don't"

The shouts came from all around. People were on their feet, calling up to him, begging him to continue. Philip smiled, but shook his head, taking off his microphone as if preparing to leave the stage. People stamped their feet, and a roar started to build in the theatre. Philip watched, not-quite astonished, and then raised his hands for quiet. The stamping and shouts sputtered out.

"Thank you, thank you," he said. "Your support really means so much to me. I couldn't leave such a wonderful audience!" He attached the stage microphone back into his ear, as the audience erupted into cheers. Philip smiled into the applause, and when it had faded, he spoke again.

"This has been a difficult session, and so, to help me through the rest of the night, I'm going to call on the assistance of my spirit guide, who first helped me when I was only fifteen."

The audience sighed, and there was some more clapping. Isis couldn't see a spirit guide on the stage, of course. There were no spirits with Philip at all, it was just more of his performance.

The ghost/woman made a little noise, almost a whimper.

Isis turned, and saw Mandeville sitting stiffly inside the woman, her hands clamped on the armrests.

"Now you should pay attention," he muttered through her mouth.

On stage, Philip Syndal brought his hands together. "All right, if anyone else has a loved one they'd like to contact?"

Arms shot up, and Philip peered out from the spotlight, deciding who to choose.

Isis sank back in her seat.

"He's just another fraud!" she whispered.

"No, he isn't," said Mandeville quietly. "But he is a waste of his talent." Isis looked at him, surprised, and Mandeville turned the woman's head stiffly towards her. "He was never as good as you, my dear, but he had real psychic ability, once."

She felt like he'd just turned everything upside down, she was struggling to follow things. "But... you just told me his show is done by tricks!" she said.

Mandeville nodded. "Now it is. But when he was your age, he was a bright fire."

Isis stared back at Philip Syndal. Was he really psychic? If he was, why would he pretend not to be? Or was Mandeville playing tricks as well?

She turned to the ghost. "You said all real psychics go mad! He doesn't seem mad at all."

Mandeville smiled sadly with the woman's mouth. "As I said, my dear, you should pay attention."

Isis looked at Philip Syndal, but she couldn't see anything. Then, at the back of the stage, she saw a flash in the deepest blue. Only for an eye-blink, the colour taking on the form of something huge, shapeless and billowing.

Were those wings beating?

She watched, carefully, and saw the blue shadow again. Moving from the stage, shifting every time she blinked, until it reached the top of the theatre curtains. It hung there, shimmering in and out of focus, barely visible.

Were they using a projector? Was this part of the show?

Isis craned her neck, staring up. The shadow faded and reappeared, like the flicker of leaves on a windy day. It started heading further upwards, and Isis followed it with her eyes, straining them, trying to focus on it.

Still there was no reaction in the theatre.

Deep violet, shadowy wings drooped from the ceiling, flaring out above the audience. Narrowing her eyes, Isis could see something gripping onto the gilded plasterwork.

Hands? Claws? There were definitely eyes, staring down at Philip Syndal.

He was at the far left of the stage, talking to an elderly woman called Mavis.

"Edith says George is fine, and he sends his love." Philip smiled at the white-haired lady, squashed into her wheelchair. She was parked at the end of one of the rows, handbag on her lap.

"I'll be seeing them soon, I shouldn't wonder," she said cheerfully.

Philip Syndal looked sideways at nothing, then chuckled.

"Edith says there's no rush. Take your time and enjoy the grandchildren."

The audience laughed. A few people called out, "Ah bless" and "Sweet".

Philip thanked Mavis and walked back to centre stage, turning to the audience. He opened his hands.

"Now I think the time really has come to draw this seance to a close. Those departed friends who wished to speak have done so, and we are nearing the end of the night…" People groaned in the audience, and Philip shook his head, as if sorry to disappoint them. "There is just one last spirit I want to call on." He paused. "Julian Chambers."

There was a cry at the back of the theatre.

"Me! That's me! Oh thank you! I'm here, I've been waiting! I need to speak to my Greta, I didn't say the things I should have…"

Isis turned, astonished. The shouts were coming from one of the ghosts at the back of the theatre. A short, barely visible man, with straggly grey hair and wearing an old-fashioned corduroy jacket. He rushed forwards, heading to the stage, pushing through the oblivious crowd. People shuddered in their seats, shivering as he passed straight through them. An elderly lady was half-standing up, her hand raised.

"Here, Greta! I'm here!" the ghost shouted at her, waving his arms, almost jumping with delight. "Just wait another moment and I'll be speaking to you again, after all these years!"

On stage, Philip Syndal was staring out into the theatre. He put his fingers to his forehead, slowly, and stayed in pose for a few moments. Then he dropped his hands, shaking his head.

"I'm sorry. It seems this spirit isn't with us tonight after all."

"No! NO! I *am* here!" the ghost shrieked, wading

down the slope of the audience. The elderly woman sat back down again, clearly not sure if it had been a mistake, while the ghost looked torn between reaching out to her and continuing his rush to the front.

Next to Isis, Mandeville was observing the frantic spirit with a pitying yet scornful expression.

At the front of the theatre, Philip Syndal opened his hands. "So, I think we've come to the end of the show."

"No! I'm HERE!" screamed the ghost, flinging himself towards the stage and Philip.

Isis saw a flutter of violet, high up on the ceiling. Shimmering wings pulled back, a grip loosened from the carved plaster. She heard a soundless sigh, like an inward rush of breath, and the something dropped in shifting blue. Straight down, straight for the audience below. A splash of colour landed on the stage. A swirl of violet poured upwards from the puddle, filled with eyes and open mouths, folding itself around Philip Syndal and the ghost right in front of him. The living man didn't even notice, but the ghost's pleading to speak with Greta was cut off with a cry.

There was another soundless sigh, like a breath being exhaled, and violet-blue barely visible wings flapped upwards. Philip Syndal was unharmed, unaffected, but the ghost of Julian Chambers was carried away. His head and body were lost in the ooze, only his legs stuck out from the flickering nothing. They kicked weakly as the creature flew back into the air. When it reached the ceiling, it faded into the plaster and disappeared.

On stage, Philip Syndal smiled, then stepped out of the spotlight. It winked off, and in the same moment all the house lights came up.

Wild clapping poured around the theatre. People whistled and whooped, crying, "More! More!" Cally was on her feet, clapping madly. Everyone was cheering, except Isis. And the middle-aged woman next to her.

She was blinking into the light, rubbing her eyes and looking around.

"Has he started yet?" she asked.

Her eyes and her tired face were her own again. The ghost who'd been squatting inside her was gone.

Chapter Thirteen

Gray

I knew it was getting serious when Dad invited them on one of his chasing trips. I mean, he never did that before, not with any of his other girlfriends. I came into the kitchen and he was on his mobile, asking Cally.

I stopped dead in the doorway.

"Dad, you can't!" I cried, but Dad just cut his hand in the air to shut me up, and when he put the phone down, he said, "That was really rude, Gray. Luckily Cally didn't hear you."

"You can't bring them along!" I said.

Dad turned his frown up a notch.

"Why not? It'll be fun. Anyway, Cally wants to see what I do, and I want to show her."

"But it won't be the same if *they* come."

Dad opened a bag of bread that was on the worktop, and took out some slices.

"If you don't like it, Gray, you can stay at home." He went to the fridge and shoved things about until he found the butter and the cheese. "Or, I can rearrange it for one of the weekends you're at your mum's."

"If that's what you want!" I stamped into the living room, turning the telly on. It was some stupid bloke playing stupid golf, and I didn't even turn over.

Dad followed me in a minute later, holding two plates. There was a cheese sandwich on each of them.

"Here's your lunch." He put my sandwich on the arm of the sofa. "Are you going to waste electricity watching that?"

I didn't answer, just stared at the golf. Dad started eating his lunch.

"I'm not changing my mind," he said, chewing. "Cally's coming with me. You can join us, or not."

Like I said, that's how it is with Dad.

"Is Isis coming?" I asked.

Dad nodded. "Of course. You won't be on your own or anything. She'll be there to keep you company."

Which just showed how much he knew.

Cally and Isis were late. We'd already set up the gear, and the camper was parked as out of sight as Dad could get it. Which wasn't very, cos Dad's calculations had got us to the middle of this big, flat, open field. There were a couple of straggly, half-dead trees, but mainly it was just wheat and the sky. Not even any hedges, just a barbed-wire fence running either side of the track we'd come along. We climbed through, so Dad could take readings out in the field, and it was like wading into a swishing, rustling sea.

We'd timed it to get there late, just before sunset, because the only thing to hide in was the dark, but Cally and Isis hadn't turned up. Dad kept looking back down the bridleway, then checking his watch and peering at the low-down sun.

"If they don't get here soon, they'll struggle to find us."

"Yeah, that'd be terrible," I muttered, plonking our camp chairs on the grass next to the dusty track, and letting Dad's fall over.

"Keep your attitude to yourself," snapped Dad. That was when we heard wheels running on dirt, and I spotted their dirty orange car heading our way.

Dad ran to meet them, shouting directions about

where they should park. And when Cally had finished scraping her car up onto the grass, he didn't even wait for her to get out. Just squashed his head in through the open driver's window and started kissing her.

The passenger door whacked open and Isis shot out.

"Hi," she said to me.

"Hi."

We didn't really speak apart from that. I mean, what was there to say?

Eventually Dad stopped snogging Cally, and helped get their stuff out. Not that they'd brought any proper gear. Isis had this thin, flowery sleeping bag, and Cally didn't even have that, just a coat and a blanket.

"We don't really do camping," Cally said, smiling at Dad. "I thought we could all go in your camper van if it starts raining."

"There are only two beds," I said to her. "Dad took the others out so he could fit more boxes in. You'll have to sleep on the floor or something."

Dad glared at me over Cally's shoulder.

"You and me can squeeze in together," he said to her, and she giggled.

"Is it going to rain?" Isis asked me.

"I really hope not."

Isis was holding two garden chairs, those cheap canvas fold-out ones you buy in garages. She clunked them along a bit further, then dropped them onto the grass.

"Are you going to light a fire?" she asked.

"You joking?" I said. "We might as well call the police ourselves, and ask them to come and arrest us."

She looked at me blankly. Of course, she didn't know about farmers or anything. How they hate people camping on their land. How they really hate UFO spotters like me and Dad. We've got chased off a few times – Land Rovers turning up at two in the morning, filled with shouting blokes and a gang of dogs running after.

Dad was showing Cally all the monitors, and the laptop and everything.

"I'm really confident about my predictions now. I'm getting much better results than the early days. I found a link to fractional fluctuations in the electromagnetic field, and developed an algorithm that can predict the levels in advance..." He yakked on, and Cally picked up one of the EM field monitors, turning it upside down to look at it.

"I think it's wonderful, the work you're doing," she said. "Do you study patterns of ley lines too? I'm sure everything's connected with places where the earth's energy is strong. The ancients knew that; Stonehenge isn't that far away from here, is it?"

"About twenty-five miles, I think," said Dad, taking the monitor off her, recalibrating it and putting it back in place. If I'd picked it up like that, he would've really shouted at me. "But you're right, there are some very unique electromagnetic fluctuations in this part of the country. We hardly know anything about it really. Most scientists won't touch this kind of work, because the government always cuts funding for any research that shows the truth about aliens."

"It's just the same with the spirit world," said Cally. "All these so-called scientists, trying to discredit psychics. Phil says it's because they're frightened of what we know. Did you know he was investigated by one of the newspapers? They said he was conning people out of money, that he's a charlatan. But actually, he never even charges for private readings. People just give him money, and he can't help it if they want to give him thousands of pounds, can he?"

They carried on like that for ages, agreeing with each other, standing a bit too close together. When I couldn't take any more, I walked over to my camp chair and bundled my stuff into it. Then I picked the whole lot up and started heading off down the track.

"Hey, where are you going?" Dad called. I turned round, looking at him over the top of my gear.

"I'm going that way," I said.

Dad glared, and put his arm around Cally. "Do what you want, Gray."

"I *will*," I said, and started walking again. Fast, kicking up the dust. I didn't stop, even though I'd got this really awkward grip on the chair and one of the hinges was digging right into my hand.

Then I heard feet thumping after me, and I dropped the lot, ready to sort things out with Dad. But it wasn't him, it was Isis. She was running after me with her garden chair and her rubbish sleeping bag, feet tripping on the pot-holey track.

"Can I come too?" she said.

I didn't answer. She probably saw what I thought on my face.

"Don't go too far, Isis!" Cally called out to her, waving. "Keep where we can see you."

Me and Isis both looked back. Now Dad had his arms

around Cally's waist, pulling her tight to him.

"I can't stay with *them*, can I?" said Isis.

I sighed, then nodded. She had things worse than me, really. I could always get a break from them at Mum's.

We walked along the track into the twilight, until we got far enough away. Then we put down our chairs and got settled in. The sun dropped behind the horizon, the wheat stilled, and the only sound was a plane roaring at the far end of the sky. There weren't any swallows or sky larks, not even any bats darting. You never see anything flying over those big fields, because there's no insects for them to eat. There's this birdwatcher who writes in *Wildlife Monthly,* and he says those massive fields should be called green deserts, because there's nothing living in them but wheat.

Anyway, me and Isis sat in our chairs, watching the world get darker and the stars get brighter. Me and Dad always used to talk through that time. Like, he'd ask me how things were going at school, or tell me about school when he was a kid. Talking about stuff was half the reason I went out with him, you know?

It wasn't the same with Isis, and we sat in silence for ages, hours probably. I got in my sleeping bag, she got in hers. I played some games on my DS, she watched the stars. I was actually nearly falling asleep when she said quietly:

"I'm sorry."

I twisted round in my chair. She was looking at her hands.

"I'm sorry for laughing about your dad thinking it was aliens." She fiddled her fingers together. "My mum's weird too."

"My dad's not…" I stopped. Who was I kidding? "It's all right." I shrugged. "Mum laughs about it all the time."

Isis looked up.

"Is your mum nice?" she asked.

I shrugged, then I smiled. "Yeah. She's not bad."

"Do you think she minds?" Isis nodded her head towards the camper van. Dad and Cally were lit greeny-white from all the monitor screens. They were both squeezed into one chair.

"About them two?" I nearly laughed. "I don't think Mum even keeps track any more."

Isis winced at that, turning away.

"But," I said, "I think it's different this time. With Cally. I think it's serious."

I wanted her to feel better, you know? Only Isis said, "Oh," and I couldn't tell if she thought it was good or bad. She moved in her chair, creaking it.

"Can your mum really see them?" I asked. "Ghosts, I mean."

Isis creaked her chair again.

"I... don't know. She says she can hear them." She looked at me again, like she was studying me.

"Have you seen any UFOs?" she asked.

"Yeah, I have actually! It was amazing, and I filmed it. You can watch it on YouTube if you want."

"Do you just tell people? Don't they think you're... mad or anything?"

I shrugged. "I filmed it, didn't I? People can see for themselves."

"Oh, yes. You have proof." Isis went silent for a bit. "What if you didn't, would you still tell?"

I shrugged again. "It depends who."

"Would you tell me?"

I thought about her mum, and how Isis keeps herself to herself. How she'd said sorry for laughing at my dad.

"Maybe. Probably."

Isis was quiet for a long time after that.

"*I* can see them," she whispered, at last.

"You can see what?"

"Ghosts." She looked down at her lap. "I see them all the time."

WHAT?

Oh, I shouldn't have raised my voice. I was surprised, that's all. No, don't struggle, don't try to get up. You are feeling relaxed, feeling safe. Lie back, that's right. You trust me, you want to tell me all about her.

Chapter Fourteen

Isis

Her heart was beating a frenzy, the aftershock of telling him. Gray was staring at her, eyebrows drawn together, like she was a puzzle he had to untangle.

But he wasn't laughing.

"You serious?" he asked. She nodded. "Are you sure it's not like..." he waved a hand "... seeing shadows from the corner of your eye and not really knowing what they are?"

Isis glanced at her lap. Angel was snuggled into the sleeping bag, her blurry little head poking straight out through the fabric. She wasn't a shadow at the edge of Isis's vision; she always made sure she was the centre of attention.

"I can see them." Isis looked at Gray. "Like I can see you." She took a deep breath. "I'm not crazy or anything.

We went to see this therapist, me and Mum, and she said I was really normal." She was talking fast, trying to convince him.

Gray blinked. In his sleeping bag he looked like a caterpillar. "A therapist? Was that cos of your dad leaving?"

"Not just my dad. It was Angel too. My little sister. She was run over. Killed…"

Gray nodded. "Dad said, but not anything else…" His eyes were wide, his face a question.

Isis took a deep breath. She'd gone too far to stop now. And she'd had to tell the tale before, anyway. To teachers, to the school counsellor. She'd found a way of telling it, so it didn't hurt too badly.

"Mum took us out to the countryside, she wanted to show us this standing stone, I think. I can't really remember now. But we had to walk along the road for a bit, to reach the start of the footpath. And Angel…" A small, nearly see-through face looked up at Isis – Angel, round-eyed, listening to the tale about herself. "She ran on ahead, wouldn't stop when Mum shouted. I tried to catch her, but this car…"

Isis had been complaining, that was the part she didn't tell. How she'd been moaning about having to walk, about having to go out. She'd wanted to go home; she said it over and over, watching her mum get crosser and crosser.

Why had she made such a fuss? Why couldn't she have just been good that day? Isis couldn't remember, maybe it didn't matter anyhow? Except it did, more than anything.

She'd stepped in a puddle when they'd been about halfway between the lay-by and the start of the footpath. The mud and water had slopped cold inside her sandal.

"I can't even walk now!" she remembered crying, furiously, and shaking her sodden foot. Cally had finally lost her temper, shouting back, yanking at Isis's sandal and pulling off her mud-stained sock. Neither of them had noticed Angel, running on ahead.

"She was only three," Isis whispered to Gray. "She didn't know to stay off the road, not really."

Angel had been playing a game, jumping on and off the grassy verge, and it had led her away from them. Not far, only a handful of metres. But it was where the lane curved away round a bend, where a tall, blowsy hedge blocked any sight of what was coming.

It was Isis who'd seen her first. Isis who'd raced, one foot bare, to catch her.

"Angel!" she'd shouted. "You mustn't go on the road!"

Cally had gasped, dropping Isis's sock.

"Stand still both of you!" she'd cried, running behind Isis. "Get on the grass!" But Isis had ignored Cally, and Angel had ignored them both, hopping up onto the verge, then back onto the tarmac.

Isis had just reached her when the car came round the bend.

Its brakes were already screeching when it hit, and Isis remembered the driver's face, rigid with horror. She remembered the strange, shattering sensation of being hit, and seeing Angel fly over the bonnet.

When she'd opened her eyes, she was lying next to Angel in the road. Angel was staring at her, but even though dazed and filled with pain, Isis could see how terribly wrong Angel was. Her head was twisted one way, her body the other. Isis stretched out her hand, and took hold of Angel's.

"Her eyes were open," Isis said to the night and the sleeping wheat. Next to her, Gray was silent. "And then she died."

Like a sigh, like some invisible change.

She remembered how much it had hurt. She remembered Cally, screaming and clinging to Angel. The driver of the car running over and gabbling into his phone, begging for an ambulance to come quickly.

"And then, Angel got up. Her body was still on the ground, but she was sitting next to me as well, still holding my hand. Like she'd just... stepped out of herself." The little ghost on Isis's lap nodded.

"I do that," said Angel.

Isis smiled down at her. "It was her ghost, you see? I knew she was dead because I could see her ghost."

She looked across at Gray. His eyes were white against the dark, his mouth open.

"And... then what?" he asked.

Isis shrugged, her sleeping bag slithering off one shoulder. "She just sort of... hung around. And I started seeing other ghosts." With one hand, she pulled the sleeping bag back up again. "Maybe I'd seen them before that? I don't remember though."

Gray twitched, looking around quickly.

"Are there any here?" he whispered.

"Me!" cried Angel.

"Yes," smiled Isis.

Gray pulled into his chair, going very still.

"Where are they then?" he asked. His voice was too loud, a challenge.

"With me," said Isis. "It's just Angel. She's around most

of the time actually." She looked down. "Don't you have anywhere else to go?" she teased.

Angel leaned up and kissed Isis on her chin. Like being brushed by spider's silk.

"I lub you and I lub Mummy," said Angel. "That why I here."

"I love you too," whispered Isis, and turned back to Gray. He was staring at her.

"You've got a ghost sitting on your *lap?*" he asked.

Isis nodded.

Gray jerked backwards in his camping chair, nearly knocking it over. Then he steadied himself, and started laughing.

"You're winding me up, aren't you?" he said. "That's a good one, especially out here." He sat down in his chair again. "You're weird, you do know that?"

"I'm not joking!" said Isis. A sudden desperation filled her, just to have someone she could tell, someone who believed her!

"Yeah, right," said Gray.

"I'm not!"

Angel started wriggling, pulling herself out of the sleeping bag, her wisp of a body emerging through the cloth.

"I here!" she shouted at Gray. "I here!"

Angel scrambled onto the ground, a cold shiver in the summer night. Flowery-sandaled feet stamped soundlessly on the dirt, little fists sat on Angel's hips as she planted herself in front of Gray. The white dust path showed clearly through her.

"I HERE!" she shouted, in a voice that would have woken the field, except only Isis could hear it. "I HERE!"

There was the tiniest of flickers on Gray's face, his only reaction. Angel glared at him, her lip wobbled, and she started to cry.

Isis unzipped her sleeping bag and got out of her chair. She crouched down next to Angel, and carefully took hold of one of her hands, like unfolding a baby's whisper. Isis focused on her own fingers, using them to find the nothing-fizz of Angel's cheek, and stroke away invisible tears.

Gray pushed back in his chair. Its legs caught in the grass and it toppled behind him.

"What are you *doing*?" he asked.

Isis stayed kneeling.

"You upset her. She's crying now."

"I upset a ghost?"

"She's only three."

Gray's sleeping bag was puddled around his knees, and his arms were out, as if he were trying to ward her off. Isis ignored him.

"Are you all right?" she whispered to Angel. The little ghost head bobbed a yes. Isis stood up, keeping hold of Angel's hand.

Gray's arms thumped to his sides.

"You are *really* weird."

Isis's heart was beating more slowly now, the calm pulse of hidden anger. He didn't believe her, he thought she was weird. Well, so did everyone else.

"Just forget it," she said. "You were right, I was only joking." She smiled, trying to look happy. "I had you going though, didn't I?"

His face was a blank, confused.

"You were joking?" He was looking at her fingers, still curled around Angel's. He shook his head.

"Are you holding hands with it?"

"I not IT!" shouted Angel. "I a girl!"

Isis started laughing, she couldn't help it.

"What are you doing now?" snapped Gray.

Isis caught her laughter, pulled herself back.

"Nothing," she said.

Gray kicked his way out of his sleeping bag, staring hard at the space next to Isis's hand, slightly off where Angel was standing.

"I can't see anything," he said, squinting and frowning.

But he was trying.

"You looking WRONG way!" cried Angel, darting towards him. Isis felt a weightless pull on her arm, her fingers still linked with Angel's. The ghost swiped with her free hand, trying to slap at Gray. Isis waited for the shiver, for the brief, unnoticed cold as the ghost passed through him.

"Whuh?" Gray was staring, eyes wide. Angel's hand was stuck to his.

It only lasted for a moment, a heartbeat – Angel holding hands with Isis, and holding hands with Gray. A stretched-mist child, linking them together.

But it was like a jolt of electricity. It was like when she first saw Angel, back at the roadside.

Gray let out a wordless shout, amazement and fear working his face. He jerked backwards, his feet catching in the sleeping bag, and tumbled over his fallen chair, tripping on the thin metal legs. He landed heavily on the ground, his hand out of Angel's.

Chapter Fifteen

Gray

I saw her! I know you aren't going to believe this, but I did.

This girl, this little ghost-girl, with curly hair and big brown eyes. She was see-through, but not like a skeleton or anything, actually she was sort of chunky. And she was wearing this pink dress and sandals with flowers on. I mean, she was right there, looking at me – but not, at the same time. Like she wasn't quite in the right place, or your eyes couldn't get focused or something.

I'm not making it up. I was holding onto a ghost! I could see her fingers in my hand. I could see my hand through her fingers.

Then I think I might have made a noise or something, cos she let go.

And the next thing I was flat on my back on the grass, and the only person I could see was Isis.

Angel? You saw her?

I do believe you, Gray. You couldn't make it up, even if you wanted to...

But who will look after my little Angel, now Isis is gone?

Chapter Sixteen

Isis

Gray got to his feet.

Isis hobbled back a step. Angel was clinging to one of her legs, freezing it into numbness.

Gray turned his head from side to side, staring down, searching the dark grass. He picked up his chair, looking underneath it, then lifted his sleeping bag, opening it to peer inside. He turned to Isis, his eyebrows scrunched.

"Are you okay?" asked Isis. "Did you hurt yourself?"

He shook his head.

"She's got curly hair," he said.

Isis stared at him.

"And she's wearing this pink dress, and sandals with flowers on."

The world fell into silence. The wheat stopped growing

and the stars froze onto the night. There was nothing, anywhere, except her own breathing.

"You saw her?" she whispered.

Gray nodded.

"He SEE me!" shouted Angel. She flung herself away from Isis's leg, jumping up and down without actually touching the ground.

Her numb leg gave way, and Isis sat down heavily on the grass.

"I can't see her now," said Gray. "It was only for a second. Just now."

Isis turned the moment over in her mind.

"When her hand was in yours?" she asked.

Gray nodded.

Angel's dance turned into an aeroplane flight, arms stretched wide as she flew around them.

"Will you hold Gray's hand again?" Isis asked her. Angel shot behind Isis, pulling her arms in tight. She peered round at Gray, then shook her head.

"No."

"But you just did!" Isis pushed herself up to standing.

"I not want to *now*," said Angel, putting her hands behind her back. "He too big."

"Please, Angel, don't you want him to see you again?" Isis made a move for Angel, but the little ghost skittered away, shaking her head even harder.

"No no! I not *want* to!"

"What's going on?" asked Gray, looking blankly around.

Isis stood still, and sighed. "She's being awkward, like usual."

"I not orkard!" Angel's mouth fixed into a pout, she started fading.

"No! Angel, don't!" Isis lunged for the little ghost, but she'd already misted into nothing. Isis turned to Gray. "I think she's gone a bit shy."

They sat in their chairs, looking up, letting the star-filled night press down on them. Cally and Gil were near the black lump of the camper van, surrounded by a pattern of blue and green lights, some along the track, some glowing out of the field. Gil's UFO monitors, relentlessly measuring.

"Will she come back?" asked Gray.

Isis shrugged. "Usually she sulks for an hour or so, but I don't know about now. She's never been seen by anyone else before. I think it scared her. She's always saying it's what she wants, and she was really happy. But then she just vanished."

Gray stretched out his legs, nylon-whispering his sleeping bag.

"Has your mum seen her?"

Isis shook her head.

"Have you told your mum you can see her?"

Isis shook her head again. "After Angel died, she got really depressed." Lost in a dark world, unreachable. "I wanted to tell her, but I... couldn't."

Her dad had been around, for a few weeks after Isis got out of hospital, but he and Cally had filled the air with fighting and crying. When he went away again, the house had seemed too quiet to speak in, too empty. The words had sat on her tongue every day, the imagined answer to everything her mum said.

"Did you have a good day at school?"

Angel's still with us.

"What do you want for tea?"

I see her all the time.

She'd never said them, of course. She'd never known if they'd make things better or worse. Not long after, Cally had said she was going to become a psychic, and even at not-quite eight years old Isis had understood what a fragile strand her mum was clinging to. She'd known then she definitely couldn't say anything about Angel.

Isis watched a star twinkle in reds and yellows, just above the horizon.

"And now it's been so long, and she says *she's* the psychic."

Gray was watching her, frowning.

"What does that matter? Won't it make her happy?"

Isis stared at him, then shrugged. "She *is* happy. Since she met your dad."

Gray went quiet, looking away.

"How long did you see Angel for?" she asked him.

His eyes turned back to her. "Like I said, just a second."

He didn't seem special, or gifted. Especially not swaddled in his sleeping bag.

"I just don't understand why it happened," said Isis. "No one else has ever seen her."

"Maybe I'm psychic too?" said Gray, hopeful sounding.

"Maybe."

But Isis remembered the first time she'd seen him, back in the garden. Angel had touched Gray then, kicked him actually, and he hadn't noticed. This time, Isis had been holding onto Angel as well. Was that the difference?

"We should wait until she gets back," said Gray excitedly,

"then we can try again and…" His eyes flashed with a sudden reflected light. His face was bleached by it, every curl of his hair gleaming like wire. The flowers on Isis's sleeping bag leaped into colour, and she squinted against the brightness. In the distance, Gil was shouting.

Gray leaped up off his chair, scrambled out of his sleeping bag and ran for the camper van.

Isis stumbled to standing, still caught in her sleeping bag, putting her hands up against the blinding light. Looking down, she saw the grass lit into luminous green.

Then, darkness.

She couldn't see a thing for a moment, her eyes struggling to adjust. She could hear Gray's feet on the track, running away from her.

"It's happening!" Gray called back. "Come on, Isis!"

"Oh!" she gasped, her heart flinging into fast-drumming excitement. Stray blobs of colour floated in her vision as she ran after Gray. Ahead of her, Gil was a tall shape, moving quickly between the lights of his equipment, and Gray was already helping, confident and sure. Cally stood awkwardly by herself, forgotten.

"Look at these readings!" shouted Gil. "There were spikes twenty minutes ago. It must've started but we didn't see it!" He put a pair of binoculars up to his eyes, surveying the night-time field. A new breeze rustled through the wheat. "We should have been paying more attention."

Gray was bending over a laptop screen, his finger pressed on the return key as he scrolled through some kind of graph. "The readings aren't very strong. Not like last time."

More lights blazed into the sky, flickering above the field. Isis squinted, trying to judge where they were, but it was hard even to focus on them, as if they were moving, or she was seeing them through a filter.

Gil dropped his binoculars. "The readings are weaker because it isn't centred here!" He ran for the camper van, yanking open the door and jumping in the driver's seat. He started the engine, then looked back at the others. "Come on!"

"What about the gear?" Gray yelled, following.

"Leave it! We'll come back for it after."

Gray pulled open the side door and scrambled inside the camper.

"Come on, girls!" shouted Gil. "Don't you want to see a UFO up close?"

Isis and her mum shared a glance, then they dashed for

the camper, laughing as they tumbled in. Gil wrenched at the gearstick, and the van's tyres spun over dirt.

There were no seats in the back. Isis had to cling to a rope dangling down from the roof, and Gray hung onto a cupboard handle. They crashed into boxes and each other, as the camper bumped and jolted along the bridleway. In the passenger seat, Cally peered at the track ahead, lit by the van's jittering headlamps.

"Don't you think you should go slower?" she said to Gil. "The children aren't strapped in!"

"If I slow down we'll miss it!" he shouted, hurtling the camper over another pothole, sending Isis and Gray flying upwards.

They rattled on, driving for where the sky was brightest, where the strange lights were most densely packed in the sky. Light poured in through every window of the van; they were being surrounded.

With a screeching crunch, Gil slammed the van's brakes on.

"It's too narrow to drive further," he yelled, opening his door and jumping out. "We're running from here."

"Are you all right?" Cally leaned over her seat, stretching her arm down to Gray.

"Yeah!" He jumped up from where he'd fallen, leaping out the door after his dad.

Cally climbed through to Isis, helping her out of a squashed cardboard box and looking happy, excited.

When had Cally last been like that?

Isis took her mum's hand and they scrambled from the camper, running along the dusty gravel path. Lights blazed and danced around them, throwing criss-crossing shadows. Ahead, Gray and Gil squeezed between the strands of the barbed-wire fence, pushing out into the silvery, shivering wheat.

"I didn't think it would be so bright!" cried Cally.

"Me neither," laughed Isis. It was nothing like watching Gray's film on the computer.

They reached the fence. Gil and Gray were wading dark trails into the crop. Gil had some kind of flashing box up over his head and Gray was holding a camera.

Cally put her feet onto the bottom strand of the fence, wobbling on the wire as she tried to climb over. She fell backwards, laughing.

"How do we get over this?" she shouted.

Lights flashed everywhere. The wheat flamed in gold, the metal fence glittered.

"Not over," called Gil from the field. "Climb through it!"

Cally tried again, this time bending down and squeezing between two strands, trying not to get caught by the barbs. Isis pulled the top strand up, making a wider gap for her mum.

"Look at that!" yelled Gray, just as Cally climbed into the field.

Isis looked up.

The lights were drifting upwards, just as she'd seen on Gray's film from the time he saw a UFO with his dad. She'd watched it half a dozen times on the computer, she knew what to expect.

Except, she could see now, here in real life, that they weren't just blobs of floating light. If she concentrated, she could see other shapes hidden inside. The dazzling rays lengthened into beating wings. Shards of colour grew into heads, beaks and fluttering tails. No longer drifting, the light-birds were flying upwards, circling. A flock on the wing. Gleaming like stained glass, they filled the heavens in a vast, rising spiral. Singing in a deafening cloud, piping out their songs as she watched them for a heartbeat, for a lifetime.

Then, all at once, they dropped like stars tumbling from the sky. A chaos of falling, their silver wings missing each other by the smallest ruffles of air. The sky emptied, as the great, shining flock plummeted into nothing…

Isis gasped in the sudden darkness. Cool air filled her lungs, her hands were clutching the wire fence. She was back on the ground again, the grass soft-brushing against her ankles.

In the field, Cally was a black silhouette near Gray and Gil. She turned around, waving at Isis.

"Come on," Cally called. "What are you waiting for?"

"Uh…" Isis swallowed, tried again. "I'm just coming." Her voice sounded strange and wobbly, but no one noticed.

She checked the fence for barbs, then carefully gripped the wires. They gleamed molten between her fingers, the field pulsing into a headachy orange-red. Looking up, Isis saw a huge ball of light growing out of nothing.

She saw it explode.

Streamers of silent fire flew outwards, engulfing Gil, Cally and Gray, dissolving them into orange-sparkling vapour. Isis tried to scream, but the light poured through her, past her, carrying her voice away. Yellow haze swirled and blew in the air. It flowed between her ribs, streaming from her fingers and out through her eyes. Now ribbons of light drifted and tangled in the dark, pouring upwards, collecting together into a vast, single shape.

A bird.

A creature out of myth, with dazzling wings wider than the sky. The light-bird swooped above the fields, covering the world beneath with a golden shadow. Its thundering wingbeats seemed to sweep up the stars and it lifted its head to let out a silvery cry. A single booming version of the flock's piping chatter. The sound echoed across the wide, flat wheat fields, and for a moment Isis was sure she was standing amongst the greys and greens of a sparkling marshland. She heard the chuckle of water, smelled the saltwater scent of an incoming tide. Then the bird called again, and the ghost-marshes dried to bare earth, the sea smell turning to sewage and smoke.

"I don't understand," Isis whispered. The enormous, shining bird flapped with slow, sad wingbeats into the night and let out a last lonely cry, telling of death and the distant wash of time…

"ISIS! Where are you?"

She gasped, trying to remember where she was. Her hands were still on the barbed-wire fence, the metal biting into her palms. She unclenched her fingers, she'd been clinging on so tightly they were almost numb.

"Isis!" Cally shouted again.

She tried to answer but she couldn't get her tongue to make words, instead birdsong filled her mouth. She put a hand to her face, but her mouth was the same as normal. She just couldn't remember how to speak.

A sound was creaking and crackling all around. The stems of the wheat were snapping, folding over as if a scythe were cutting through them, falling into widening patterns of circles.

Opening and shutting her mouth, Isis managed some gasps, and then eventually two words.

"I'm here," she croaked, desperate for someone to hear her, to come over and check if she was all right.

But Gil and Cally were running across the field, chasing the waves of toppling wheat, while Gray stood filming, his face blue-lit from the camera screen. As Isis watched, the crop fell into silence. Gil ran to a stop, surrounded by the pattern of the crop circle, punching his arm in the air.

"Did you see that?" he shouted. "Did you see that? We're going to blow things wide open! We got it all this time: the UFO and the crop circle it made! No one will say crop circles are hoaxes and aliens don't exist, not after this!"

Chapter Seventeen

Gray

It must've been four in the morning by the time we got home, but it didn't matter. Everyone just bundled inside, all talking at once.

"I'll download the film," I said, heading for Dad's computer.

"Who wants a drink?" he asked.

"A cup of tea would be nice," said Cally, going with Isis into the living room.

"I mean a proper drink!" Dad said, coming from the kitchen holding two cans of lager. "This calls for a celebration."

He opened his beer, slurping it. "Is it loaded yet?" he asked me.

"Ready to go!"

We all crowded round the screen.

"Don't you think the children should go to bed?" Cally asked.

Dad laughed. "It's nearly morning anyway." He play-punched me. "And it's the holidays, so who cares?"

I leaned forwards, clicked the mouse, and the film I'd shot started playing on the screen. It looked really good, better than the last time, and I'd filmed right from the start.

"Look!" Dad paused the film, pointing at one of the lights I'd close-upped. "Do you see how it's shifting into red? That'll be the Doppler effect – they're probably travelling faster than light." He clicked the computer again, and the film played on.

"Faster than light?" said Cally.

Dad nodded. "This is some kind of travel system. Has to be."

"That's a *spaceship*?" said Cally. On screen, the lights were drawing lines, netting up the sky.

"It doesn't have to look like the Starship Enterprise," said Dad, taking a long drink from his can.

"But, could it be something else?" asked Isis.

Actually, when I said everyone was talking at once,

Isis wasn't. But that was like her, you know? Especially when Dad was around, so I didn't think much of it.

She'd got his attention now though.

"What do you mean?" he asked, his voice a bit louder. I knew he was getting ready to argue. He argues a lot with people when he gets on to UFOs.

Isis sort of shrugged.

"Are you sure it's a spaceship? It's just I thought it didn't... seem like that."

I was going to ask what she meant, but I didn't get a chance because Dad was straight in there.

"With more experience, you'll understand. If we go through the other possibilities you'll see they can all be ruled out. Firstly, the atmospheric conditions were completely wrong for a storm, and it definitely wasn't lightning. The same applies for earthlights, because those only appear before earthquakes and we haven't felt the ground shaking! Now, I know some people say crop circles can be caused by small tornados, but what we witnessed was not a tornado, plus it didn't leave a simple pattern. And it definitely wasn't hoaxers because we were right there watching..."

He went banging on like that for ages. Isis didn't say

185

anything much, just hunched up as he went on, nodding sometimes, like she was getting told off.

"So, you see?" he finished eventually. "It has to be alien technology of some kind!"

I thought Isis would've given in then, because that's what I usually do with Dad, but she really surprised me by saying, "It just didn't seem like a spaceship to me."

"Well, that's just where you're wrong…"

Dad would have given her another lecture, if Cally hadn't rescued her.

"Gil." She put her hand on his arm. "Maybe Isis means there are other aspects to what we saw."

It looked for a moment like Dad was going to start on Cally then, but you could see him getting control of himself. It showed how much he liked her, you know? He didn't tell her she was talking rubbish, he just asked, "What do you mean?"

Cally smiled. "Well, I know you have all your equipment, and of course things have to be scientifically examined. But there are other ways to test something; I myself sensed a great deal of spiritual energy out in that field. And, after all, aliens are far more enlightened than we are; they probably use spiritual forces in the way we use electricity…"

Then they really started on about aliens, spirits and all sorts of weird, completely ignoring me and Isis.

I went over to her. "Do you want something to eat?"

She nodded, and we both headed for the kitchen, leaving Dad and Cally. It was a good thing too, because they were starting to get all smoochy.

I made us some toast and peanut butter. We were both hungry, because it was gone five by then, and the last time I'd eaten was at dinner, which was yesterday!

Isis sat opposite me at the kitchen table. Chewing slowly, looking really tired, with these big purple circles under her eyes.

"What did you mean?" I asked her. "What you said to my dad."

She stopped chewing. "It just didn't look like a spaceship, that's all." And then she looked at her plate, like she was waiting for me to start on her as well.

"Because of all the lights flying around?" I asked. After all, Cally was right – nothing we saw looked much like the spaceships in films.

Isis lifted her eyes. "Did they look like lights to you?" she asked.

"Yeah, of course. I mean, they were all floating up

and stuff..." Then I stopped. I remembered who I was talking to, and what I'd seen for that second in the field, before the UFO turned up. "What did you see?" I asked.

"Birds," whispered Isis. "Thousands of them. Millions. Flying out into the sky."

I tried to believe her, but I'd only seen the rising lights, and the net across the sky, then the burning sphere. I mean, that was crazy enough, but it'd been like the time before.

"I didn't see anything that looked like birds," I said.

Isis shook her head. "I saw the lights, just like you filmed them, but the birds were there as well, at the same time."

I just didn't get it, I thought maybe she meant alien birds.

"What kind of birds were they?"

She shrugged. "I don't know, they were all the same though."

"That doesn't help much."

She thought for a moment. "They lived in the marshes," she said slowly. "There were lots of them for a long time, thousands and thousands of years. But then, not long ago, they started disappearing."

"What, like going somewhere?" I thought she meant the aliens were flying away, but she shook her head.

"Dying. They all died," she said, and she started

shivering, holding her arms tight around herself. "They kept on being killed, until none were left." She made this coughy gulp, and wiped tears off her face.

"Like going extinct?" I asked, trying to puzzle what she was saying. "You mean the aliens went extinct? But I filmed them, and their spaceship."

"Not *aliens*!" she snapped. "They were from here, from this planet."

"How can you know that?" I snapped back. "There were only lights, I *filmed* lights." It had been such a great night, and now it felt like she was trying to ruin it.

"Lots of people see lights," she said. "If they go somewhere haunted. They think they're just reflections in glass, or flickering light bulbs, but they're not. People have even filmed them."

I sucked in my breath, finally getting what she meant.

"You didn't see aliens?" I asked, and she shook her head.

"You didn't see a spaceship?"

She shook her head again.

"You filmed lights," she said, "and your dad thinks it's a UFO. But I saw the sky full of ghosts."

Oh, Isis. She was turning into such a clever girl. I always thought she'd be something special, that I'd be so proud of her one day. And now I can't even tell anyone about her, because I'm not supposed to be here.

Nothing personal, that was the first rule I had to swear to.

I know I should never have got involved, but I did... so involved my real identity was close to being revealed. And even after I gave all of them up, I couldn't stop myself from watching.

Chapter Eighteen

Isis

"It's not quite what I expected," said Cally, looking around.

Why not? The thought fizzed angrily in Isis's mind, but she kept her mouth shut. They'd had a fight last night, and they were still barely speaking to each other.

Early morning sunshine dazzled through the glass roof of Wycombe's main shopping mall, bouncing off the gleaming, tiled floor and glinting over the shopfronts with their logos and displays. The shop doors were all still closed; a woman in one of the windows was fiddling with the clothes on a mannequin. Angel helter-skeltered past, transparent in the bright light, unseen by anyone but Isis.

Cally put her bag down and stared at the tall, striped tent in front of them. Its door flaps were pulled open, and a banner taped across the top read FORTUNE TELLER. Nearby, a young man with a shaved head and patchwork trousers was laying out some juggling clubs. A bit further off, an older man dressed in a black evening suit was carefully placing various items onto a small table. A top hat, a handkerchief, a deck of cards, a wand.

Isis heard the crackle of a walkie-talkie and the centre manager bustled over to them. She was smartly dressed and thin faced, with short, grey hair and bright pink lipstick.

"Is everything all right?" she asked, but not as if she cared.

Cally pointed at the banner.

"I'm not a fortune teller," she said. "I'm a clairvoyant."

The woman was already looking past them, at the juggler. "Isn't it the same thing?" she said.

Cally shook her head. "I speak to the spirits, but they only communicate future events if they choose to."

The woman's gaze came back to Cally, eyes flicking up and down, measuring her. "Well, I'm sure no one will mind. And a fortune teller fits in much better with our circus theme." She pointed one finger at Cally's purple dress. It looked washed out, almost pink, in the bright sunshine.

"Is that your costume?"

Cally nodded. "It's what I wear for performances."

"It's not very *gypsy* though."

"That's because she's not," said Isis.

The woman regarded Isis, then asked Cally, "Who's this?"

"My daughter, Isis."

The manager's walkie-talkie crackled, and a voice garbled through about an obstruction in the bins area.

"I have to go," said the manager. "But could you try and look a bit more... ethnic? Buy a tasselled shawl or something." She glanced at Isis. "And we have very strict rules about young people loitering. Please remember that."

Her heels clicked on the floor as she walked away.

"Don't worry 'bout Mrs Parkes," said the juggler, smiling at them. The studs in his bottom lip gleamed. "She's like, high stress. But if you do all right, she'll keep on with the bookings."

Cally didn't answer, just smiled back awkwardly and opened up her bag.

"I'm not sure I want to do this any more," she said quietly.

"I never wanted to at all," said Isis.

"Are you part of the act or something?" the juggler asked Isis.

Isis looked at her mum as she answered. "No, I'm just here for the humiliation."

The young man grinned, and Cally folded her arms.

"I couldn't leave you on your own, Isis."

"Yes, you could!" snapped Isis. "Other people's parents leave them at home. Gray's dad does it all the time!"

Cally tutted. "So now you think Gil's wonderful, do you?"

"At least he doesn't treat Gray like a baby."

Cally turned to the juggler. "Do *you* think I'm being overprotective?"

He held his hands up, shaking his head. "I ain't involved in your stuff."

Cally turned to Isis.

"Gil does his thing, I do mine. I thought you understood, that after what happened…"

"Angel died," hissed Isis. "That's 'what happened'. But it was on a road, not in our flat. A car isn't going to drive up the stairs and crash into the living room!"

Cally went very still. The juggler got suddenly busy, sorting through his gear.

"Why are you being like this?" Cally asked.

"Haven't the *spirits* told you?" asked Isis, turning round

and stamping off, her footsteps echoing in the empty shopping centre. When she reached the entrance, where the glass roof gave way to sky, she stopped, wrapping her arms around herself. In front of her were two free-standing noticeboards, each one with a poster tacked onto it.

> # CIRCUS at the Garden Shopping Centre
>
> Jugglers! Clowns!
> Magicians! Fortune Telling!
> *All day, August 12th*

A security guard ambled by, followed a minute later by two early customers. An elderly lady, holding onto the arm of a middle-aged woman.

"Oh, that sounds fun," said the old lady, pointing at the noticeboards.

"Yes, Mum," said the younger woman, not even looking. "Now the first place we need to go is Debenhams, get you some vests."

Isis thought about just carrying on. Walking all the way home, then on until she reached the railway station. She imagined getting on a train, and heading for…

Where would she go? The longing for her dad cut through her. In his last email he'd said he was in South Africa. The train wouldn't get her there.

Next to the entrance was a bakery. One of the bakers brought a tray of pastries out from the back of the shop and started loading them into the glass-fronted display. A wisp of toddler-shaped steam drifted above the cakes, but the baker worked on, oblivious to the small ghost floating around him.

Isis heard footsteps behind her.

"Isis," said Cally, "I need you to come back to the stall. Remember what the manager said about loitering."

Isis didn't move.

"I'm sorry you don't want to be here," said Cally, "but I have to earn money."

Isis turned round. "You could get a job in a shop."

"What's wrong with you?" said Cally. "Why are you being so… difficult?"

"I'm not!" Isis snapped. Except that was a lie, because difficult was exactly how she felt.

Ever since that night, out in the field. It was like she'd been filled up with ants, biting and nipping her from the inside. Her skin was itchy, the way her arms moved felt wrong. She picked things up then dropped them, because her hands were suddenly wings, her fingers feathers. And every night she dreamed of flying, only to wake heavy and miserable in the morning. She was sure she'd lost something, something really important, and she couldn't even remember what it was.

She felt cross with everyone and everything. Even Angel.

Cally narrowed her eyes, examining Isis.

"It's since we went out that night with Gil and Gray, isn't it?" she said.

Isis's cheeks flashed hot. *Did she know somehow?*

"I know you're not very keen on me being with Gil…"

Isis shook her head, relieved, but also irritated. Did Cally ever think about *anything* else?

"It's not about him," Isis said, scornfully.

Cally winced.

"Then what is it, Isis? Can't you tell me?"

But she couldn't, that was the problem. Because she didn't know what was wrong, because even to start explaining would take her into places she couldn't go. So she tried to smile, pointing at the Danish pastries in the bakery window. "I'm probably just hungry," she said.

Cally frowned at her for another moment, then went into the bakery. She chose a cheap iced bun for Isis, and nothing for herself.

By 11.30 a.m., Isis was hungry again. She'd spent the morning sitting on a wooden bench with a book in her hand, as far away as Cally would allow her to be, next to a small shrubbery of plastic plants in the middle of the glass-covered atrium. Two weeks ago she could have read for the whole day, but now it was a strange torture. Her legs jittered, she shuffled and shifted on the bench. Her mind was even worse, leaping from each printed word to some random thought and then, inevitably, to the fluttering of wings.

"Restless?" A voice rasped next to her ear, a dusty whisper.

She shut her book with a snap, not moving her head but feeling the sudden chill down her side.

"Go away," she said through almost-closed lips.

From the side of her vision, she saw the crossing of

tweed trouser legs, a shower of mould spores falling onto the polished floor.

"I am sure I will, eventually," said Mandeville. "Even phantoms seem to fade in the end. In the meantime, I enjoy your modern world. Take this covered parade of shops. So vibrant and busy. I remember it was merely a market garden, in my day. Vegetables and so on, no doubt grown by surly and ignorant peasants." He stopped speaking, but he didn't leave.

Isis turned her head, trying to look like nothing was happening.

"What do you want?" she whispered.

Mandeville flicked his hand lazily in the air. "Company, my dear. Conversation."

"I can't talk," Isis said through her closed teeth. "People might see."

"Amiable silence then," said Mandeville, resting one arm on the back of the bench. Where he touched it, the varnish began to crack, green fuzz growing out of the wood. "I see your mother is busy."

Cally was in front of the fortune-teller's tent, sitting on a metal, fold-out chair. A young-looking, dark-haired woman was seated opposite her. Isis couldn't hear what they were saying, but by the tilt of her head she knew Cally was 'listening with her spirit ear'.

Mandeville glanced around the shopping centre. "I am afraid news has spread of your mother's charlatan ways. She no longer attracts spirits to her performances."

Isis slapped her book down on the bench, right through Mandeville.

"Manners, please," he said.

"There's a ghost over *there*," hissed Isis, flicking her eyes towards a pale figure moving through the mall. A thin, faded woman with a pinched face, wearing a long drab dress of rough brown material, a piece of sack tied around her shoulders as a shawl. She was walking knee deep through the floor, bending to pick up things only she could see. As she reached the shoe shop she faded into the window, a moment later reappearing where she had started, repeating her walk and bending at all the same places as before.

"The potato picker?" said Mandeville. "She has no interest in seances. She'll take no more notice of your mother than she would me, even if I were cavorting in front of her. I used to try and engage with her type, but I gave up long ago. They are frozen to their tasks, locked in their patterns. Memories of a place, or perhaps echoes in time."

Isis gave up trying to ignore him.

"Are there lots of types of ghost?" she whispered, despite herself.

Mandeville arched one of his eyebrows. "Have you observed nothing as a psychic?"

She shook her head, minutely. "I try to ignore any ghost I see. I don't want them noticing me."

Mandeville chuckled. "Oh, they notice. But to answer your question, I have categorised many forms of spirit, referenced their form and awareness. Apart from those like our bending lady, there are the phantoms who lurk in graveyards and crypts, chattering their last words. One can't get any sense out of them either. Then we have the screaming-heads who melt out of walls. I *have* managed simple conversations with them, but they don't have much to talk about. I suppose you wouldn't, stuck in a wall. And of course there are the classics, such as white-clad ladies and headless horsemen. They can converse, but it's all rather melodramatic. Curses and cruel fate, that sort of thing. Then—"

"What about birds?" said Isis, cutting him off.

He looked at her in surprise. "Are you asking if birds have ghosts?"

She nodded.

"Well they have spirits of course," said Mandeville thoughtfully. "The after realm is filled with the flutter of life turning endlessly into death. But birds as ghosts? I wonder if they would even have the desire to? As I have said, ghosts are driven by their own tragedies. Only some of us join in the haunting."

Mandeville pointed one of his fingers at an area of the shopping centre near the escalators. "Like your little ghostling."

Mandeville's withered finger was aimed in the direction of Angel, who was flitting amongst the to and fro of shoppers, near the bottom of the escalators. A toddler-shaped shadow, standing still with her arms out. Every time someone walked through her, shivering in the unexpected chill, Angel let out a shout of delighted, noiseless laughter.

"Rather childish behaviour, I must say."

"She *is* a child," said Isis.

Mandeville turned his blue gaze back to Isis.

"No, she is a phantom. And she can be devoured, like the rest of us."

He dropped the words like pieces of ice. Isis forgot there might be people watching, and spun on the bench to face him.

"Is that a threat?" she hissed.

"I am only pointing out what could happen, if you do nothing."

Isis felt a shiver at her back, like something was already watching, and she wanted to rush over to Angel, grab her into safety. But she didn't move. "I can't help you," she whispered.

"Won't, you mean," said Mandeville. "I know you *could* help, if you chose to. Your power is so strong, your mind so clean and open."

Isis turned away, and the ghost stood up from the bench, sending a plume of murky dust into the air.

"Please," whispered Mandeville. "By saving us, you would be saving yourself."

"You caused the problem, not me." she whispered back. Mandeville sighed, and then he funnelled down into the tiles, leaving only a fading stain.

Isis sat motionless, her heart thrumming. For some reason she kept glancing up at the glass ceiling.

"Hello, Isis." A voice from behind her. She spun round,

knocking her book from the bench onto the floor. Gray was standing a metre away, holding a carrier bag with a shoebox inside it.

"What are you doing here?" he asked. Isis blinked, trying to bring herself back to normal, but before she could answer, Gray noticed Cally over by her tent, and the sign saying FORTUNE-TELLER.

"Oh…" His face was sympathetic.

Isis hunched a little. "She made me come along…"

"Because she couldn't get a babysitter?" Gray finished the sentence for her.

Isis smiled. "That's right."

She looked past Gray. "Are you here with your friends?" She tried to ask it normally, even as her stomach twisted at the thought. If anyone from school saw her, if they saw Cally…

Gray shook his head.

"I'm here with Mum. She said I had to get new school shoes." He pointed with his bag, and Isis saw a slim black woman near the shoe shop, talking into her mobile. It was instantly obvious she was Gray's mum – her features joined up all the parts of Gray's face that didn't look like his dad. She was wearing a blue patterned shirt and linen trousers, and her straightened hair was cut into a bob. She looked fashionable, respectable, the kind of mum who just brought you out to buy shoes.

Isis was filled with a sudden urge to rush over and ask if she could move in.

"She looks really nice," she said.

"Suppose so," said Gray, not even looking back. "Is Cally telling people's fortunes then?"

Isis nodded, wanting to crawl underneath the bench.

"I didn't know she could do that," said Gray, sounding impressed.

"I don't think she can," said Isis. "But I don't think she can do spirit readings either, so what difference does it make?"

Gray laughed, swinging the carrier bag against his legs.

"You're so lucky," said Isis, staring enviously at Gray's mum. "I have to drag after Cally all the time, doing this stuff."

"It's the same with my dad and his UFOs," said Gray.

"No it's not!" said Isis. "No one sees you, your dad doesn't make you sell tickets!" She was nearly shouting, shocking herself.

Gray's carrier bag came to a stop. "Are you all right?" he asked, narrowing his eyes a little. "Is this girl stuff or something?"

"No!" She took in a breath.

"It's since we went out to the field—" she started, but a crash echoed across the mall, cutting off her words. The chat and shuffle of the shoppers stilled for a moment, as people paused their shopping and looked around.

In front of the fortune-teller's tent, Cally was picking up her knocked-over chair, the cause of the clatter. She was staring, red-faced, towards the entrance. The neat figure of a man was walking confidently towards her. Philip Syndal.

What did he want?

"Hang on a minute," Isis said to Gray, and set off towards Cally, her pace getting quicker. He was a liar, a fraud – he'd proved that at the theatre.

Cally didn't notice Isis, instead she smiled brightly at Philip, walking a few steps to meet him.

"Phil. How wonderful." But it wasn't quite convincing.

"I heard from another member of the society that you'd be here," said Philip. "So I thought I'd come along, see you at work."

Cally's smile wavered. She fiddled with her dress and her newly bought shawl.

"Of course," she said. "Um, they led me to expect something slightly more… professional when I agreed to the booking." She gestured at the shoppers, the tacky little tent.

Philip lightly touched her arm.

"It's always this way when you start out," he said kindly. "I worked the nightclubs. At least everyone here is sober." He turned his head, spotting Isis. "I see you've brought your lovely daughter along."

"She always comes to my performances," said Cally, throwing a 'behave yourself!' look at Isis.

"Even on school nights?" smiled Philip.

Cally gave a slightly ashamed laugh. "Well she can do her homework in a corner. And if we get back really late I always let her sleep in. I just tell her teachers she isn't feeling well."

Isis blushed. Cally made it sound way worse than it was. She'd only lied to the teachers twice.

Philip didn't answer, looking at Cally intently for a moment. Then he turned away.

"You know," he said, "they do a very good cappuccino in the coffee bar here."

But now people had started noticing him. Two middle-aged women were pointing. Another woman, carrying four shopping bags, pushed in front of Isis, then waved some more people over. A little crowd started to form around Philip and Cally, mostly made up of women. The noise level was rising, the same excitement as had filled the theatre. Isis was getting pushed away from her mum.

Gray tapped her arm. He was behind her.

"Who's your mum talking to?" he whispered.

Isis looked at him in surprise. "Don't you know who Philip Syndal is?"

"Is he famous or something?"

"He's a psychic. He's been on telly!"

Gray shrugged. "I've never seen him."

A woman pushed in front of them, then another, driving them back to the edges of the crowd. Philip was transforming himself for the growing audience, smiling and looking oddly handsome in the sunshine. He'd separated, ever so slightly, from Cally.

"He looks taller than just now," said Gray, staring. "How's he done that?"

"It's called stage presence," said Isis. "Cally says all the best stage psychics have it. It's like an act, sort of."

On the other side of the crowd, a red-haired woman wearing a stripy dress pushed her way towards Philip, holding out a scrap of paper and a pen.

"Can I have your autograph?"

And with that, the crowd was unleashed. Closing in on Philip, surrounding him with a solid wall of backs and jostling elbows. People jumped up and down to get a better look, holding up their phones to take pictures, their excited cries echoing back from the shop windows.

Gray tried to peer through, but there wasn't even a crack in the scrum.

"Wow," he said. "Look at them going for him!"

"Is Cally all right in there?" said Isis.

"Wouldn't it be cool," said Gray, "if your mum got to be a celebrity like him." He stood on tiptoes. "You'd have loads of money."

Around them people were stopping to watch the scramble for Philip, pausing the flow of shoppers around the mall, adding to the people-jam.

"Who is it? Who's in there?" said a woman with blonde hair and a long summer dress, trying to shove her way through.

Gray jumped a few more times, then gave up.

"He must be really good at seeing ghosts," he said.

Isis shook her head. "Me and Mum went to one of his shows. He couldn't see them at all."

Gray looked at her. "Then why…?"

Isis glared into the crowd. "What he's really good at is fooling everyone."

Gray didn't question how she knew. Since the night in the field, the balance between them had shifted.

"Mandeville says he pretends the spirits tell him things, when really it's stuff people have told him before the show."

"Who's Mandeville?" asked Gray.

Isis startled, her face reddening.

"Um… he's a ghost," she mumbled. "I met him at one of Cally's seances, and a couple of times since."

Gray widened his eyes. "You have the weirdest friends."

"Mandeville isn't my friend!" said Isis. "He's really old, and mouldy too."

Gray laughed. "Sometimes you sound crazy, you know?"

Isis folded her arms. "Why don't you go back to your mum then?"

"Crazy is good!" said Gray, smiling. "Like seeing UFOs. Or your sister!"

"Angel!" Isis spun around, suddenly worried, scanning between the shoppers for a sight of the little ghost. "She'll get frightened by all these people."

"*She'll* be frightened?"

"Of course!" said Isis. "She's only little."

She pushed through the still-spreading crowd, heading for the escalators where she'd last seen Angel. But there was no sign of her. She scanned the nearby shops. Bright red banners shouted SUMMER SALE! and *30% OFF!*, but there was no little ghost. Isis looked up the escalator to the upper floor, most of which was a large coffee shop. A group of older teenagers were lurking around the top of the stairs, peering down and laughing at the commotion below. Slouchy boys in low-slung trousers, and spiky girls wearing bright make-up and too-tight jeans.

Squeezed between two of them was a small faded figure.

"Can you see her?" asked Gray, looking in completely the wrong direction.

"There," said Isis, nodding up at the teenagers. One of the girls was rubbing her arms against the cold, and looking confused.

"Are you going to get her?"

Isis looked at Gray. "Oh yes. I'll just pop up there and say, 'I'm here for my little sister. Don't worry if you can't see her, she's a ghost.'"

"*Okay.* I was only asking," said Gray.

"If I wait, she'll come down…" started Isis, but her attention was caught by a gleam of blue on the clear curve of the glass roof. Too dark to be the sky, and too close.

The gleam moved. Pouring itself along the white steel frames that held the glass, flowing like water. It oozed towards one of the roof supports, collecting into an impossible puddle.

It spread its wings across the windows. The sun shone through them without touching. Something like a head turned and looked down.

Straight at Angel.

Chapter Nineteen

Isis

"*What's* up there?"

Isis could see Gray was struggling to understand. She tried again.

"I've seen it before at the theatre. It sort of dropped onto Philip Syndal and grabbed away this ghost he'd called up to the stage."

"Hang on, I thought you said Philip was a fake?"

"He…" Isis faltered, trying to think. "Mandeville said he was using tricks, but he's psychic too." She wavered. If Philip Syndal had any talent, why hadn't he spotted Angel in his own home?

"Mandeville the ghost?" asked Gray, looking more confused.

Isis nodded. "He was at the theatre too. Inside a woman."

Gray opened his mouth and shut it again. He squinted up at the glass roof. "And now this… ghost grabber is in the shopping centre?"

"It's at the top of that pole," said Isis, "by the glass."

"Up there?" Gray pointed.

"Don't!" hissed Isis, slapping his arm down. "It might see you!"

"Are you winding me up?" said Gray.

"No! That thing is stalking Angel. Mandeville called it a Devourer. He said it eats ghosts or something."

Gray paused, then turned to look up at the escalators. "And is Angel still up there?" he asked.

Isis nodded. The teenagers were bunched together at the entrance to the coffee shop, getting told off by a security guard. "Legitimate shoppers feel intimidated with you here…" he was saying loudly.

"We're legitimate shoppers," said one of the boys, waving a drinks can. "I bought this."

Angel, the pale sprite, was still playing amongst them, unnoticed by everyone. Except for the blue-wash creature above, watching her with its many eyes, and gathering itself to strike.

Isis stood still at the bottom of the escalators, hesitating.

"Go on then," said Gray.

The ridged metal steps trundled up with a constant rumble. At the top of the escalators, the teenagers moved just enough to placate the security guard. Angel went with them, and the slime of blue slipped along the ceiling, keeping track.

Isis turned to Gray.

"I can't get to her without them noticing," she said.

He shrugged. "So?"

So they'd see her talking to the air. Then they'd see her arguing with the air, grabbing hold of it and dragging it away. Her stomach tightened at the thought. The insults and laughter, the sly punch to put her in her place. She faced it every day at school – she didn't want to face it here as well.

"They'll think I'm a freak," she said quietly, hating herself for being afraid.

But the overhead blue was spreading now, getting deeper, as if the whole shopping mall were a submarine descending into water. What the teenagers might say didn't matter, nothing mattered but Angel.

Isis took a breath. "You stay here," she said to Gray.

"Why?" he said, his heavy eyebrows shadowing his eyes.

And he stepped onto the escalator, rising smoothly away from her, his hand on the moving rail.

Isis stared, then jumped on after.

"They'll think you're a freak too," she said.

Gray shrugged. "I don't care."

"What shall we do?"

He shrugged again. "I don't know. Something."

They were carried upwards, the air thickening and flickering into a blue only Isis could see. As if she were really, dizzily, diving down into the sea. The sky was obscured by the vast, spreading bulk of the creature. It filled the top of the mall, its multiple shifting eyes focused on Angel.

If it took her away, like it took the ghost at the theatre...

"We have to hurry!" cried Isis, one fear overcoming another. She pushed past Gray, running straight off the escalator towards the teenage gang. They were chatting together, drinking from their cans and eating crisps. All of them ignored Isis, except for one of the girls; arms crossed under her crop top, one hip pushed out. She glared at Isis from under scraped-back hair.

"You want something?"

Angel's head poked out through the girl's jeans, as if her legs weren't there. Isis wanted to grab the little ghost, but she couldn't imagine what would happen if she stuck her hand between the girl's legs.

"Isis! I here!" Angel called, before vanishing again.

The girl rubbed at her goosebumpy bare arms.

"What's wrong with this place?" she snapped. "Why can't they sort the temperature out?" She glared at Isis again. "And what's up with you? You got something wrong with your eyes, or is it your brain?"

Isis realised she was squinting, trying to see through the gloopy depths created by the blue-wash creature. She shook her head, opening her eyes.

"Nothing. I'm fine," she managed.

Gray caught up, and the girl flicked a scornful glance over him.

"Hello," he said, very loud and bright. "My name's Gray. Who are you?"

The others turned challenging stares on him. Four boys and three girls, spreading out into a loose semicircle around Gray and Isis.

One lad was slim and good looking, holding himself like he owned the place. He pointed his can at Gray's carrier bag.

"You come up here to give me a present? What is it?"

The others laughed.

"It's his shoes," Isis said. "They wouldn't fit you."

The air darkened a little more. The creature was wrapping itself around the mall like silk.

"Then why is he giving them to me?" said the good-looking lad, making a grab for the bag.

Gray whipped it out of reach. "I'm not," he said.

"Go back to your shopping," said one of the girls. "Buy yourselves some dollies or whatever."

Gray ignored her, and pointed down the escalator, to the floor below where the crowd was still milling about. To Philip and Cally, caught in the middle of it.

"Do you know who they are?" he asked.

"Do I look like I care?" answered the girl.

"Are they famous?" asked one of the boys.

Gray nodded. "Famous ghost hunters. That's what they're doing here, looking for ghosts."

The boy rolled his eyes.

"Yeah, right."

But the others were already peering past Gray and Isis.

"You serious?" asked the girl with the scraped-back hair. "Like, really ghost hunters? Like on TV?"

Gray nodded, then pointed at Isis. "And she's one too."

Isis jumped, staring at Gray in panic.

The good-looking boy laughed.

"*I see dead people,*" he said, mockingly.

Overhead, many eyes were focused on Angel. The deep blue shifted into an eye-aching violet.

"She really is psychic!" said Gray. Isis glared at him, but he took no notice. "One of the best there is."

"If she's the best, why is everyone mobbing that bald man down there?" asked the scraped-back-hair girl. Gray ignored her, carrying on.

"Do you know why she's up here? It's because there's a ghost with you lot. Right now." He turned to Isis. "Isn't that right?"

Isis couldn't speak. He'd just told total strangers something she'd only ever spoken of once in her whole life!

"*Go on,*" he whispered, like they had a plan or something.

Angel put her head out through the one of the boys, who shuddered.

"How Gray know I here?" she squeaked, before disappearing again.

Well she'd have to carry it on now, whatever Gray was planning.

"Have any of you been feeling cold?" she asked, her voice squeaking a bit.

The gang looked at each other, and one boy nodded.

"Yeah. It's like, really warm today, but there's these patches of cold, even in the sunshine."

"Oh my God!" squealed one of the girls. "That is *exactly* what I've been feeling."

Next thing, they were all loudly agreeing with each other, describing their own shivers and goosebumps.

"We're being haunted!" shrieked one of the girls. She looked at Isis. "Oh my God, is it a zombie or something?"

"Zombies aren't ghosts. Don't you know nothing?" said one of the boys.

Angel popped out again. "I not stombie!" she cried. "I Angel!"

Isis glanced up. Above them, claws let go of the column, wings folded back.

"*Angel*," she whispered, focusing on her hand. She whipped her arm forwards and grabbed the little ghost, right from next to one of the teenagers.

"Hey!" shouted the girl. "What you doing? Don't you even *try* and touch me!"

Isis pulled Angel towards her, trying to shield her from

the creature gathering above. The air fizzed into a whining, crackling blue, like it was electrically charged.

"Have you got Angel?" asked Gray.

"Angels?" said the good-looking boy. "You said it was ghosts!"

Isis put her arms around Angel. Everyone was turning into shadows, lost in the ink-washed gloom.

Angel let out a high scream.

"It's here!" cried Isis, trying to run. But the air had turned to glue, she was wading through it. Teeth filled the dark, biting at her from strange angles. Clawlike hands took freezing hold of her shoulders, shaking her.

"Isis!" wailed Angel.

"It's all right," she whispered, "I've got you." Trying to keep her mind focused, trying to keep her arms around Angel's nothing-form.

"What's she *doing*?" laughed one of the teenagers.

"She's not a ghost hunter, she's just mental!"

More hands poured out of the creature, out of nowhere. They gripped Isis, trying to force her arms open. Angel screamed and was lifted off the floor, numberless hands pulling at her feet, gripping her ankles, tugging at her clothes and her hair.

Isis willed every thought into her hands, focusing on holding Angel, gripping as tight as she could. But the little ghost was being pulled away from her – she could feel her hold slipping. Endless fingers pinched particles of light out of Angel, carrying them back to a thousand hungry mouths. Angel's screams grew frantic.

Somewhere, distantly, Isis could hear the shrieks and laughter of the teenagers, still in their otherworld of bright sunshine and shops. The creature roared in a breath through many mouths, like a storm bending a forest. Angel jerked almost out of Isis's grasp, and she gripped harder, feeling her nails bite into her palms. But Angel's substance was falling away, Isis was losing even the shape of her. All she had left were their tight-held hands as they desperately clung to each other.

"Isis!" Angel's thin wail fell upwards. "Mummy!"

"Angel!" Isis's tears turned to ice on her cheeks. Angel was unravelling into spider silk, her scream a breathless whine.

"I can't hold her!" Isis cried out, but no one came to help. No one could even see what was happening. The only reply was mocking laughter, from somewhere beyond the flickering ocean of blue.

Isis felt her fingers get warmer, as Angel slipped through them.

Chapter Twenty

Gray

That girl was right, Isis did look mental. Holding onto nothing, yelling. She had tears rolling down her face, and she was screaming, "Angel! Angel!"

Everyone sitting at their tables, drinking coffee, they were all staring. The gang of kids were laughing their heads off.

I guess I would've thought she was mad too, except for what I'd seen before, in the field. She'd said there was a ghost, and there was one. So now, if she said something was in the shopping centre, I believed her, you know? The trouble was, I couldn't see what she could. I didn't know what was happening.

I ran over. "What? What do I do?"

She looked at me and her eyes were blown pure black. She was freezing too. "Help me hold her," she said, and her voice sounded miles away. "Help me hold Angel."

How do you hold a ghost?

I swiped my hands through the air, flapping them about until they hit cold. Ice in the air. That was Angel, the shape of her, frozen out of nothing. Like, you know when you're holding something, your hands make the shape of it? Well if you took away the thing, and left your hands in the right place, that's what holding Angel was like.

The gang started shouting stuff at me too, but I didn't care, because as soon as I got a grip on Angel, everything changed.

Like a dream got laid over my eyes. Or the world was a dream, and I woke up.

Out of nowhere, there was this... monster. I mean, really, a monster. It's hard to describe, because it didn't exactly have a shape, but it was a deep, dark flickering blue, like the bottom of the ocean, or a shadow at night. It filled up the top of the shopping centre, oozing into everything, pushing right up to the roof. And even while I could see it, right there, I could see all the people just carrying on, like it wasn't.

It had teeth all over – thousands, millions – but no mouth. Then sometimes it would flicker, and it was nothing but mouths. It had hundreds of eyes as well, all over, and when it flickered the eyes all crunched together into one. Like a whirlpool spinning into its body. Every time that happened I thought I was going to fall in, just go down and down. I stared at the monster, with my brain going, *"You're not seeing this! You can't be!"*

I think I screamed.

And Isis headbutted me.

Not hard or anything, just enough to get me out of those whirlpools.

"Don't look in its eyes!" she cried.

I managed to pull my eyes off the monster, to what we were both holding. Isis had a grip on one of Angel's hands, and it turned out I had hold of Angel's shoulder. I nearly let go then, nearly screamed again, because Angel didn't look like this plump little ghost-girl any more. She was all stretched out and up, with these hands on her everywhere, pulling her into the monster. Her feet were already stuck inside it. Around her ankles, the blue watery stuff was rippling and sloshing, trying to suck her in further. Her eyes were open, and she was saying,

"Mummy, Isis, Mummy, Isis," over and over.

"Take both her hands," cried Isis. "I'll get hold of her waist." In the weird blue light, she looked like a photo, like all the shape had been taken out of her.

To get a decent grip of Angel's hands, I had to let go for a second.

And everything went back to normal.

No monster, no Angel. Only me and Isis, on the top floor of the shopping centre, screaming and holding onto air. The gang were still laughing, everyone was staring.

No wonder.

I hardly even noticed though, I just felt for the cold, and grabbed hold of Angel again. Soon as I touched her, the normal world faded and I was staring straight at that night-watery monster. And it was scary. I mean, wet-yourself-scary. Not because it was huge and freaky and trying to eat Angel. It was scary because…

Well, there was this time me and Dad got caught in a thunderstorm, out in this really big field. The lightning hit a nearby tree with this massive crack, and it exploded into flames and smoke. We watched it burn, the thunder crashing around us, and I knew there wasn't anywhere to hide. Then Dad said, in this really calm voice, "We're going to get down on the ground, Gray, and make ourselves as small as possible." And I curled up next to him, nearly burying myself in the dirt, while the rain pelted my back and the thunder boomed on forever, shaking the ground under us.

The thing in the shopping centre was like that storm. You knew it'd roll right over and kill you without even noticing.

Me and Isis pulled on Angel, trying to get her out. The monster let out this roaring, and the ripples glopping around Angel's feet turned into waves. She slid through our hands, sucking further into the monster. I tried to pull her back, but my feet were slipping on the floor, my fingers so cold I couldn't even feel them.

One of the monster's whirling eyes slid down its body, until it was right above Isis. Staring at her, like it hated her. She gripped harder around Angel, and made this crying, grunting noise, heaving even harder. From where Angel's feet were, all these sploshes and ripples started spreading out across the thing's body. It let out this gargling scream, and all the shops and people, everything that was normal, they all got even fainter. Like it was trying to pull us out of the real world. It was really, really cold. Our breath was puffing frozen in the air.

I was terrified by then. My heart was hammering, my arms were going numb with cold.

"Let her go!" Isis screamed, heaving at Angel. The monster shuddered in slow-motion ripples, and, just like that, Angel's feet popped right out.

She pinged through the air, straight through Isis's arms and into mine. Like getting a bucket of ice chucked over me. For one weird second, I was back in the sunshine, back in the real world, then Isis ran at me, and as soon as she touched Angel, we were all three into the underwater blue again. Angel was crying and gasping in my arms, one hand around my neck, one hand reaching for Isis.

The monster roared – it was like getting hit over the head. It reared up, into this tidal wave of blue. A wave filled with eyes and mouths, like a school of sharks crashing in. Everything got darker, the real world faded into foggy shapes.

"Everything's still there," Isis whispered. "Remember, everything's still there."

Except, we weren't.

Above us, the monster's mouths and teeth were collecting into this huge, jagged circle. Champing, gleaming and licking its lips. What wasn't mouths, was its eye.

Spinning, circling, trying to suck us in. I wanted to throw myself in it.

"Turn around," cried Isis, "Stop looking at it!" But I couldn't, I couldn't even speak. "Turn around!" yelled Isis, yanking me round by my arm.

I was able to think again.

"Run?" I gasped, and we scrambled for the escalators, sort of hugging each other around Angel, trying to protect her. We must've looked crazy – clumsy-running down the steps, barging past a woman with her shopping. But we got away from the dark fog of the monster, slipping out from underneath it.

At the bottom, we ran into the crowd, which was still hanging around Cally's psychic mate. There were hundreds of people in front of us, milling about like idiots.

"'Scuse me, 'scuse me!" I shouted, trying to push us through, but no one even moved.

"It's following us," cried Isis.

I looked up. The monster was blue-oozing across the ceiling, covering the sky like a storm.

"It want to bite me!" sobbed Angel. She was so cold, sucking the heat out of me. All the hair on my arms was stood up straight, every one in a goosebump.

"What do we do?" I asked Isis.

She looked at Angel, and you could see how much she loved her. "Can you leave?" she whispered. "Can you hide?"

The little ghost shook her head.

"It bited me," she said. "I too tired now." I could see right through her, like she was made of glass.

I started to shiver, Isis was shivering too.

"Can't we kill it or something?" I asked.

"Kill it?" said Isis. "Is it even *alive*?"

"I don't know!" I snapped. "You're the one who knows about all this stuff."

She shook her head. "Not this."

The air was getting darker, colder. The crowd all around us were fading into paper cut-outs, and the bright shopping centre was turning misty, like a fog was soaking into it. The thing had covered the whole glass roof.

"We'll have to h-hide," said Isis, her teeth chattering now. The monster was sucking the warmth out of the world, and holding Angel was like standing in a tub of iced water.

"Where?" I asked. "It's a-already oozed over everywhere."

"All right, run then," she said. "Is there another w-way out?"

I nodded. "T-to the c-car park."

Isis looked at me. "You'll have to g-get her out."

"Me? What about you?"

"I'm going to try and hold it off," whispered Isis. She looked really scared then, but like she was trying to be brave.

I stared at her. "It'll p-pull you in! Eat you!"

She shook her head again.

"I'm not a ghost," she said. "I'll be okay."

Which goes to show, even she didn't know everything.

I have seen that moment, Gray, it is on footage taken by security cameras at the shopping centre. If she's gone somewhere, I always retrieve the tapes. Keep an eye on her.

I was worried by what I saw in them. Calista should've taken better care.

But, it's my fault as well. I've got too used to being at a distance. I should have stepped in. I should have done something.

Chapter Twenty-one

Isis

Blue. Spreading and thinning in front of her, unfolding into the wide open space above the shops. Shimmering with eyes, endless reflections of each other. Countless hands descending, by scuttle or finger walk, down the walls, clinging to the glass shopfronts, clutching and pulling at the unheeding shoppers.

Her mouth tasted of dry paper, her heart was beating out of her chest.

She remembered words, suddenly. *These other bodies can't see me. But you can.*

Someone had said that to her once, but she couldn't think who.

The creature carried on pouring out of nowhere, a slow

tide filling the shopping centre. Her legs were shaking, but she stopped herself from running. She had to stay here, she had to stop it from leaving and chasing after Gray. She had to give him time to get away, to get Angel to safety.

The creature rippled like water, the head and outstretched arms melting and stretching, turning into something like tentacles. One whipped through a family coming down the escalator. The parents were instantly sliced into shattered, sparkling pieces, their shopping bags exploding into shreds of plastic snow.

Isis gasped the start of a scream, but stifled it. No one else in the mall had even blinked. Not the crowd around her, nor the other people trundling up the escalator. The children carried on down, sucking their drinks, unaware of their parents' destruction. The tentacle whipped back, and the atoms of the man and woman swirled together again. Utterly untouched, utterly unconscious of what had happened.

Your sister will not be so fortunate.

More remembered words, loud and vivid in her mind. Who'd said them?

"What happened to those people was just a trick," she whispered, trying to reassure herself. But a voice drifted out of her memory, half-remembered, like a dream.

Are you so sure?

The creature reared upwards, covering her with twilight. It was going to crush her, drown her into emptiness! She cried out, her arms going up over her head, squeezing her eyes shut. Cowering, waiting for the end.

Nothing.

She opened her eyes. A middle-aged man wearing a neat white shirt and ironed jeans was staring at her.

"Are you all right?" he said.

Isis swallowed and put her arms down.

"Fine." She croaked the word out.

The man frowned.

"Really, I'm fine." This time she managed to sound almost normal, despite the rippling wall of violet-blue rising up behind him, and the dozens of hands reaching out of the air towards him.

"Okay," the man said, but like he didn't quite believe her. He walked away, and Isis took in a deep breath.

The creature folded itself in again, disappearing some of its strange, shimmering body.

A child-ghost is only a small meal.

With a jolt, she remembered when she'd heard those

words before. It was a few years ago, when Cally used to read her bedtime stories. Cally had closed the book after reading them, and turned off the light. Then she'd kissed Isis on the forehead and said sadly, "*I am so hungry.*"

Her mum had never said any of that!

"Get out of my mind," hissed Isis.

Then how will we converse?

Isis winced, trying to drive away a sudden memory of Cally, singing these words to her as an eerie lullaby. She glanced towards the exit. Was Gray outside now? Was he running through the sunshine, holding an invisible Angel?

Your sister.

Her mum, younger and happier. Sitting in a neat hospital bed and smiling down at a tiny baby, wrapped in a pink blanket. This was a real memory – Isis had gone to visit them with Dad, after Angel was born.

"You can't have Angel," Isis whispered now.

But in her memory, her mum looked up from Angel's sleepy, red-squashed face. "*She is already dead.*"

"Cally never said that!"

The creature shifted. Without moving, it had got closer. Isis forced herself to stay still, keeping herself between the creature and the way out.

All around her, people were carrying on with their shopping, or milling about in the crowd. Men, women and children, ambling between the stores, squinting in the bright sunshine, passing in and out of the twilit body of the creature. None of them noticed it, none of them even shivered.

"What are you?" she whispered. "What do you want?"

I am hungry. I want to eat.

And now Isis remembered hunger. Those days upon days when Cally had been too depressed to buy food, driving Isis to search through every empty cupboard again and again, so hungry she'd even eaten dry pasta pieces scattered in a dusty corner, crunching them between her teeth in desperation.

"That never happened!" she cried. "Cally always made sure I had something to eat."

The creature rippled a hundred heads. Was it sighing?

Isis's mind filled with memories of food. Slices of toast she'd had for breakfast, the iced bun Cally had bought, the spaghetti they'd had for tea last night. Fish and chips Dad used to buy on a Friday, Angel's second birthday cake. Angel eating an apple in tiny bites, Angel with ice cream smeared around her mouth. Cally spoon-feeding Angel from a bowl of mashed banana. Food and Angel, Angel and food.

Isis clenched her fists, stopping the flow.

"You can't have her!" she whispered, glaring at the creature. She opened her fingers, and put her hands out in front of her. They were trembling.

"I can hold onto ghosts, hurt them even," she whispered. "Maybe I can do the same to you?"

Laughter ripped through her life, a mocking soundtrack to every memory.

Was Gray far enough away by now? Were he and Angel safe? Could she run now?

A sudden pressure, a cold poking at her thoughts.

Where?

She took a step backwards, bumping into a woman overloaded with shopping bags.

"Watch what you're doing," said the woman.

Isis opened her mouth for an automatic sorry, but what came out was, "I live at Flat 2b—"

She slapped a hand over her mouth. She backed away, not from the frowning, head-shaking woman, but from the huge, bluely invisible creature, stalking her like a cat.

Where?

She pressed her hand even harder against her mouth, trying to stop herself from screaming out her address. And now she wanted to run away even more, run straight home without stopping…

Something else. She had to think of something else.

One times seven is seven.

Two times seven is fourteen.

Three times seven is Flat 2b…

The creature grew a long, impossible neck, weaving it through the shops, encircling Isis like a snake.

She jumped to the names of the planets.

Mercury, Venus, Earth, Mars, Wentworth Ro…

"No! I won't."

The creature roared soundlessly, rising up into a straddling arc of violet-blue, a dark rainbow. Its eyes collected into a single whirling orb – a black hole sucking in the sunshine, pulling every gleam from the shop windows.

Desperately, she thought of anything she could, panicking her thoughts through random jumps. Grandma Janet's house. Going with Cally to the Welkin Society. Walking in the woods with Gray. Gil and his UFO hunting. Walking out into the night-time field, and the lights rising up into the darkness. She remembered having wings and seeing all those birds. She wanted to be like them, to fly away!

A soundless flash, the crack of an unseen whip. An eye leading to infinity, right in front of her face. Fists everywhere, slamming, thumping and smashing onto the floor tiles.

Tell me!

Isis staggered, falling to her hands and knees, her breath coming in gasps. The whirlpool circled faster, and she screwed her eyes shut, trying to force her thoughts away from Angel. She focused again on the night in the field, reliving every moment, every strange detail of the lights swirling into a strange sun, of the flock of ghostly, doomed birds.

When she reached the end of the memory, her mind was still.

She opened her eyes.

A swirl of blue, curling around the shopping centre, softly undulating. Gentle as a coil of smoke, covered in slow smiles.

Your bargain is good. You can keep your sister.

Isis stared at it, shaky with disbelief. She'd beaten it! She'd kept it from Gray, from Angel; they were safe and away, running down normal, sunlit streets. She laughed, almost hysterical, and pushed herself to standing. An elderly couple glanced at her, then looked quickly away. She put her hand to her mouth, tears trickling down onto her fingers.

Then, you will feed me. You will be my feast-giver.

The words froze into her mind, spoken by everyone she'd ever known.

A weightless wind blew through the shopping centre, and the creature oozed into the air. It rippled through the main hall, rising above the heads of the shuffling shoppers, shooting straight up and crashing out through the glass roof, splintering the windows into a million shards of crystal.

Leaving them perfectly whole, and undamaged.

The sound of footsteps brought Isis back into the noise and chatter of the mall. The middle-aged man in the white T-shirt and jeans was leading Cally towards her. Behind them was a security guard, and trailing after was Philip Syndal.

Cally rushed for Isis, grabbing hold of her.

"What happened to you? What's the matter?"

Isis stared at her, a blank in her mind where words ought to be.

"Uh… I was here…" she managed. Her voice sounded strange, as if she were speaking a foreign language.

"A fit," said the man in the T-shirt. "She was definitely having a fit or something. Talking to herself, shaking, eyes rolled back in her head."

"Oh God!" Cally pulled Isis into a tight hug.

"I wasn't…" Isis said into Cally's shoulder, but she wasn't listening.

"She's ill! I have to take her home!" said Cally. She turned to Philip. "Please, could you explain to the centre manager for me? I really can't continue the readings after this."

"Of course," said Philip. He turned to Isis with genuine concern on his face. "I hope you feel better soon."

And the world darkened around them, the sun overhead hazing and cooling. In dread, Isis looked up and saw an arrow of darkness, a swarm heading straight for them out of the sky. It plummeted downwards: a falling fountain of deep blue water, filled with eyes and laughing, biting mouths. She was frozen by fear; it was too fast to avoid. The cloud was a dagger, heading right for her. A scream opened her mouth, but came out as a gasp. The dark swarm, the many eyes and hands, they funnelled neatly into the top of

Philip's head, as if there were an open hole in his skull.

He continued to talk with Cally as the raging swirl rushed into him. When it had finished, he shut his mouth, and Isis saw him swallow.

"Don't worry," he said. "I'll sort everything out."

Chapter Twenty-two

Gray

When I got back to the shopping centre, it was Mum I ran into first. Of course, then I was in loads of trouble. She yelled at me twenty minutes straight for not telling her where I'd gone. She wouldn't listen to a word I said, just marched us both out of there, which meant I never got to look for Isis or find out if she was okay.

Later on, Mum tried to get Dad into being cross with me, but luckily he didn't care.

"I always hated going shopping with you, as well," he said. "All that hanging around while you tried stuff on."

"You never *came* shopping with me," said Mum, "and I wasn't shopping for myself today. I took your son to buy new shoes, which he needs. Not that you think about that kind of thing!" And then they were into a whole new round of fighting, so I sneaked off.

Normally I hate it when they go for each other, but this time I was glad because it meant they never asked me why I'd run out of the shopping centre in the first place. I mean, I couldn't exactly tell them I'd been saving Isis's dead sister from a ghost-eating monster.

Not that I actually knew if I had. Without Isis, I couldn't even see Angel, so when I was running for Isis's place I didn't know if I'd got Angel or not. Except I was freezing. I was running through town on a really hot day, and I was so cold it hurt. When I got outside the flats where Isis lives, I stood in the street, shivering and wondering what to do. In the end I just said, "Go home now," to thin air.

I stopped being cold, so Angel must've gone.

But I didn't see Isis for days after that. I was dying to talk to her, and find out what had happened, but I couldn't because the whole thing timed with Dad and Cally cooling off each other, or something.

I mean, before, Dad was desperate to see Cally. Now she phoned and blew him out on a date, and he didn't even seem bothered.

"Okay then, see you another time," he said, like it was

no big deal. If she'd known him better, Cally would've been worried. His girlfriends usually only lasted a few weeks once he got that way.

"Aren't you seeing Cally?" I asked.

Dad shook his head. "Isis isn't well. She was taken ill yesterday."

"She was?" And I was even more desperate to find out then. I was scared, wondering what that monster had done to her. "What's wrong with her?"

Dad looked at me. Smiled a bit.

"Have you got a thing for her, Gray?"

"No!"

"You certainly like spending time with her."

"No way!"

Dad shrugged. "Whatever you say."

Trouble was, I couldn't tell him what was really going on, so he got all the wrong ideas.

"The doctor thinks it was just a bit of heatstroke," said Dad. "But you know the way Cally is about Isis." He rolled his eyes. "She's probably got her on a twenty-four hour nursing watch."

I knew it wasn't just heatstroke, whatever the doctor said. But Isis was strong, even though she looked like a twig.

I think being strong is how she held on so long, at the end…

So I had to wait to find out how she was, because I couldn't ask Dad without him winding me up, and he wasn't chasing Cally any more. Actually, when I think about it, he wasn't exactly cooling on her. It was just that things were going really well for him then, with his UFO stuff.

The latest readings, and my film, they were good, you know? As soon as he posted them on the Network, his mobile started ringing, and he said his email was clogged with messages. It wasn't just other UFO freaks either — the film clip got forty thousand hits in the first week! Dad got a call from a TV company, and from some professor in America who asked him to go and talk at a conference over there. Dad was turning into a name in the Network, and he was loving it.

It wasn't until the Saturday I got to talk to Isis, when Cally invited us over. After a week of not seeing her, I knew Dad would be trying some way to get rid of me and Isis.

"How about the cinema?" he asked, when we were walking over to their place. "There's that film you want to see. The one with all the robots."

"I went last week, with Dipan and everyone."

Dad looked at me, surprised. "Did your mum pay for that then?"

I nodded. "She wants me to go out with my friends."

Dad just grunted, and walked a bit faster. He was cross I'd said that, but it was still true. When I'm with Dad, it's just me and him. Or me, him and some girlfriend. He's never even met most of my friends, it's like the rest of my life doesn't exist.

Dad slowed down again. "Isn't there something else you want to see?" he asked.

I shook my head.

"You could go with Isis," said Dad, "And I could go for a walk with Cally, or something."

I didn't even want to think what the something was.

So that's how me and Isis ended up watching *Merlin Wakes*. Don't bother, by the way, it's rubbish. But it was the only thing neither of us had seen.

We were in seats right at the back, in the noisy, flickering dark.

"Thank you," she said quietly, as soon as we sat down.

I looked at her.

"You saved Angel," she said.

I shrugged like it was nothing, even though I was really pleased.

"What happened?" I asked her, and she started telling me.

"It spoke inside your mind?" I asked, when she'd got a bit of the way into it.

Isis waggled her head — not yes, not no.

"More like I was remembering what it said. Like someone else had said the words to me, a long time ago." There was a catch to her voice, and she went really still and quiet, staring at the film. A woman in a medieval-style dress was running around this stone castle, carrying a sword like she didn't know how to use it. She smashed it into a massive wooden door, and the door broke open.

"That'd never happen," I said. "You'd need a chainsaw or something."

The woman rushed into some kind of dungeon and set about freeing a white-bearded old man who was shackled to the wall. *"Merlin!"* she cried, then they went into this stupid long chat where they explained the plot of the film to each other.

"There was another thing," Isis said, and her voice sounded weird. Scared. "Philip Syndal came over with

Cally, afterwards. And the thing came back, out of nowhere, and… poured right into him."

I stared at her. "Poured how?"

"Through the top of his head."

"Did he…" I didn't know what to ask. Did he drown? Ice over? Did his head explode?

"He didn't do anything," said Isis. "He didn't even notice, I think."

"How could he not notice a monster going into his head?"

Isis took a sip of her drink, the ice clunked inside the cup. "No one else at the shopping centre even knew it was there. It exploded these two people, then put them back together, and no one even blinked." She put her drink down on the arm of her chair. "Mandeville said Philip was psychic, but he never noticed Angel at his house."

"So is it… still inside him?" I asked.

"I don't know."

We watched the film for a bit then, both thinking hard. Merlin and the woman left the castle and rode through these random bits of countryside, asking the peasants if they'd seen King Arthur. All the peasants were really clean, and they had nice white teeth.

I turned to Isis. "Do you think it could've been an alien, maybe? Like, with advanced technology, so no one could see it? A cloaking device?"

Isis frowned. "An alien hunting ghosts and possessing people?"

"Maybe. Aliens do all sorts of things."

She shook her head.

"No," she said, firmly. "It didn't have anything to do with aliens, or your dad's UFO stuff." The light from the film flickered over her face. "It felt like pure… wanting, or hunger or something. Mandeville said it was from before humans could even speak."

She wrapped her arms around herself. "Mandeville said something might happen to Angel, and then next thing the Devourer appeared."

"Devourer?"

"That's what Mandeville calls it," she said.

Now I can see he practically told Isis what was going to happen, especially giving it a name like that.

Isis looked at me. "He wants me to save the ghosts from the creature, but how can I even do that? I don't know how to fight it, and I don't want to see it again, not ever!"

"Do you think it's still hunting after Angel?"

Isis shrugged, looking miserable.

"It said something about a bargain, that I could keep her. But then it said…" She stopped, and sort of shuddered. "I don't know what. I didn't agree to anything though, I'm sure I didn't."

I thought about it, but I couldn't work it out. Not then, anyway.

"Where's Angel now?" I asked.

Isis sighed. "Hiding inside the sofa. She hasn't come out for days – I think she's recovering."

"Well that's good, isn't it? She's safe for now."

Isis stared at the film, her eyes reflecting the cinema lights. I could see how scared she was.

"We'll think of something," I said. "Angel will be all right."

But the thing is, we hadn't fitted it all together properly. We'd forgotten all the other stuff we were caught up in.

I wish I'd thought harder. I wish I'd been cleverer.

Other stuff. Well, there is certainly that. But would knowing about it have helped Isis? I doubt it, Gray.

That's why we are here, to deal with the 'other stuff'.

Even your father is only scratching at the surface. And Stuart Bradley may call himself the Keeper, but the only secrets he'll ever find out about are the ones we want him to.

Chapter Twenty-three

Isis

Cally led the way through the trees, along a narrow path, brown-patterned with last year's leaves. A little way back they'd passed a wooden footpath sign, faded and green-stained with moss.

"Are we there yet?" asked Isis.

"*Nearly*," said Cally.

Isis rolled her eyes at Cally's back, trudging on between the trees. What was the point of this?

There was a flicker of movement just off the path, leaves in the sunshine maybe. Isis half-expected the small, familiar shape of Angel, but she wasn't there. She hadn't been in the car with them either; she'd barely been in their flat. Angel still spent most of the time inside the sofa.

Hiding or hurt, Isis wasn't sure which.

"Please, just let me see you," Isis had whispered into the cushions.

"No! I not coming out," was the only reply.

Isis had watched a whole morning of *In the Night Garden*, and asked Cally if they could make a cake. Nothing would tempt Angel out of the upholstery, but then, after what had happened at the shopping centre... Isis wished she had a sofa she could hide inside as well.

She followed after Cally, pushing past the thin stems of a straggling bush.

"Are you sure this is the way?" she said. "It's a bit overgrown."

Cally paused next to the gnarled trunk of an ancient tree. Its canopy spread above them, a roof of dusty-dark leaves.

"We'll be there soon," she said, "and then you'll see."

"See what?" asked Isis, but Cally just started walking again.

A bit further on, they passed into a patch of sunlight, a clearing created by the falling of another tree. Its rotten trunk lay shattered on the ground, covered in earlike fungi, only a dead, jagged spike of wood marking where it had stood. The corpse was surrounded by green-spray ferns and young saplings – new trees growing out of the leaf mould.

Cally paused next to the stump, taking in a deep breath and tilting her head back a little.

"Shut your eyes," she said. "Just listen."

Isis frowned, watching Cally breathe herself into the peace of the sun-dappled woods. A breeze rustled the leaves, and a hidden bird sang a short, repeating song.

"Isn't it wonderful?" sighed Cally. "Doesn't it make you feel calm?"

But Isis felt too scratched inside to be calm. If she closed her eyes she might see dark blue filled with faces, a shadow pouring into Philip Syndal's head, Angel screaming for help, or impossible birds flying into the night.

Cally opened her eyes and saw Isis's frown.

"Oh, Isis," she said.

Isis walked past, taking the path out of the clearing. "When can we go home?"

"We have to get there first," snapped Cally.

"Where is there?" cried Isis. "Why are we even here?"

These woods, this walk Cally had insisted on. Not asking Isis, more like threatening and cajoling, all morning long, until at last she'd given in just to keep the peace. Staring silently out of the car window as Cally drove them into the countryside.

Now, in the clearing, Cally seemed to be studying Isis.

"You've been so... odd, lately," she said. "Won't you tell me what's the matter?"

Isis sighed. "The doctor said. It was just a bit of heatstroke."

"I don't mean that," said Cally. "You're so distant... You've changed so much recently." Her eyes glistened, tearful, and her voice was croaky. "You were always the one I could rely on, Isis. When I was on the edge, it was having you that kept me sane. You do know that, don't you?"

Isis nodded, her throat felt full and fat.

Cally brushed her hair back from her face. "So why are you... like this? Are you angry about something? Or scared? I can't help you, if you won't tell me what it is."

A bird flew over their heads, wings swishing in the air. If Gray had been here, he could've told them what kind it was. Isis didn't have a clue, but she still felt the ache of feathers she didn't have. She wanted to leap upwards, and join it in flight.

She shook her head a little, trying to clear her thoughts.

"Oh, Isis," said Cally. "Please."

And suddenly she wanted to tell her. Like on telly, when girls tell their mums their problems. The words were on her tongue, she was already speaking them in her mind. The ghosts, the night in the field, the creature in the mall, Angel...

Her heart went still. Not Angel. Telling about Angel would smash the bit of happiness they'd reached these last months, and if she left out the little ghost, how could she tell the rest?

Cally sighed. "Do you know what Grandma Janet thinks? She told me you're turning into a teenager, and I should expect you to be horrible for the next five years."

Isis laughed. "That sounds like Grandma."

Cally answered with a small, hesitant smile.

"I'm fine, Cally," said Isis. "Really I am."

Cally's smile pinched off. "When did you stop calling me Mum?"

Isis shrugged, it had been years ago.

"I know how hard it's been for you," said Cally. "Losing Angel, and then your dad. And I know I wasn't... the best mum, for a long time." She put her hand out, touching Isis's cheek. "But things are better now, aren't they? I've got Gil, and the Welkin Society. I'm so much stronger. I think... Maybe it's my turn to help you?"

Isis tried to smile, but it turned into tears. Everything that had happened, all the secrets she was keeping, they were bursting to get out. She couldn't hold them; she was going to burst into crumbled pieces like the fallen tree.

Just a part of it, that's all I'll tell.

"Something did happen," she said, more quietly than the rustling leaves. "That night when we went chasing UFOs, with Gil and Gray."

Wings fluttered at her back, her bones were light as air. She looked down at the strange, lumpy shapes of her body. Her wrong body, which wouldn't fly.

Cally stared at her, then gasped.

"Oh, God!" she cried, pulling Isis into a tight, crushing hug. She whispered in her ear. "Did Gray… did he try and *touch* you?"

Caught in a dark curtain of hair, it took Isis a moment to realise what Cally meant.

"*No!*" Isis pushed out of the hug, shaking her head. "It was nothing like *that*."

Cally rubbed a hand across her eyes. "Thank goodness. For a moment I thought…"

And Isis plunged in. "It was the lights," she said, watching Cally's face, trying to gauge her reaction.

"The lights in the sky?"

Isis nodded. "When I watched them, I saw them turn into birds. And I felt like... I had wings, and I was flying." She swallowed. "It wasn't a dream. It was as real as this."

Cally frowned. "And that's why you've been out of sorts?"

"I can't get it out of my head." It was a bit of truth, enough maybe.

Cally's frown slowly turned into a delighted smile.

"Isis!" she cried, "Why didn't you tell me before? Don't you see? This isn't bad, it's wonderful! You've inherited my gift! I'm sure you were frightened, but it was only the spirits speaking to you. I said it to Gil, didn't I? There was spiritual energy all around the UFO!" She reached out, taking Isis's hands. "It's very unsettling, the first time they communicate, but you'll get used to it."

Isis opened her mouth, then shut it again. Cally didn't understand her better now – if anything, it was worse. And how could she put her right without telling a whole lot more? Things she *couldn't* tell.

Cally laughed, hugging Isis.

"I'm so happy, Isis! And this makes today even more important!" She let go, keeping hold of Isis's hand, her smile as bright as the sunshine. "Come on, we're nearly there."

Another clearing, but larger this time and lawned with fine grass. A purposeful space, not just an opening in the trees. Tended by a warden who came each spring to mow back any encroaching gorse and bracken, and in the centre, a standing stone. Iron-grey, dappled with lichen, and shaped roughly like a pointed leaf. Around it was a low fence, with a small sign reading THE DEVIL'S SPEARHEAD.

"This is it," Cally said quietly.

Isis's chest was tight, as if a hand had closed around it.

A standing stone in the woods, half an hour's drive away from Wycombe.

"Is this where…?"

Cally's mouth was a flat line, her cheeks pale in the sunlight. She looked as squeezed as Isis felt.

"It's where we were going, the day that Angel… died." Cally took a deep breath. "But I brought us in by another way. I couldn't bear to take the main path, or drive along that road again."

Isis stared round. "Why did you want to come *here*?"

In answer, Philip Syndal walked into the clearing from a path on the other side of the standing stone. He was pink-faced and sweat-glistened, wearing shorts that revealed his hairy, fat-calved legs. He looked like somebody's uncle, innocently out for a ramble, but the hand tightened its grip on Isis's heart. Why was he here? Was the shadow still inside him, a darkness waiting to pour out?

"Cally, Isis," he said genially, "so good to see you." His habitual smile faded a little as he got closer. "Is everything all right?" he asked Isis. "Has your mother explained why I asked you here?"

"I didn't know if it would be right to," answered Cally, awkward and guilty.

Philip's smile returned. "It was my suggestion we meet at this place. It's important we work somewhere with resonance. Somewhere strongly linked to your troubles."

"What work?" asked Isis, fear building inside her.

"Phil's very kindly offered to cleanse your aura," said Cally.

"My aura?"

Cally nodded. "You know, darling, the field of psychic energy around your body. Phil can see its colour, he can clean it up."

Isis stared at them. Was this a joke?

"I'll clear away the darkness, the stains of sorrow and trouble," said Philip. "You'll forget all your unhappiness."

She shook her head. "I don't want to do it."

Philip reached out to her. "Your mother told me how unhappy you are. She thinks you're suffering from delayed trauma about your sister."

The word on his lips held strange echoes. Isis backed away.

"It's got nothing to do with her," she said.

Cally caught her hand. "I talked with Phil, and he explained it so clearly. *Everything* for us is about Angel." Her voice was quiet, trembling. "What happened to her changed us both so much."

If only Cally knew! But Isis couldn't tell her, not with him here.

"Please," said Cally, "I just want us to be happy again. We've been through so much, and now we can be better. Phil can work on our auras, right here in the sunshine."

Isis shook her head again, looking around for escape. But there was only the path, and it wouldn't take her anywhere; at the other end was a just small car park in the middle of fields.

"I don't want to," she repeated.

"I promise, it won't do her anything but good," said Philip, looking at Cally, who nodded. The two adults agreed between themselves, ignoring Isis.

Philip sat down on the ground, crossing his legs. They squeezed out of his shorts, the colour of uncooked pastry.

"My spirit guide wants to help you," he said, looking up at Isis. "Why not think of it as a spring clean for your soul?" He patted the grass. "Please, sit down."

Cally immediately knelt down on the grass next to him.

"I've worked on auras hundreds of times," said Philip, "and people always tell me they feel better afterwards."

Now Cally grabbed Isis's hand and pulled her down. The grass was soft as lace.

Surely someone else would come into the clearing? A sightseer or dog walker, interrupting them and bringing this all to an end.

But no one did.

Cally took Isis's hand and put it into Philip's. His grip was fleshy, warm and as tight as a manacle.

"Now," he said, "we're here today, in this special place, to find healing for you both." His voice oozed with calmness. "Your auras have been clouded by sad events, but with help from the spirits, we can clear away the darkness and send you forth refreshed and sparkling."

Isis studied the top of his head, watching for anything spilling in or out, but there was nothing apart from his shiny-bald skin under thinning hair. Did he even know what was hidden inside him? The woman at the theatre had no idea about Mandeville's possession of her.

Philip turned to Cally, without letting go of Isis's hand. "Cally, can you use the meditation technique we've been practising at meetings?"

Cally nodded and gazed upwards, her eyes unfocused, breathing deeply through her nose.

"Shut your eyes," Philip said to her, "and find your third eye."

"Her what?" asked Isis.

"It's my psychic portal," said Cally, her voice low and sleepy. "It connects me with the spirit world."

"That's right," said Philip, soothingly. "And now you're drifting out through your portal, into communion with the spirits. Isn't it beautiful? Too beautiful to see or hear anything else."

Philip started to hum tunelessly, first whining the sound though his nose, then dropping into a beelike rumble. Even as she tried to stay alert, Isis began to feel sleepy, while Cally's breathing grew even slower and deeper. After a little while Cally began to snore gently.

Isis pulled herself out. "Cally, wake up!"

Cally didn't react, not even a flicker of her eyelids.

"Don't worry," said Philip, giving Isis's hand a squeeze. "She's just in a deep trance. She's having a lovely dream, really enjoying herself. Your mother's a wonderful subject, very open to suggestion."

"You've hypnotised her?" Isis stared at her mentally absent mum.

Philip nodded. "One of my modest talents. How else could we speak privately?" His grip on her hand tightened a bit, scrunching her fingers together and hurting her. "Calista would never let us talk by ourselves. She's so protective, hardly lets you out of her sight." He chuckled. "Not like your sister... she doesn't pay *her* the slightest attention."

Isis froze.

Philip glanced around the clearing. "Where is she, by the way?"

"You can see Angel?" whispered Isis.

"I could hardly miss her. Prancing about on the table like that!" He smiled at the memory. "Very sweet, if a little awkward, since the others couldn't see her."

Angel said *none* of them had seen her. But then, she was too young to tell if someone was pretending.

Philip looked at Isis. "We're the same, you and I. Hadn't you realised that?"

"You can see ghosts," said Isis. Mandeville had been right.

"Did you think I was a fraud?" grinned Philip. "Fake, like everyone else in the Welkin Society?" He shook his head. "I suppose it *is* surprising to find a real medium in the society. When Norman asked me to join, all those years ago, I knew they didn't have an ounce of psychic ability between them. But he was a very wealthy man, and if he believed in you... well, let's just say he helped me a lot. Of course, that all changed these last couple of years." He paused, then shook it away. "You probably think the people at my house were all charlatans, or liars. But they're not, they're just exceptional believers, even fooling themselves. It's why they make such good hypnotic subjects."

Isis looked at her sleeping mum. Could she shake her awake? Was it dangerous to shock someone out of a trance? "Please, wake Cally up."

Philip ignored her.

"The meetings are pretty awful though. I have to stop myself from laughing when they start on about the wisdom of the spirits. You and I know what ghosts are really like!"

Isis stared at his smile. Was he trying to be her friend?

"What about the theatre?" she said, remembering all the tricks he'd used, the lack of any ghosts and the creature at the end.

Philip tilted his head. "I knew *you* wouldn't be fooled by my stage show. The trouble is, despite what people want to think, the spirit of dear Aunty Ethel almost never appears at a seance just because her niece wants it. Ghosts are unpredictable by their very nature." He leaned towards her. "Norman could never understand this, even though I tried to tell him. He couldn't face the truth that ghosts aren't whole people like us. They're just leftovers. Longings and cast-offs. I never tell the punters this, but I think ghosts are just bits shaved off our spirits when we squeeze our way to the next life, whatever that is." His voice was oddly high-pitched. "Dropped socks of the soul, I call them."

Isis didn't say anything. She didn't know what she thought ghosts were.

Philip smoothed his hair with his free hand. "Anyway, people want to believe their loved ones are watching over them. *I* can't tell them Aunty Ethel couldn't even be bothered to turn up. So yes, I use tricks."

Isis almost nodded, it all made a kind of sense, more

than Mandeville's hints and mutterings. Except, there were lots of spirits waiting to be called at Cally's performances, she just hadn't been aware of them. If Philip was a real psychic, why didn't the ghosts clamour to be at his shows?

"Norman just didn't want to understand what it's really like," said Philip to himself. "I *tried* to show him."

He looked back at Isis. "I know the Welkin Society has no talent, but they do have influence, money and connections. Not long after joining, I learned the techniques of hypnotism." He smiled. "I told the group it was a special meditation, and they lapped it up! Soon I could drop them all into a trance with just a few words." Now Philip chuckled. "I even used hypnosis to get my first big break. In one of my *meditations* I told Ian to take me on tour with him. He'd never have done it otherwise – he knew I'd steal the show."

She'd thought Philip was a fake, but this was worse. He was using people, manipulating them.

Isis tried to pull her hand out of his tight, sweaty grip, but she was snare-caught, like a rabbit.

"Don't worry," said Philip, squeezing her hand a little tighter. "I wouldn't do anything like that to you. Your mind has to stay open, untainted."

There was something in the way he said it. An expectation.

"Why did you invite Cally to join the Welkin Society?" Isis asked carefully.

Philip chuckled again. "Well not for her talent, obviously!" His pupils were wide and black, even though the day was bright. "For *you*, Isis. I invited Cally for you."

She pulled frantically, trying to get away from him, but he held on firmly, stopping her from standing up.

"Shh," he said, "you don't need to be frightened." Like a hunter calming his prey. "I could hardly believe it when I heard about you, so I invited your mother to join the society."

Heard?

"Who told you about me?" Isis asked.

Philip smiled, a little sly. "I have my means. Perhaps my spirit guide told me. And you're such a clear psychic, the ghosts must flock to you!"

"No," said Isis.

Philip looked smug. "You should probably thank me for that. They're more respectful these days, and there aren't the numbers there used to be."

She felt a shiver at the back of her neck, as if someone

were watching. But apart from Cally, there was no one else in the clearing, living or dead. Only the trees and the plumed tiers of ferns.

"It was worse when I was your age," said Philip. He frowned, remembering. "If I woke at night, they'd be around my bed. At school they blocked my view of the teachers."

Isis nodded, surprised by a shared understanding.

"I did really badly," said Philip, "left without passing any exams."

"It's hard to concentrate," said Isis, thinking of her problems in the Victorian parts of her school.

"You know, don't you?" Philip put his other hand over hers. "All the pressure, all the wanting. Filling up your life, creeping into your mind." His voice cracked a little, he was struggling not to cry. "Imagine how much worse it was for me, when there were so many more."

"What happened to them?" Isis asked.

Philip shook his head, not answering. And his next words were quick and aggressive. "It's their own fault, if they insist on coming! And it's *much* easier to hold things together when there are fewer ghosts to deal with." His gaze shifted, pinning to her. "But I need to stop now, to rest. I've done my time, now it's someone else's turn."

You chatter. She remembered the words, spoken long ago. *But I am hungry.*

A frightened prickle ran up Isis's spine, lifting the hairs at the nape of her neck.

"It was small at first, but it just kept growing," Philip smiled at her. "You're young and empty; you'll be able to hold it, no problem. And it's only fair, don't you think? I've had it for twenty-five years, that's a long time."

The leaves of the trees washed into purple, as if dipped in ink, and the sound of wings hushed in the air.

"What will I be able to hold?" Isis asked, almost whispering.

Philip smiled. "*You know.* Try to think of it as a friend, as your protector. It's already extending over you, and soon…" He tapped her forehead. "It'll fit right in. Plenty of room."

Isis gasped, her breath running ragged. "I don't want it!"

Philip tutted. "Well it's all decided, so there's no point fussing. I'm getting tired, and it needs someone new. I'm sure it's looking forward to the move."

"I won't! I'll fight it!" She imagined the dark cloud pouring down into her head, grasping hold of her memories and pulling them apart with its fingers.

"You have to take your *turn*!" snapped Philip. "Someone

has to keep the ghosts down, otherwise they multiply like vermin. It's your go, I've done enough."

She shook her head desperately.

"Selfish," Philip muttered. "I put *my* life on hold, never did the things I wanted to. Do you think I wanted to be a stage psychic, and have ridiculous middle-aged women constantly asking me about the afterlife? I wanted to be a vet when I was your age."

Isis looked around, trying to see, straining to hear. But only the ferns in the clearing were whispering, speaking a breeze.

Philip sighed. "All right, I didn't want to say this, but you really are forcing me. I give personal seances, and one of my clients is a poor woman who lost her husband. Very good hypnotic subject, works in the council's social services department. Well, last week she gave me your file, not that she remembers doing it." He flicked a glance at Cally, lost in the false safety of her dreams. "You should see the letters your teachers have written about you. And the replies from social workers." He looked at Isis. "Are you aware how close you are to being taken into care?"

Isis glared at him.

"There's nothing wrong with me and Cally!"

Philip pulled his face into a sympathetic expression. "We naturally defend our parents, but your file says otherwise. A chaotic and neglectful lifestyle. Cally dragging you all around the countryside on evening performances when you should be at home doing your homework, or in bed. People in the audiences reported it. And then your teachers are worried about how small and underfed you look. Turning up at school without the proper uniform, and no packed lunch. Apparently your concentration is really quite terrible. Of course they blame that on poor parenting, not ghosts." He pulled Isis towards him a little. "Think how easy it would be for me to get you taken away from your mother. A nudge here and there. Perhaps a few concerned phone calls?"

Isis's heart was pattering in panic. Was this true? Could it be?

It probably wouldn't take much, now she thought about it. The deputy head already asked Isis questions like, "How's your mother doing?" and, "How are things at home?" Isis had thought she was just being nice, but maybe she wrote down Isis's answers and sent them off to a social worker?

"My dad," she said. "He'd stop you!"

Philip's mild expression flicked into harsh. "And where is

he, then? Oh yes, he left you. Do you really think he cares?"

The grass felt like rock beneath her. She could hardly breathe, the air stolen from her lungs. "Please," she begged. "Don't take me away from my mum."

Philip gazed at her. "I don't want to... I loved my parents too. Even when they called me lazy and stupid, even when they turned me out of the house at fourteen." His voice was cold, tinged with bitterness. "I ended up in a care home, run by a man who *cared* for us with an old snooker cue. I still have the scars from his beatings." He squeezed her hand tighter, so her fingers almost felt numb. "I don't want that to happen to you."

"Cally would never let them take me!"

Philip narrowed his eyes. "Even if she found out the truth? About Angel, and how you've been lying to her all this time?"

He looked up. The sky was a circle of blue, lined by the soft ruffle of the surrounding trees.

"Do you know why psychics are so rare?" he said quietly. "Because it's a defect. Like two heads, or a heart on the outside of your body – it's not supposed to happen. That's why people with psychic ability suffer so much." He looked back at Isis. "And you see ghosts very clearly, don't you? Which is unusual, even for a psychic — they all look quite blurry to me. So you're at the extreme end of defective, don't you see? You really need protection, or you'll be gibbering before you know it." He smiled. "You'll get used to having it in your mind, after a while."

Isis tried to breathe, tried to think. Mandeville had said the Devourer started as a protection, but now it was out of control. Had it somehow attached itself to Philip, was that what Mandeville meant?

"I won't do it," she whispered, trying to hold out.

"Well you will," he said calmly, letting go of her hand at last. Blood prickled back into her fingers.

Isis stared at him for a second, then she sprang up, grabbing Cally's shoulders, shaking her out of her trance. "Wake up! Wake UP!"

"Wha...?" said Cally, bleary, her eyes barely open.

"We have to go!"

Cally rubbed her eyes.

"We have to leave right now!"

"*Isis*," said Cally, turning to Philip. "I'm sorry, Isis is being *so* rude today."

Philip smiled calmly. "It's really quite all right. Everything will be sorted out soon."

Violet colour fluttered through the trees.

"No it won't!" shouted Isis. "Because Cally's leaving the Welkin Society! We're never seeing you again!"

"What are you talking about?" said Cally, standing up, frowning. "I'm not doing any such thing."

Isis opened her mouth, but how could she even start to explain?

"The Welkin Society is... just a big con!" she said. "Philip said you were doing a meditation, but really he was hypnotising you!"

Philip chuckled, as if Isis were joking, and Cally narrowed her eyes, her voice shivering with contained anger. "Philip is one of the greatest healers in the country," she said. "I think you should apologise."

"Maybe this has been a little overwhelming for Isis?" Philip said to Cally, with what sounded like concern.

Cally shook her head. "That doesn't excuse her behaviour."

"It's not just me who thinks you should leave the Welkin Society!" shouted Isis, desperate. "Gray thinks the same. And Gil!" Anything to get Cally away from here, away from Philip. "He says it's a cult! He thinks you're stupid for joining!"

She stopped, watching the blush rise in Cally's cheeks.

"I think maybe it *is* time for us to go home," Cally said coldly.

"Please, don't worry about this," said Philip. "Sometimes people react in odd ways to a cleansing. I'm sure she'll think about it later, and see this is the right thing for her."

"Come *on*," said Isis.

Cally didn't answer, her face was grim.

They walked back to the car, not speaking. The trees seemed menacing now, and Isis kept looking up, watching for a shift of hue. For the leaves to change colour, and gather into a shadow.

Chapter Twenty-four

Gray

It was Saturday evening when Stu came round. I know because Mum had only just dropped me off, and Dad was still grouchy after talking to her, like always. When the doorbell rang, he swore and said, "What *else* does she want to nag at me about?" yanking it open. His face morphed from cross to surprised.

"Keeper!" he said. "What are you doing here?"

Stu the Keeper shoved straight in, clutching this massive bag.

"I can't hang around out there!" he snapped, "Why didn't you tell me this is a neighbourhood watch area?"

Dad shrugged. "It's only local busybodies, checking who doesn't pooper-scoop after their dog."

"Don't be fooled!" hissed Stu. "Haven't you read the forums? You know MI6 is going through neighbourhood watch reports, checking for so-called terrorists? What they mean is people like you and me, those of us searching out the real truth in this world." He put his bag down, shuffled out of his anorak and dropped it on the sofa. "We're living in a surveillance state, my friend."

"Right," said Dad. "And the reason you're here is...?"

Stu tutted at him. "The *interview*. For *The Database*." He opened the bag and started pulling out bits of a camera tripod. "I thought we could start with your observations, and work through to your most recent calculations."

"What, now?" asked Dad.

Stu nodded, pulling out this really old-looking camcorder. "Of course now."

Dad pointed at me. "But I've got Gray."

"And *Doctor Who*'s on in ten minutes," I reminded.

Stu stopped getting his stuff out, and shrugged a bit.

"Oh, yeah," he said, carelessly. "Well, we could watch that, then do the interview after we've talked about the episode." Me and Dad looked at each other. Dad's told me before how Stu doesn't really have any friends; Dad's about the closest he's got, and they never do anything together apart from UFO stuff.

"I can interview Gray as well," Stu said, sort of pleading, "as an additional witness?"

I was trying to beam thought messages to Dad – *no, no, no!* But he wasn't listening.

"Yeah, fine," Dad said to Stu, who looked really happy, his face going all crinkly under his grey stubble. He pulled this fat, tattered book out of his bag.

"*Doctor Who Encyclopaedia*, 1978 to 1999. Let's see if there's any cross references in this new series."

"Can't we just watch it?" asked Dad.

Stu flicked a look at me. "Your dad's not really a fan, is he?"

Which made me laugh, cos Dad's the most obsessed person I've ever met about aliens, *Doctor Who* and stuff. Apart from Stu.

Anyway, we settled down to watch telly. Me, Dad and Stu the Keeper. Once the programme started, I nearly even forgot about the smell of him smoking all the way through.

As soon as *Doctor Who* finished, Dad and Stu started talking about it. Like, all this boring stuff about what happened in the show thirty years ago, and picking holes in the science. They really got into it, and Dad ended up asking Stu if he wanted to have dinner with us. Even though I was beaming Dad the biggest thought message ever.

Of course, Stu did want to stay, especially when Dad said it was shepherd's pie and chips. Dad went in the kitchen, and got the shepherd's pie out of the fridge. I heard the crackle as he sliced open the cellophane on the packet, the oven door open and close. He shouted through to Stu, "Did you ever get any further with those deaths? The ones like Norman Welkin?"

That got my attention, but Stu shook his head. "Not really."

"No pattern then?" Through the door I saw Dad at the freezer, opening it to get a bag of chips. He clattered them onto a baking tray, putting them in the oven too. That was his cooking sorted.

Stu went into the kitchen and I followed, hanging around the door.

"I've checked against all the standard variables," said Stu. "Unusual weather, distance to a nuclear power plant, meteorite strikes, UFO sightings, chemical spills and so on. I even checked government activities, ours and all the other countries operating their secret services over here...

Big fat zero, I'm afraid."

Dad nodded towards me. "Maybe Gray was right then?" he said. "Maybe it was just coincidence?"

Stu leaned back against the sink, folding his arms. "Coincidence is what the government want you to think. It's what they say when they don't want you to know what's *really* happening." He looked at me. "I'll find the pattern, Gray, I just need to get the right data."

Before, I would've thought Stu was talking rubbish. But I'd seen so much, you know? I'd stopped believing in coincidences too.

It took about twenty minutes for Dad to get dinner ready. Nowhere near as good as what Mum makes, but on the plus side Dad doesn't care about me eating vegetables. We were a few mouthfuls in when I got up the nerve to ask Stu.

"You know The Database?" I said to him.

He stopped eating, fork in the air, and his eyes flicked towards the living room, where the laptop was. Like he had to check it was okay.

"Yes," he said.

"Well, you know it has all those UFO sightings, and unexplained phenomena and stuff?"

"Unexplained to current science," said Stu, waving his fork. "Current, blinkered, government science." He lowered his voice. "What's *really* happening... that's in The Database." He pulled his eyebrows together, glaring at me. "All triple locked, with password protected encryption." Like I wanted to break into it.

"I just wondered about something that might be in there," I said.

Stu looked pleased. "You know, you're a lucky boy," he said. "Growing up with your dad. You aren't being brainwashed by the government and corporations, like most kids." He turned to Dad. "You haven't let him have a mobile phone?"

Dad shook his head. "I stopped Jenice from giving him one as well."

Jenice is my mum. I've had loads of fights with her and Dad about getting a phone.

Stu pointed his ketchupy knife at me. "You should thank your dad for that. All those downloads and ringtones, you know there's messages inside them? Hidden ones, designed to stop you thinking about anything important. Stop you questioning what's really going on." He shoved in a forkful of shepherd's pie, carrying on with his mouth full.

"You know what I see, when I look at you kids, all wired into your phones and MP3 players? Zombies! Brainwashed and consuming whatever you're told to. They've got your generation licked — you're just lambs to the slaughter." He reached for the ketchup, and squirted a load more on his plate.

"The thing is," I said, trying to get him back on the point, "I was just wondering if you had anything on The Database that's... paranormal." Stu scowled at me, so I carried on quick. "Like, stuff about... ghosts."

I knew by their faces I'd gone too far.

"Ghosts?" said Dad coldly. "Are you trying to be funny, Gray?"

"The Database isn't a joke!" shouted Stu, spraying gobs of chip onto the table. "It's for holding evidence about the *truth*, not superstitions!" He'd gone red, and the veins in his neck were sticking out.

"Sorry, I was only asking."

"You should be sorry!" said Dad. "I'd have thought you'd know better!"

Stu calmed down, and put his hand on Dad's arm. "It's all right, Gil, you don't need to fight my battles. Combating ignorance, distinguishing the real, that's what I do this for."

He looked at me. "If you want to know about ghosts, they're the effect on our brains of natural variations in the earth's magnetic field." I opened my mouth, but he didn't give me a chance to answer. "They did an experiment a few years ago, where they strapped magnets to people's heads. Half the people taking part thought they'd seen their dead relatives, floating around in the room. Which proves it."

Dad smiled, but his frown at me wasn't gone. "Why did you even ask, Gray?"

I shrugged. "I was just wondering, that's all." Trying to keep it casual.

But Dad wasn't put off so easy.

"It's Cally and Isis, isn't it? You've been listening to them."

I shook my head.

Stu looked a question at Dad.

"Cally's my new girlfriend," Dad said.

Stu smirked. "How long has she been around then?"

Dad went a bit red. "A couple of months."

"Five," I said. "Five months."

Stu whistled. "Serious."

Dad went even redder. "She's got something about her, you know?" He glared at me. "But she also believes in ghosts, fairies and any nonsense that comes her way." He sighed. "She even joined some club, where they all get together and talk about contacting the spirits. A right bunch of nutters, if you ask me."

Stu rolled his eyes. "Women!" Like he knew anything about them. He turned to me. "So, that's where you got this ghost stuff?"

I hunched down in my chair. All I wanted by then was to get out of the kitchen.

"It doesn't matter," I said. "It was just a question."

Stu studied me, pressing his finger onto one of the bits of chip he'd spat on the table. Popping the smear of chewed-up food into his mouth.

"Ghosts aren't real, Gray. All those ghosts hunters and mediums, they're just spooking themselves in old houses. Bumps in the night, that's all it is. They're always going on about having evidence and taking pictures, but the best they get are those 'orbs'. Circles of light, floating in shot, which anyone can tell are just camera glitches and reflections."

Stu ate another bit of sprayed chip.

"Whereas what you and your dad filmed, now *that's* real. And real film of it too, not just some wobbly little blob of light."

Dad nodded. "Don't listen to all Cally's stuff about ghosts."

It's funny really, because Isis had said ghosts can look like balls of light, and Stu had just agreed with her even though he was saying they didn't exist.

Dad took the empty plates and dumped them in the sink. He raised an eyebrow at me. "Washing up?"

I sighed and got up, while Dad went to the fridge and took out a couple of cans of beer, handing one to Stu, who pulled a fag out of nowhere and lit it up. They cracked the cans open, gurgling the beer into their mouths. I started running the water into the sink.

"Ghosts and the afterlife," sneered Stu. "It's just fantasy. Wishful thinking."

Dad did a long burp. "People should focus on what's real."

Stu burped back. "It doesn't even make sense! If you can get ghosts of people, why not cats, dogs or whatever? Animals die too, but you never see those TV mediums contacting a dead orangutan. If there's really ghosts, the spirit world ought to be crammed to bursting with the ghosts of all the pigs and chickens we've killed, and the trees we've chopped down!"

They finished their cans – both of them could really pour it down – while I scrubbed the plates and stacked them on the draining rack. Because Dad doesn't even have a dishwasher, if you can believe it.

Stu put his empty can down on the table. "I mean, we've caused as many species to go extinct as an asteroid hitting the planet."

Dad got up and went to get two more beers from the fridge. "I wouldn't blame them if the aliens didn't want to come down and talk to us. Probably waiting to see if we wipe ourselves out too."

"They've *tried* talking to us," said Stu, taking a can. "That's the problem. America, Russia. Plenty of evidence they had secret alien contacts. But it all gets hushed up by the military."

"I'm going to try and start communications next time," said Dad.

"Good idea," said Stu, nodding. "That's what the lights in the sky are – they've got to be trying to tell us something."

I was standing there with the washing-up sponge in one hand, a ketchupy spoon in the other, and what Stu said just… slotted it all into place.

He was right about the extinctions, I'd read loads about it in my wildlife magazines. We're making hundreds of species go extinct, every year. Like that giant tortoise, Lonesome George, from the Galapagos Islands. He was the last one of his kind, living all alone. When he died, his species went extinct.

They all died, that's what Isis said.

I mean, Lonesome George died in a zoo, but most wild animals get killed when a forest's chopped down, or a river's being polluted, or they're hunted or whatever. Thousands and thousands of deaths, and when the last one goes...

Both times we saw all these tiny lights, coming together into one.

"Do you think?" I asked, my words coming out slow. "Do you think when the last of some kind of animal gets wiped out, and it goes extinct, there could be a ghost for its species?"

Stu and Dad both looked at me.

"Well," said Dad. "I suppose if you believed all that stuff. A species is kind of alive, so extinction is a kind of death."

Stu nearly choked on his beer. "I just explained why ghosts don't exist! And even if they did, a species is millions of individual organisms, living over millions of years."

"That'd make it a big ghost then," said Dad, grinning at him.

Stu glared back. "Oh yes, and what would it look like, this ghost of a species?"

Dad laughed, and shook his head.

But I know. I've thought about it lots. The ghost of a species would look like itself. Like millions and one, at the same time. Birds or insects or fish or wild animals. Except most of us can only see them as lights.

You see, Stu and Dad had it wrong. It isn't aliens who are trying to tell us something.

Hey, who's there?

Shh. Gray, be still.

Someone's knocking at the door.

You will stay completely silent. You won't be able to move a muscle. It's just someone searching, probably for you. A boy doesn't go missing from Accident and Emergency without hospital staff looking for him. But the doors to this storeroom are locked, and by the time they find another key, we will be finished.

No, don't try and leave, don't panic. Just look into my eyes and lie back down on the trolley... that's right... tell me what happened next.

Chapter Twenty-five

Gray

Stu never got to do his interview. He nearly did, he even set up his camcorder, but then everything just kicked off.

It was probably about eight o'clock. I was at the top of the stairs, going into my bedroom, when the phone rang.

"Gray! Can you get that?" Dad yelled up from the living room.

"You're nearer than me!" I shouted back.

The phone kept on ringing. Dad swore and came out of the living room.

"Yes," he snapped into the phone, then, "What, what is it, Cally? No, stop crying, I can't understand you... Of course, come round then..."

He put the phone down, a crinkly frown between his eyebrows. He glared up at me.

"What have you said to Cally?"

"Nothing," I said, but Dad looked like he didn't believe me.

About a minute later the doorbell rang. Cally must've phoned from her car, when she was already driving round.

Dad opened the door and made to kiss her, but Cally pushed past and turned on him. Her face was really white, and her eyes were red and teary.

"What do you think you're doing?" she cried. "Interfering with my life, trying to turn my own daughter against me!"

In the living room, Stu froze. Dad backed up against the sofa.

"Cally, darling. What's the matter?" He had his hands out to her, and his voice was... well, it's the way he sounds when he's got an angry girlfriend to deal with. I've heard it often enough.

Behind Cally, Isis was in the doorway, looking miserable. I went down the stairs and sneaked over to her.

"What's going on?" I whispered to Isis. "Why are you here?"

"I tried to stop Cally," Isis whispered back, "but she's really mad at me."

Dad had his hands on Cally's shoulders, stroking them.

He always does that to women when they're yelling at him, it distracts them or something.

"Why are you upset?" he said, in his calming voice.

"I'm upset because you're poisoning my daughter's mind!" shrieked Cally. "Because you're using her against me!"

"What's happened?" I asked Isis. She gripped onto her sleeves, stretching them down, like she was cold.

"I had to say something," she whispered. "We went to these woods, and Philip Syndal was there. He told Cally some rubbish about cleaning our auras, but really he…" She looked at me. "He knows all about the ghost-eater. And…"

"I thought you loved me, Gil!" shrieked Cally, and she started sobbing.

In the living room, Stu was packing his camcorder away.

"Love you?" Dad's hands stopped for a second, then he started stroking again. "I mean, it's early days…"

Cally slapped at his hands.

"You're just using me!" she cried. "I should have known! That woman in the bar, the one you said was an 'old friend'. She warned me, but I ignored her."

"Anna?" said Dad. "Don't believe anything she says."

"I don't believe anything *you* say!" wailed Cally, tears running down her face.

Stu lifted up his bag, and shuffled for the front door.

"Right then, I'll be going," he said, pushing past me and Isis to get out. "We can do the interview another time." And he was off down the road, only his smoke stink left behind.

"Who was that?" whispered Isis.

"One of Dad's UFO mates." We climbed up the stairs a few steps. Isis had her jumper sleeves scrunched up in her hands.

"Philip Syndal knows about me," she whispered.

"What?" I mouthed, my eyes wide.

"He saw Angel, one time at his house, but he pretended not to. And he…" she was shaking, white as anything, "he says it's going to leave him, and go into me."

"The ghost-eater?" I asked, not quite believing.

She nodded.

"No." I shook my head. "No way. He's trying to scare you or something, that's all. I saw you fight it! You'd never let it in."

She looked away, at Cally, then spoke so quietly I could hardly hear her. "He said if I didn't, he'd…"

"CALLY, just CALM DOWN!" shouted Dad, drowning out Isis. "I don't even know what this is ABOUT!"

"It's about you trying to stop me going to the Welkin Society!" screamed Cally. "Because you're jealous of my friendship with Phil!" She whipped her hands through her hair, messing it up, going crazy-looking. "I was a doormat once!" she yelled. "But I won't let you control me! I won't go through that kind of thing again!"

"I'm NOT trying to control you!" shouted Dad. "I've never tried to stop you seeing Philip Syndal or his club of nutters!"

"*Nutters?*" shrieked Cally. "Am I a nutter too? Is that what you think of me?"

"No! That's not what I meant!"

They carried on like that. The front door was wide open, I bet the whole street was listening in. Me and Isis went further up the stairs, but I wished we could just leg it like Stu had.

"You *have* to tell your mum about him," I said to Isis, when we got to the top step. "If Philip Syndal's trying to set that monster on you, then he's…" Dangerous, I should've said. A murderer.

"I can't tell her," she said, "I'd have to tell her so much to explain it properly. I'd have to tell her *everything*."

"So?"

She sat down on the landing, pulling her knees up.

"I keep thinking, about all that darkness just pouring inside him." She looked scared. "I don't want it inside me."

Her knees were poking out from her skirt. They were grass and mud stained.

"You have to tell your mum, even some of it!" I said. "You have to get as far away from Philip as possible!"

She only shook her head, not looking at me.

Dad and Cally were still fighting. Cally yelled out, "Yes, you are!" and whacked Dad in the chest with a flat hand. It didn't look like it hurt much.

"You're crazy if you don't say something!" I snapped at Isis. I was getting angry with her by then; I thought she was just being stupid, you know?

"I did!" snapped back Isis. "I told Cally she should leave the Welkin Society. That's what all this is about!"

I frowned, I didn't get it.

"I said your dad wants her to leave too," she said guiltily.

"Oh." That explained all the freaking out – it was exactly the kind of over-the-top reaction you'd expect from Cally.

"I didn't say your dad was jealous, that's her own stuff."

We realised at the same time they'd gone quiet downstairs. Cally and Dad were looking up at us.

"Isis," said Dad, "could you come down here please?"

Isis looked at me, then got up slowly and started down the stairs. Dad had his arm around Cally, and she was leaning into him. United.

I followed Isis, two steps behind.

Cally ran her hand through her hair. "Isis, why did you lie to me?"

"I don't know what you're talking about," said Isis, calm as anything.

Cally huffed. "You know perfectly well. Why did you say Gil doesn't want me to stay in the Welkin Society? Why did you say he's jealous of Phil?"

Isis didn't answer.

"Isis," said Dad, "are you unhappy that I'm dating your mum?"

Isis shrugged. "I don't mind."

Cally glared at her. "Isis," she said, "you can't drive Gil away by lying."

"I didn't lie," said Isis. She was always full of surprises. I don't think I could've stayed so cool.

A blush rose up Cally's neck, and her eyes flashed dark. "Isis Dunbar, you're in serious trouble!"

And that's when I said it. Because I had to help Isis;

Dad and Cally didn't even know what was going on.

"It's true," I said to Cally. "Dad *doesn't* like your psychic club." Dad widened his eyes at me, but I took no notice. Anyway, I've covered up for him loads of times, and I was sick of it. "He said so, just today. That it's all a load of rubbish. I heard him say it to Stu."

"What?" Cally pulled away from Dad.

"That's not true!" lied dad, trying to catch her hand back, but she wouldn't let him have it.

Dad looked daggers at me, but Isis smiled a thank you.

"I knew it!" Cally shouted at Dad. "You *are* jealous! Of my interests, of Philip." She put her hand to her head. "I don't know what to think!"

"Don't listen to Gray!" said Dad. "He's lying!"

Cally turned furious. "That's the third person you've accused of lying about you! I wonder if I know you at all!" She pulled herself up, took a shuddering breath. "Maybe we aren't right for each other. Maybe we should stop seeing each other…"

Isis gasped. I went still, wondering what'd happen if they split up.

But Dad… he turned pale, then red, then he sort of sagged.

"Cally, no!" he croaked out. "I'm sorry if I said the wrong things. I'll do anything to make it up. I couldn't bear to lose you." He held his arms out towards her. "Because I do… love you."

I never heard him say that before. Not to any of them.

Cally burst into tears and flung herself at him.

"I won't go to the Welkin Society again," she sobbed. "Not if you don't want me to."

Isis grinned at me.

"No!" said Dad. "I want you to carry on. It's important to you."

Isis stopped smiling.

"I'll prove I'm not jealous," Dad said, looking all gooey at Cally. "You know my next chasing trip, this Friday?" Cally nodded. "Well I want you to invite your Welkin Society. They can investigate the spiritual energy you felt last time."

"Oh, Gil!" Cally kissed him.

"Dad, no!" I cried. "They're dangerous! Nutters, like you said."

"Shut up, Gray!" snapped Dad. He looked so angry with me, it felt like getting slapped. He turned back to Cally. "I never said that," he lied again. "But since Gray is so disapproving of them, he can miss out on this trip."

So me and Isis were both in trouble. Not long after, Cally took Isis home. It was only later I remembered that I hadn't even told Isis what I'd realised about the UFOs... I mean the ghosts in the sky.

I wish I could turn back time, and do everything another way.

Even we can't do that, Gray, and we can do a lot of things. If turning back time were possible, I would have done so already, believe me. Gone back to the field, back to the house, back to the roadside.

We've made our mistakes, and they can't be undone. That's why Isis is lying in the mortuary.

Chapter Twenty-six

Isis

"I don't want to go!" shouted Isis. It must've been the twentieth time she'd yelled it. They'd argued round in circles, grinding down to a stony stalemate. Cally wouldn't budge about going on Gil's UFO hunt, Isis hadn't been able to convince her not to. The only way would be to tell her the truth, all of it. But that was impossible.

She couldn't even speak to Gray and get his ideas on what to do. Cally had banned her from talking to him. Isis had heard her on the phone to Grandma Janet, saying he was a bad influence.

Cally stood by the front door. Coat and car keys in her hands, their blankets and chairs bundled up on the floor.

"You are coming with us," Cally said coldly. "If there was any other way, I'd happily leave you at home."

"Do that then!"

"I'm not leaving you by yourself for a whole night. Who knows what might happen?" Cally's phone rang and she answered it, the anger clearing out of her voice. "Yes, of course. We'll be down in a minute."

She looked at Isis. "It's time to go, and I expect you to be civil to Philip. It was incredibly kind of him to forgive you, after the way you behaved." She opened the front door, waving Isis through, and they heard footsteps in the stairwell. Philip Syndal coming up to meet them.

"Everyone set?" he called, jovial and merry. "Shall I follow your car, Calista? Here, let me help you with your things." He took the camping chairs from Cally. She glared at Isis, pulling her by the arm and locking the door behind them.

You must come.

The memory fluttered up from deep inside Isis's mind, but she couldn't remember who'd said the words to her. Shuddering, she knew no one had.

Shadows were deepening over the field, the sun gleaming

red across a western roll of hills. This was a different place to last time, the location down to Gil's calculations. And even after they'd found Gil's camper van, parked up on the roadside, it had been a long walk to get to the field. Now they were all standing on a rough, nettle-strewn strip of grass next to a hedge.

A breeze fluttered through Isis's hair, then hissed across the wheat. Cally shivered, drawing her cardigan around her shoulders.

"It's chillier than I thought it would be."

"You're always cold!" said Gil, smiling at her. "You need someone to keep you warm."

Cally giggled, but Isis said nothing. She'd seen the real reason for Cally's chill: Angel had been running in circles around her legs. Recovered now, and back to her chubby, invisible self.

"I with Mummy!" she laughed.

Philip Syndal looked pointedly at Angel, then up to Isis. He winked.

"Go home!" mouthed Isis, but Angel took no notice, only plopping onto the ground and running her hands through the grass without moving it.

Gil set about putting out his monitors and scientific

instruments: unrolling long strands of wire back to his laptop, weaving a black, straggling electronic web around the field, lecturing them all as he worked.

"It's to do with fluctuations in the electromagnetic field – they're very unusual in this part of the country," he said, as he set out a large grey metal box. "This is an EM field generator. I'm going to try communicating with them."

Cally and Philip followed after him, asking questions, but Isis couldn't pretend to care. Over the hedge, she saw the tops of three heads. Voices drifted in the evening air as more people headed their way.

Philip called out, and started towards them. Gil stood slowly, watching as the small group huddled on the other side of the field gate, seemingly baffled as to how to open it. He turned to Cally.

"More of you?" he asked.

"You said I could invite anyone from the Welkin Society," she said.

"Yes, of course," said Gil quickly, wilting a little under Cally's challenging stare. "It's great that they're here."

Cally headed off to the gate, but Isis kept back as a man and two women joined Cally and Philip in the field, all of them talking excitedly. Instead Isis watched for any strange flutters in the sky, or a shivering sweep of blue.

Philip introduced Gil to an elderly woman called Jean, a tall soft-voiced man called Ian and a round, blousy woman wearing draping layers of clothing, who loudly announced herself to be Andrea Simms. Isis recognised all of them from the meeting at Philip's house.

Almost straight away they gathered in a huddle, arguing about how to create a 'psychic circle'. Isis stayed close to Angel, who was running about on her short legs, chasing after a moth fluttering along the hedgerow.

"Please go home, you'll be safe there!" Isis hissed at her. But Angel only shook her head.

"No. I not doing that."

If any of the adults had been watching Isis, they might have wondered at her odd wanderings up and down the field edge. But they weren't paying her any attention, caught up with their own concerns.

"Just stick to the tramlines," Gil was saying to the others, "and it'll be easier to move around the crop."

"What are the tramlines?" asked Jean, turning her grey-haired head towards the field.

"It's where the tractor drives when they're spraying

the crop," said Gil, pointing at the long thin gaps in the wheat, heading straight into the field.

"This is wonderful," said Philip, brightly. "I am sure we are going to have a most interesting night. I'd like us to start by calling on the spirits to come and assist us."

Isis glared at him from a distance – he was such a hypocrite, leading the others into another of their sham seances. There were no spirits out here, except Angel.

"There are six of us," said Philip, "so we can make a very effective circle."

Gil shook his head. "Not me. I'm not included."

"I thought you wanted..." started Cally, but Gil stood firm in this.

"I have my own work to do."

There was a small moment of tension between them, ended by a smile from Cally. She turned to Philip. "It'll have to be the five of us."

Andrea Simms waved her arms, flapping several layers of her tentlike dress.

"No, no! Five is a terrible number. If the spirits draw lines between us, think of the shape..." She lowered her voice dramatically. "The dark star, the pentangle. We want to draw down angels, not *other things*."

Ian snorted. "If you draw lines between five people, the shape you get is a pentagon."

"It's the same thing!" snapped Andrea.

"Actually, no," said Jean, "a pentangle is an extension of a pentagon, so we'd need more people to form it. If there were ten of us, and we took up staggered positions..."

"The spirits are perfectly capable of making any shape they like!" cried Andrea dramatically. "Dark spirits will be attracted the instant we take our places, and before we know it we'll be drawing in all sorts of evil!"

"I'm sure it will be all right," said Cally, trying to calm her.

Andrea folded her arms. "I refuse to take part in anything involving five people."

"Well we can't just use four," said Jean, "we'd make a rectangle or square. They're very un-mystical shapes."

Ian sighed. "If only three of us take part, then two people are left with nothing to do. Why don't we just stick to what we have, and use the five of us."

Andrea opened her mouth to argue, but Philip Syndal held up a hand to stop her. "We don't just have five." He pointed at Isis.

She froze.

"Isis could take a part," he said. "Then we'd be six, which is a very pleasing number for the spirits."

"A child?" said Jean. "Would that be safe?"

"The spirits wouldn't hurt her," said Philip, confidently.

"But does she have the gift?" asked Andrea. "She's rather small to be a channel."

"She *is* gifted!" said Cally, bristling. "My daughter had a very strong psychic experience recently."

"So she'll be perfect," said Philip.

"No!" Isis said, her heart pounding. There was no way she was doing anything he wanted. Whatever this was about, he couldn't be trusted.

"*Isis.*" Cally spoke her name as a warning, but Philip gave Isis a kind, gentle look.

"It's all right," he said quietly. "I understand if you're nervous."

"I was scared the first time I heard the spirits," said Andrea, speaking loudly and slowly, as if Isis were stupid. "However, once you face the truth of your gift, you'll find there's nothing to fear, really."

Isis kept her eyes on the adults. She had to get out of this, and so she let a little bit of fear creep into her voice. "Ghosts do scare me," she said, hoping they'd believe her.

Philip's mouth twitched, as if they were sharing a private joke. "We'll all be with you," he said.

Isis shook her head.

Cally held her hand out. "This is really important to me."

"You can stay with your mother," said Philip, his kind-sounding words reminding her of his threats.

Isis looked at Cally. "I don't want to," she said desperately, needing her mum to understand, to stand by her, even if she didn't know the reason why.

"I expect Isis wants to text her friends," Ian said, "or play a game on her phone. So sad how children these days aren't interested in anything."

Cally winced. "I don't let Isis have those things," she said quickly, before turning to Isis. "Will you stop being so difficult?"

"I'm not!"

"Yes you are!" cried Cally, her temper flashing. "You're always difficult these days! You won't do one thing for anyone else!"

Philip took the few steps towards them, his hand resting on Cally's elbow. "Now there's no need to shout," he said, pulling Cally away from Isis. The other adults watched, looking a little awkward. Apart from Gil, who was absorbed in his electronics.

"She's just going through a difficult stage," said Cally.

"She is?" asked Philip quietly, sympathetically. "Could it be between the two of you perhaps?"

"What? I mean we do argue, but…" started Cally. Behind her, Isis saw Andrea and Jean exchange meaningful glances.

"I always say teenagers need extra attention, not extra discipline," said Andrea loudly. "Parenting is so much more important at their age."

"I do give her attention," said Cally to Philip. "Although I suppose it's less since I started seeing Gil."

Philip nodded, his eyes on Cally. But when he spoke it was loud enough for everyone to hear. "Children act out what they see around them, especially if their parents are absent or unpredictable. But screaming and shouting at them never helps, I think we can all agree on that."

"She wasn't screaming at me," said Isis.

"Bringing up a child on your own can be very challenging," said Philip.

"But you must restrain yourself," Andrea told Cally. "Put her needs first."

Cally stared at her. "I do!"

Andrea raised her eyebrows, and glanced at Philip.

Suddenly Isis understood; Philip had already started laying the groundwork on his threat. He'd obviously told the others his 'concerns' about Cally. There was an almost invisible smile on his lips as he listened to Andrea lecture Cally about childcare, and watched Cally's growing irritation.

"I'll help," said Isis loudly. She looked at Cally. "You were right, I was being selfish."

Cally blinked, then smiled at her. "Thank you, darling." Her anger was gone like it had never been, and she kissed the top of Isis's head, unaware of the cold, scrutinising stares of the other adults.

They walked out into the wheat, Philip leading the adults and Isis following reluctantly after. As they trod the narrow tramline into the crop, Jean dropped back so she was walking with Isis. She didn't say anything for a moment, then she put her thin-boned hand on Isis's shoulder and gave a little squeeze.

"Don't worry, dear," she said. "Things may be difficult with your mother, but I hope you won't have to put up with living with her for much longer."

Chapter Twenty-seven

Gray

On my own.

It was the first time in years I hadn't gone out UFO-chasing with Dad. Each time I thought about it, everyone out there without me, it made me feel sick inside, you know? And I was worried about Isis too.

I said sorry to Dad, of course I did. Loads of times, actually. I asked if I could go with him. I reminded him Friday was one of the nights I was meant to be at his place, and how Mum would go mental if he cancelled because she'd already arranged a meal out with Brian. I tried anything I could think of, but he wouldn't budge. I didn't say anything to Mum, cos I hoped he'd change his mind in the end.

Friday, about half past five, Mum dropped me off at

Dad's. I got out, ran to the door and waved back at her, like everything was normal. I didn't want Dad to have a chance to talk to her. I rang the doorbell, and by the time Dad answered, Mum was already driving off.

He was holding one of his monitors. It was covered in bubble wrap, ready to go in the van. He frowned at me, so I pointed at my rucksack.

"I'm packed."

Dad peered out of the door, but Mum had gone. He frowned at me again, all serious.

"I've already told you, Gray, you can't come along, not this time. Cally wouldn't like it, and I don't want any more arguments. I need to be able to concentrate on my work."

"Isis is going to be there. If she can go, why can't I?"

Dad shook his head. "I don't decide what Isis does. Anyway, Cally said Philip Syndal specifically asked for Isis to go." He rolled his eyes. "Apparently Isis has got psychic powers now, or whatever." He looked at me. "But you haven't."

"Please!"

"No. You're staying here. Watch a film or something, stay up as late as you want."

I plonked my rucksack on the floor. "You're not allowed to leave me on my own all night."

Dad snorted. "Are you a baby? You've been on your own loads of times."

Which was true, and another thing I never told Mum.

Dad put the monitor into a cardboard box. "Look, Gray. I can't risk things with Cally. Not now, when she's already threatened to break it off."

"But you've had loads of girlfriends!" I yelled. "And the chasing trips were always *our* thing." About the only thing we ever did, just the two of us.

Dad didn't even stop packing up.

"This is different!" he said. "Cally's important, you know?"

More important than I was.

"If you won't let me go with you, I'm going to tell Mum!"

Now Dad stopped, staring at me. "Tell her what? What are you on about?"

My hands were in fists.

"I'll tell her," I said, "about the times you dragged me along on your dates. And the times you left me here on my own, so you could go and meet a girlfriend. And the times you told Mum you were helping me with my homework, when really I was helping you on a gardening job." It hung there in the air. Mum'd flip — Dad would be back to Sunday afternoon visits, like when I was little.

Dad folded his arms.

"What are you up to?" he said, and his voice was as cold as the Arctic. "First you try and split me up from Cally, and now you want to ruin our time together? For what? Spite?" He was holding himself really still; I could see how angry he was. "If that's how you want things, fine. *Do it!*" He slammed off into the kitchen, bashing and crashing as he packed up the last of his gear, marching to the front door.

"There is no way you are blackmailing me into anything, Gray!" he shouted, yanking the door open. "Me and Cally are for keeps, so you'd better get used to it! Phone your mum. Tell her I'm irresponsible, tell her what a useless dad I am! If you want to stop our visits, that's up to you, but you're NOT coming out tonight!"

And he stormed out of the house, driving off without me.

I sat on his sofa. I might've cried for a bit.

I thought about phoning Mum, but I didn't want to tell her that stuff, not really. Like Dad said, she'd stop me staying with him.

I got up, and went into the kitchen. Dad never gets in any food on UFO-chasing nights, because we're always out in the countryside somewhere, eating Super Noodles. So there was only breakfast cereal, and some milk in the fridge, which nearly made me cry again. But instead I sat down with a big bowl of cornflakes, and thought about stuff.

Like, how my dad is.

Like, how other kids have dads who stay with their mums, and do stuff like swimming and football at weekends. Dads who don't introduce a new girlfriend every few weeks, and expect their kids to be fine with it. Dads who aren't obsessed with UFOs and think that's more important than anything.

By the time I'd got down to the mushy-sweet milk at the bottom of the bowl, I was back to thinking about everyone else being out there on Dad's UFO-chasing trip, without me. The sick feeling inside me actually hurt.

"I wish it was last year!" I said, out loud. "I wish Dad never met Cally!"

Except, then I wouldn't know Isis, and she's one of the best people I've ever met.

Was. Was one of the best.

I drank the milk out of the bowl, then what was left in the carton. Dad was probably there by now, setting up his gear. Over by the phone, the coordinates of the field were written on a bit of paper. Every time he goes on a chasing trip it's somewhere different. He used to just think of places, like where the fields are really big and flat, or where there'd been crop circles before, but now he's got this computer program he worked out. He puts in things like weather, sunspots, geology and UFO sightings. He says it can predict where the next sighting is going to be, so now if we see a UFO, Dad says it's because of his computer program. Even though we've been out loads of times, and only seen stars.

I cheered up a bit. Probably none of them would see anything, even with their seances or whatever.

But it was still bad. Weird, when I thought about it. Cally had said Philip Syndal was desperate to go on Dad's UFO hunt, once she'd told him about it. Why would he care about UFOs?

Except they weren't UFOs, were they?

And he couldn't know that – I'd only just worked it out and I hadn't even told Isis.

I banged my head with my hand, trying to think, but everything kept rushing around. I tried to remember what I knew about Philip Syndal.

He was a real psychic, but Isis said he used tricks and

lies in his shows. He'd pretended not to see Angel, so Isis would think he was a fake. He had a ghost-eating monster living inside his head, and now he wanted it to go into Isis.

My brain went crazy in panic for a moment then, thinking what would happen to Isis if that thing got inside her. It was so massive, like frozen darkness. If it got in her head… she'd be a puppet, or a zombie or something.

I flapped about in my mind for a few minutes, then I got a grip.

Philip Syndal couldn't do much with everyone there, could he? I mean, it wasn't just him and Isis. Dad and Cally would be on the UFO hunt, plus all the nuts from the Welkin Society. They'd see him if he tried anything.

The Welkin Society.

It seemed ages ago, I'd almost forgotten about it, but the Welkin Society was part of it all too. I mean, Norman Welkin dying was what got us all together in the first place. Dad had said there was some fighting going on in the society, that Norman had been suspicious about some of the other people in it. And I bet he'd meant Philip.

He was covered in ice, like frost. That's what Isis had said, afterwards in the pub. I'd thought she was being over the top, back then.

I ran to Dad's computer and switched it on. As soon as it was online, the instant messenger started blinking. There he was, like always. Stu the Keeper, ready for a chat.

I clicked on the chat box and started typing.

> Hi Stu. Just wanted to ask a question
> about Norman Welkin's death.

Blink blink. Then a reply straight away.

> Hi Gil. Your latest totty let you have a bit
> of time off then? You tired her out?
> Ha ha.

"Yuk," I said, looking at the screen. But Stu was probably going to tell more if he thought he was talking to Dad, so I typed.

> Yes, ha ha.

Which was the best I could do without actually being sick. Then I typed:

> Have you got any more on Norman
> Welkin? Cause of death?

Blink blink.

> Do you ever read anything I send you,
> Gil? I emailed the coroner's report
> last week.

Blink blink.

Fancy another Doctor Who night
some time?

I didn't bother to answer, and I don't care if Dad falls out with Stu. Instead I opened up Dad's email and typed in his password, which he doesn't know I've worked out, but it was easy to break because he uses my name and birthday for everything.

Anyway, I scrolled through Dad's emails and there it was: one from Stu saying 'NWelkin coroner's report – we were right!' Dad hadn't even looked at it. I opened it up, and started reading. It took a bit to understand it, but I found a line that read 'cause of death' and next to it, 'hypothermia'.

Norman Welkin didn't have a heart attack at all, he'd frozen to death.

On a sunny day in March. I remember, I wasn't even wearing a coat. He couldn't have got frozen going for a walk in his garden.

Except I knew he could. Because I'd got caught in that freezing blue, shivering so hard I couldn't speak, my hands going numb. And all on a boiling hot day in the shopping centre. The ghost-eater, the Devourer, it was as cold as deep space. If me and Isis had been caught for any longer, we probably would've frozen too.

Isis had tried to tell me something, back when Dad and Cally were fighting – the reason she wouldn't tell her mum what was really going on. She'd never finished telling me, but now I was sure what it was. I felt like my heart stopped.

Philip Syndal had used the ghost-eater to kill Norman Welkin, and he was going to use it to kill Isis if she didn't do what he wanted.

I sat at the computer, still as a statue.

Isis was out there with a murderer. I was the only one who knew, and I was fifty miles away.

You need to hurry, Gray. We haven't got much more time. I expect a few staff are already starting to wonder about the doctor they'd never seen before, the one who took you away from your treatment room.

I can't risk getting caught, because if they find out I've gone personal again, they'll make me forget all about her. And I can't bear that, not when all I've got left is memories.

Chapter Twenty-eight

Isis

Philip Syndal dropped the members of the Welkin Society into a trance as quickly and easily as he'd hypnotised Cally. He led them down the rustling tramlines, deep into the wheat, then asked them to push out into the rough stands of the crop, taking up positions in a straggly circle. Isis followed them, taking her place five or so metres from Cally. She didn't want to do anything that might spark an argument, and so give Philip more ammunition against Cally.

"Ian," Philip called, "can you move a pace to your right? Jean, just come forwards a step or two."

As if any of it mattered, thought Isis. This was just another trick, like the ones he used at the theatre. She checked the distant hedgerows, which looked like dark walls under the fading-gold sky. There was no sign of anything. Not yet.

"Now," said Philip, "shall we start our meditation?" Isis saw his eyes glitter as he looked her way. "You too, Isis. Just shut your eyes and do what I tell you."

Close your eyes.

Words, half-remembered from a non-existent memory, forced her lids shut. Philip Syndal started talking, a soothing murmur that quickly lulled the others into quiet, then sleep. After a while he stopped, and began humming in his off-key whine. The noise blended with the hushing wheat and the distant whir of a combine harvester. Isis fought against it, but with her eyes closed her mind started to drift, a sleepy cloud covering her thoughts.

Small, freezing hands grabbed her arm, pulling at her.

Isis snapped awake, looking down to see Angel staring up.

"Wake up!" said the little ghost.

Isis smiled a thank you, but put a finger to her lips.

"You have to be careful," she whispered. "He can see you, remember?"

"He dint see me," said Angel, looking pleased with herself. "I play hidey-seek." As Isis watched, the small figure scattered herself into the shadows between the ripe wheat, vanishing.

Now Isis only pretended to close her eyes, keeping them open a crack, ignoring Philip's strange humming. He finished, and there was silence for a minute. Then the rustle and crack of footsteps through the wheat as Philip moved around the circle. She watched him stop next to each of the hypnotised adults and murmur words to them she couldn't hear.

Isis held still, eyes nearly shut and heart fully pounding, as he crunched her way.

"Are you awake?" he whispered to her.

She didn't move. He laid a heavy hand on her shoulder, pushing a little. She swayed gently, not resisting the movement, but not falling either. Was that what a hypnotised person would do? She hoped so.

Philip leaned in, breathing next to her ear.

"You will stay here, in this circle, until I tell you to open your eyes," he whispered. "You won't hear anything, or remember what I say and do."

She tried to stay motionless. If he was giving her commands, then he must think she was hypnotised like the others. She breathed slowly and steadily, as if she were sleeping, while his footsteps crunched away from her, becoming more and more distant. After a little while, when she was sure he'd gone, Isis opened her eyes properly.

Around her the adults were standing motionless in the wheat, arms at their sides, heads tipped forwards a little, like sleeping scarecrows.

"He stinky," muttered Angel, flickering like moonlight from behind the wheat stems. "I glad he gone."

"Where did he go?" whispered Isis, trying to see. Fifty metres away were the screens and bright dots of Gil's computers and monitors, his tall figure moving between them, oblivious. The rest of the field was fading into shades of grey, as the last of the sunset slipped out of the sky. She couldn't see Philip anywhere.

"He over there," said Angel, pointing at a distantly dark and gloomy corner of the field, where Isis could only see the shadow of an overreaching hedge. "He talking."

Isis stared at her in surprise. Who else could have come into the field?

"Who's he talking to?" she whispered.

Angel shook her head, and pressed her lips together.

"Please?" asked Isis.

Angel folded her arms. "I not tell. He horrid."

Isis narrowed her eyes, peering into the shadows. There was only one person Angel always called horrid. She took a step, and the wheat crunched and creaked loudly.

She stopped. She couldn't follow, or try and eavesdrop on Philip. He'd easily hear her crashing towards him.

Angel wafted in front of Isis.

"You not go!" she commanded.

"I can't get near him anyway. Walking though this stuff is too noisy." She stared at the brooding line of the hedges. "But if I go around…"

"Isis! Don't!" cried Angel. "Pease!"

Isis crouched down, face-to-face with Angel.

"I have to find out what he's doing, because…" She stopped, she couldn't tell Angel about Philip's plans. She didn't want to scare her. "He's a bad man, Angel."

"He a bad ghost," was the answer.

Isis went back to the nearest tramline, following it to the edge of the field. Angel tagged behind, plucking at her with cold fingers.

"You not go!" she cried. "He horrid! He stinky!"

Gil looked up from his stack of quietly beeping electronics as Isis came out of the crop.

"You had enough already?" he asked.

"I need the loo," she said.

"Take your pick." He smiled. "Watch out for nettles."

Isis headed off, down the strip of rough grass at the edge

of the field. She tried to use the long shadows and growing darkness to hide in, keeping close to the overhanging hedge.

Angel's luminous shape flitted anxiously after.

"Come back!" she cried. Isis turned round.

"Shh," she whispered. "Philip can hear you. If you can't be quiet, stay back." She crept on, until she could make out two figures standing in the corner of the field. One was Philip's slightly plump shape, the other was eerily lit, mouldy green. She crouched behind a tall clump of thistles, staying very still, hardly breathing. Listening to what they were saying.

"... even doing here? Standing around in this field." Philip Syndal was speaking, sounding irritated. "It doesn't even tell me *why* I have to do things, not any more. I'm sick of it!"

"Have some patience, my boy." Isis was surprised at Mandeville's soft tone. It was as close to comforting as his raspy old voice could be.

"I *have* been patient," whined Philip, "I've been patient for years!"

"I know, dear boy," said Mandeville, his words spoken gently. "But soon you'll be back to how you were when I first found you."

"Miserable in a care home?" snapped Philip. "Or do you mean half-mad with ghosts?"

Everything suddenly made a cold, horrible sense to Isis. Mandeville had never mentioned knowing Philip, but he obviously did. Mandeville had to be Philip's spirit guide, the one Cally was always on about, the one who helped him when he was a boy! He must have told Philip about Isis, and got her drawn into all this.

"It won't be like that now," Mandeville soothed. "So many phantoms are gone. We'll be able to work together, uncluttered. A beacon for the world."

Philip snorted. "I've already told you: when it's out, I'm done. No more Psychic Syndal."

"But I need a channel! I want it to be you. I've cared for you all these years."

"*Cared* for me?"

"I tried, at least. And think of your public, don't they deserve to know the truth about the afterlife?"

"They don't want the truth!" cried Philip. "They want Granny's old recipes and next week's lottery numbers! You're just a fame-hungry old ghost, creeping around the psychics like the rest." His voice drawled into a sneer. "Isn't that how you found Isis the wonder-child?"

Mandeville shook his head, sending out a greenish dust to glow against the dark. "Don't I even get a little gratitude?"

Now Philip laughed. "For *what*? You gave me to a monster. You said it would scare the ghosts away, well it did more than that. And it didn't just find a little corner of my mind, like you said it would. It's everywhere, in every thought! I only have times like now, when it's taken flight, to think in peace. My life has been nothing, a slavery. I never wanted to do the stage shows, but I have to because it's always hungry. Plus I'm a fraud; ghosts won't come near me so I have to use tricks on the punters. And even that's not enough, because I have to lure in any stupid ghost I can, just to prove I'm still useful to the thing *you* put inside me. I'm fighting for my life, for my mind, every day!" Philip was gasping, almost crying. "I would have been better off as I was. Madness would have been kinder than what you've done to me."

Behind her, Isis heard Angel's squeak of fear. She'd followed, even though she'd been told not to. Isis pulled the little ghost onto her lap, looking around for a wash of colour, listening for the flap of noiseless wings.

Out in the field, Mandeville sighed and Isis could taste the dust in the air.

"I am sorry," he said quietly, "I can't tell you how much.

I should never have removed it from the darkness. I thought its nature was to remain small and weak – I had no idea how its appetite would grow when it was this close to the living."

"So you've said," muttered Philip, "about a thousand times." Isis heard the swishing, crunching sound of Philip walking into the crop. She huddled down, praying he wouldn't see her or Angel.

"Don't!" cried Mandeville. "Please, my boy. I'm still trying to help you."

The crunching stopped, Philip turned back. "You mean Isis? Yeah, well thanks for telling me about her. I persuaded it and it likes the idea. Hop into the new girl and leave me at last. A nice new shell for the hermit crab."

Angel touched Isis's face with whisper-fingers. Isis could see how frightened the little ghost was. She clutched Angel tightly, shaking her head to show that she wouldn't let that happen. Not ever!

Mandeville made a strange wheezing noise, and green dust poured up into the air. "No! That isn't what I meant; she's only a child."

"I wasn't much past her age when you sent it into *me*," snapped Philip.

"It was a mistake! I didn't know what would happen, but you do."

"She'll be *fine*," said Philip. "Stop going on."

"It doesn't have to be that way, she can save us…"

"You just don't *get it*, do you?" Philip's voice rose into almost a screech. "I've been feeding it non-stop for twenty-five years and it's *still* hungry! I live in a slaughterhouse…" He stopped. Isis heard him sob. "I just need it out. And this way I know it will be gone."

"Please, give me one last chance to persuade her," whispered Mandeville.

"You said it yourself – she won't even try. All she cares about is her dead sister and idiot mother."

Angel wriggled on Isis's lap, wanting to scramble away. Isis held her tightly, putting a finger to her lips. They had to stay quiet and still until this was over.

"Well maybe she'll care about you too," said Mandeville, "if we can make her understand."

"Like Norman did?" muttered Philip.

There was silence, then Mandeville said quietly, "I didn't realise how fixed his views were on the nature of ghosts."

Philip snorted. "He was a fool who had money."

"So he deserved it?"

"*You* said to make him understand! I tried, but he wouldn't even listen to me! So I showed him what it's like, I helped him to see it. That's all. It wasn't my fault what happened."

"It has a heart of ice. What did you think would occur if it wrapped itself around him?"

"*I* don't freeze. Maybe it's different when it's inside someone." Philip paused. "But perhaps I should have fed it before I went to see Norman."

"And now you've taught it how to kill the living."

"No! It was an accident, he had a weak heart! The police said it was natural causes."

"Is anything ever your responsibility?" asked Mandeville.

"Isis!" Angel whispered from her lap, her small arm pointing upwards. Overhead, the sky was sweeping into dark blue, night coming in too fast.

What had she been thinking, following Philip out here? Gil and his lights were far away, Cally was even further, lost in a dream.

"We have to get back," Isis whispered to Angel. She pushed her ghost-sister off her lap, but when she tried to stand her legs were numb and stiff. Her first step was a stumble, her foot catching in the rough grass. She fell.

"Owf!" The sound pushed out of her as she landed.

"Who's there?" said Philip.

"He coming!" screamed Angel.

Isis scrabbled to get up, but heavy footsteps were already pounding towards her. She looked back and saw Philip heading for her. She set off running, his footsteps getting closer and louder behind her. Then his hand grabbed her arm, wrenching her to a stop.

"Isis." Philip was breathing heavily. "You shouldn't be out here. Anything might happen."

She tried to shake her arm free.

"I don't want it! You can't make me!" she shouted, too terrified to think clearly, or give any excuse for what she'd been doing.

Philip shook his head. "Everyone has to take shares, Isis."

"I don't want it!" she cried again.

Philip smiled kindly. "It won't hurt."

Angel flung herself at him, hitting him with her two small hands. He looked down. "You can't even make me shiver, little one."

Isis pulled her arm out of his grasp, staggering away from him. "Leave us alone!"

Philip's eyes were as black as an ocean. "I can't, you see?" Above them, the darkening sky was cut by the shape of wings, so blue they could hardly be seen.

Isis stumbled away from him, frightened and panicky. The smell of wheat and dusty grass filled her nose, the smell of mould and musty clothes.

A dirty cloud swirled around them, and the dank figure of Mandeville appeared. A tall, bony ghost between Isis and Philip Syndal.

"Leave her alone!" Mandeville roared, in a voice only they could hear. "I was wrong to bring it to you, but what you're doing is much worse!"

Philip frowned at the ghost. "You've no right to lecture me. You're just another soul shaving, another nothing, whatever you tell yourself." He looked over to the edge of the field. "Just another meal."

Philip held up his hand, signalling, and the night filled with the silent noise of beating wings.

"She can save us! Let me tell her how—" Mandeville cried, but his words were cut off as the wings smothered around him, claws and teeth ripping in. Gouts of mouldy dust burst around Isis as she flung herself away, almost falling. Mandeville's scream faded into nothing, lost in the blue-lit, glittering fog. Isis swatted at her arms and legs, as freezing bites nipped her all over. Eyes watched her out of the fog, unattached to anything.

"Angel!" Isis's scream was flat and quiet in the mist. Soft cold fluttered on her face, snowflakes falling out of the summer air.

As quickly as it descended, the ghost-eater left. Ravelling its wings into tattery swirls, dribbling into the ground, its eyes staring out of the night-blackened grass, then fading.

"Angel!" Isis spotted her little ghost-sister standing hunched by the hedge, faded and fragile as a dried leaf. Isis ran and picked her up into a freezing cuddle.

"You two are so sweet," said Philip.

Isis turned round. She would have backed away if she wasn't already at the hedge.

"Where's Mandeville?"

Philip shrugged. "He's gone." He rubbed his arms briskly. "A bit chilly isn't it? Maybe we should go back to the others, see if we can find you a jumper or something."

"What happened to him?" asked Isis, shock trembling in her legs.

Philip shrugged. "It took him of course. I always knew it would in the end."

A dark fog was oozing back out of the ground, washing around Philip's feet. Tendrils of darkness twirled onto his legs, draining into him like backwards blood. Angel squealed and tried to climb further into Isis's arms.

"Don't be frightened," said Philip, "it won't take your sister. You made a bargain, remember?"

"I didn't bargain," said Isis, staring at the fog pouring into him, trying to kick away the mist rising at her own feet.

You see more clearly than any other. You will help me take hold.

Memory words drifted into her mind.

"You see more clearly than any other," said Philip. "You will help me take hold."

Isis looked up, startled. His face was blank and empty.

I am hungry. You will be my feast-giver.

"I am hungry," said Philip. "You will be my feast-giver."

Angel squealed and dropped like a breath of ice through Isis's arms, vanishing off into the night. In the distance, Isis heard a woman shout and a man answer, as everything around them blazed into white, and lights began bursting out of the new night. Isis looked up and saw leaves. Golden-green and softly pointed, drifting into the sky, filling the air with upward leaf-fall.

She watched, transfixed, while the Devourer slid its tendrils across the ground towards her. Wrapping itself around her ankles.

Chapter Twenty-nine

Gray

I rang Mum. I mean, what else could I do?

I couldn't tell her what was happening, so I said Dad had left me on my own while he went off with Cally. Mum went nuclear. In about three minutes, her car screeched up outside the house, with her like a thunderclap inside it. Yelling about Dad the whole time. I didn't know she could swear like that.

"Where's he gone?" she snarled, like she wanted to rip his head off. I gave her the bit of paper with the coordinates on, and she punched them into her satnav. We drove so fast, it was only my seat belt that stopped me flying all over the car. The last bit was walking through fields, nearly in the dark, which only got her madder because she was wearing her best red dress and high heels for her meal out with Brian. She was screaming at Dad before we even got in the field.

"What kind of a father are you? Leaving your son on his own! Going off with some *woman!*"

"Jenice?" Dad was staring at us like he couldn't believe his eyes. "What are you doing here?"

"What am *I* doing?" screeched Mum. "What are *you?* You don't even have Gray every weekend and you *leave* him? For this?" She pointed into the field, where people were standing weirdly still in the wheat. "For *them?*"

I looked around. "Where's Isis?"

"So I left him on his own!" Dad shouted back at Mum. "Gray's not five, he can look after himself! Nothing would've happened, I was coming back in the morning."

"Where's Isis?" I asked, louder. There was no sign of her, or Philip Syndal.

"I do everything for Gray!" yelled Mum. "And you can't even look after him for *one* night? Is this the first time you've left him?" Mum swung round at me. "Gray, tell me if this is the first time."

Dad glared at me, Mum glared at me.

"Well, is it?" growled Dad, daring me to tell.

They were like zombies, the way they looked in the light from the computer screens. Sort of grey, with just their eyes and teeth showing up. Then, in a flash, they changed. I could see every line on Dad's face, every strand of Mum's hair. A light blazed from the sky right above us, a hanging spotlight. Then another, and another.

"Oh my God!" cried Mum. "What's happening?"

"It's starting!" shouted Dad.

"Where's *Isis*?" I yelled at Dad. "Where is she?"

"Huh?" said Dad. He wasn't even looking at Mum and me – his eyes were on his monitors and gear. "Oh, she went for a pee. That way." He pointed along the hedge line. "About twenty minutes ago."

I turned round, trying to see into the newly lit field.

"Twenty minutes ago!" said Mum. "What child pees for twenty minutes?"

"It's only a field, there's nothing out there."

"She could've fallen!" yelled Mum. "She could be lying with a broken leg!"

"Don't start!" Dad shouted. "Isis has got her own mum!"

I heard Cally call out, further off. "What is it? What about Isis?" But I didn't listen to the rest, because I was running along the grass beside the field, the thorny stems of the hedge whipping at my face. I ran, stopped to look for Isis, ran on again.

"Isis!" I shouted. "Isis!" I stopped again, peering into the field. The lights were pinging out all over the sky now, and everything was either blinding bright or pitch-black. Crazy, random shadows criss-crossed everywhere. I could hardly see a thing.

"Isis!" I ran out into the rustling crop, a hundred shadows dancing around me. "Isis!"

I was so scared for what might be happening to her. Shivering and cold with it. My left hand was the worst, like it was in a bucket of ice or something. Then it went back to normal. Then it started freezing again. I stared at my hand, my fingers looking strange in that strobing light. My hand was warm, then freezing again, like something cold was wrapping around it. Something about the size of a tiny hand.

"Angel?" I whispered. "Is that you?" The cold seemed to tug at my hand.

"Do you know where she is?" The cold pulled my hand, leading me.

It was really weird, getting led by a ghost. We went out of the crop, back to the grass and along the edge of the field. I wondered if I was imagining it, but I was going in a straight line, through all the flashing light and patches of black.

I couldn't see them at first, what with all the lights and shadows everywhere, but then... Philip Syndal had got hold of Isis. He was tipping her head back, trying to break her neck or something.

"Get away from her!" I screamed, running straight at them, still holding Angel's cold-nothing hand. I smacked right into Philip, but neither of them even noticed me, like they were stunned or something. I grabbed Isis's arm, to pull her away from him.

And that's when I saw.

Because Angel had grabbed hold of Isis too, connecting us up. I could see what Isis could.

The lights in the sky weren't just lights any more, they were these glowing leaves. Millions of them. You know the kind of green that leaves are in spring, when the sun's shining through them? Well those leaves in the sky were like that. But they were other colours too: golds and reds, like spring and autumn happening at the same time. The leaves fluttered upwards, swirling in patterns, and behind them the faint shapes of trees filled the night, speckled with stars. A ghost-forest glimmering in the sky.

It was so beautiful, like nothing you've ever seen. I wanted to look at it for the rest of my life, I wanted to fly up with the leaves.

But that wasn't why I started screaming. *"Isis! Isis!"*

Because it wasn't just her and Philip Syndal, staring up at the silver trees and leaves of golden light. Darkness was wrapped around the two of them. Oily slugs pulsed from the ground into their bodies, wriggling tentacles oozed back out again. Philip Syndal was sicking out this river of blue-black slime. And Isis... had ribbons of blue-dark pouring out of her eyes.

The ghost-eater was stretching itself out of their bodies. Gurgling and bubbling into the sky, wrapping itself around the golden leaves and swallowing every light it could reach. Turning them into nothing...

My head hurts. Why does my head hurt?

It's because you're fighting the trance, Gray. Just relax, it will soon be over. And then you'll have no need to worry, because you won't remember me, or any of this...

Chapter Thirty

Isis

She was deep and warm. Cradled between grains of soil, water seeping through her. She put out a single root, creeping down, searching for more water and the tang of the earth. Anchoring herself. Then, up. Pushing with her leaves, seeking the bright face of the sun.

A feast.

The sparkling touch of light fed her, giving her the strength to go further. She unfurled her leaves and burst from the soil, the sunshine tasting of honey as she tracked it through the sky. Light and dark took turns, and in the cold times she pulled herself into the earth, hiding inside her roots. Waiting for the sun's return and the tingling taste of spring.

The greatest feast.

Sap flowed, and she put out a thousand new leaves, her bark thickening, her branches reaching for the sky and the wind blowing through them…

You are my feast-giver.

"ISIS!"

She gasped, her heart pounding.

"ISIS!" Gray was shaking her by the arm. "Wake up!"

She tried to look at him, but there was something over her eyes, blurring everything into a dim murk. She could feel him slapping at her, brushing things off.

Ignore him! She remembered the command. *Look up. Take me back to them.*

"Isis!" Angel was calling her now.

She rubbed her eyes and the blur faded.

"Ugh!" An oily ooze was running down her arm, dripping and coiling onto the ground. Angel stamped on the blue-black coils with her sandals, grinding them into the earth.

"Come on." Gray was pulling at Isis. "We've got most of it off, but you have to get out of here."

Angel caught hold of her other hand, both of them trying to drag her somewhere.

What was happening?

Plants brushed against her arms and she tripped on their thick stems. A field? But why was it so bright? Why would there be lights over a field?

Look back up, lead me to them.

She started to tilt her head.

"No! Don't!" yelled Gray, pushing her head down. She saw something on the ground, a dribble of oily water trickling towards her feet. It climbed up over her shoe, heading for the flesh of her ankle.

Stop.

A breath of emptiness blew into her mind, filling her with hunger.

There is a feast.

"There is a feast." Isis heard her own mouth whisper the words.

"You have to fight it!" cried Gray.

"Pease, Isis! Pease!" whispered Angel.

Gray was dragging her. Her foot took a step, but her legs felt pinned, super-heavy.

"Come *on*!" he shouted, kicking and stamping at the tendril holding her.

It was like pulling her foot from a cold fire. She cried out with the effort of freeing herself, but the tendril lost its grip.

"It bited you," said Angel, pulling her along with cold, invisible fingers. "You got to go."

They led her away, one of her hands in Gray's warm grip, the other in Angel's freezing one. As she ran, she started to remember. Flashes of what she'd just seen and heard.

"It took Mandeville," she gasped, seeing again the ghost being ripped into pieces. She started running properly, through dazzling patches of golden-white light and sudden, dizzying shadows. But her legs wouldn't work the way she wanted them to, it felt like they ought to be burrowing down, holding her to the ground. And her feet seemed so flimsy, so... movable. She kept tripping and stumbling.

"When the Devourer touched me," she panted, "it just moved in."

"You have to keep fighting!" Gray answered, picking up his pace.

And now she understood what had happened at the shopping centre. She hadn't fought off the Devourer, it had let her go. After playing with her like a cat plays with a mouse. It had never wanted Angel, it had only been testing her; plotting the paths of her mind and opening doorways for itself.

"It's so strong," she said to Gray. "Philip said it keeps getting bigger, it never stops being hungry."

He looked back at her without speaking, but his wide eyes showed his understanding.

They ran on. In the sky, almost over their heads, light was swirling together into a blinding, whirling tower. It was impossible not to look up. Gray and Isis together, with Angel binding their sight.

This time, Isis only saw the blazing column without being pulled into a vision. Gray's view was her anchor, holding her down. And sharing Isis's eyes, he saw the golden leaves and silver trees of the ghost-forest, stretching to the edges of the sky. Together they heard the non-existent sound of chainsaws and smelled the wood smoke.

"They kept on killing the trees," whispered Isis.

"Until there were none left," answered Gray.

"Look!" shouted Angel, bringing them back.

Beneath the lights filling up the night was the dark sprawl of the ghost-eater. Still curled through and around Philip, it oozed out of his eyes and mouth, slobbering around him in the sightless colours of the deepest ocean. Its eyes stared upwards, its hands and tentacles reached up to the ghost-trees in the sky, trying to catch their glowing forms in twilight coils and pull them down into one of its champing mouths. It missed more than it caught, but each time it fed it swelled, flopping and sagging out across the field. A vast ooze, tethered to the distant figure of Philip Syndal.

Isis groaned. "The bargain."

Gray looked at her.

"In the shopping centre, I was trying to think of anything except where you'd gone with Angel. I thought about going out UFO hunting, with you and your dad. I thought about what I'd seen in the sky."

She could see Gray starting to understand. "The ghost-birds?"

She nodded miserably.

"You showed it the ghost of a whole species," said Gray. "That's what they are, I worked it out." He gasped. "The Devourer must have known what they were straight away. That's why Philip Syndal wanted to go UFO hunting so much!"

"It's always hungry," Isis whispered, remembering Philip's words. "Never satisfied."

And it was still in her mind too. Swallowing and muttering an incessant, maddening murmur.

*feast a feast a feastfeast a feastafeastafeast afeastfeastfeast
a feast a feast*

She looked at Gray, her stomach twisting inside. "I don't know how to fight it."

Her fear was reflected in his face. "Can't you do anything?"

She wiped at tears she couldn't stop from falling. "It knows my mind," she said. "It's already in me. It's going to take me over, and I'll be just like him."

They stared at Philip Syndal, barely visible, sunk inside the monster.

"You bite it!" said Angel.

"How? How can I?"

"What are we going to do?" asked Gray, but none of them had an answer.

And there was a sound of feet, running up behind them. They jumped, getting ready to run, but it was only Cally. Wild-eyed, her hair messy around her face.

"Isis! Why are you still out here? Gil said you went to the toilet half an hour ago! I thought you'd got lost or something."

"I'm fine," Isis lied, willing her to leave. Cally blinked at the strained tone of Isis's voice, then glared at Gray.

"What are *you* doing here? I thought you were at home?"

"I was looking for Isis too," he said.

Now Cally saw Philip, further into the field.

"Philip?" she called. He didn't respond. "Phil, what's going on?"

"He had hold of Isis!" Gray shouted, getting Cally's attention. "He was going to—" Isis thumped him. He looked at her, surprised, and she gave a tiny shake of her head.

"Don't!" she mouthed.

"Don't what?" asked Cally, glaring between them. "What was Philip going to do? *Tell* me!"

"Shouldn't you be in the meditation?" asked Isis, trying to sound bright, as if everything were fine. Why hadn't Cally stayed hypnotised, safely out of it?

Cally shook her head. "It's been such an odd evening, what with Jenice turning up. And those things everyone said before we started. I couldn't relax, couldn't concentrate." She put her hand out to Isis, not quite touching her. "I don't scream at you, do I? Do you think I should restrain myself more?"

Isis smiled at her mum, and was about to say no, when a voice said, "She won't answer you honestly, she's too afraid of you."

Philip Syndal was walking towards them out of the dazzling night. Calmly, as if nothing unusual were happening. Through Gray's eyes, Isis could see he looked quite normal, perhaps a little sweaty. But through her own...

A dark strand led out of his head, trailing behind him into the bloated mass of the ghost-eater, which was still trying to rip golden shapes of light from the sky and shovel them into its deep-night body.

Unfit mother.

The words echoed in her memory.

"Unfit mother," said Philip, smiling at Cally. "You're an unfit mother, and you should keep away from Isis."

"What?" Cally sounded a little stunned. "If that's a joke, Philip, it's not funny."

"Face it, Calista," he said, his smile odd and stiff. "You're a disaster as a parent. It's amazing Isis is still with you."

Gray turned to Isis.

"What's going on?" he whispered.

In a strange kind of answer, Philip staggered a step, his legs bending as he nearly fell. He managed to stop himself, but his head was bowed and his arms shook as if he were carrying some enormous weight. "It's too big," he grunted.

Now Isis remembered. Wearing shoes that were too

small, squeezing her toes. Putting on a jumper she'd grown out of, squashing herself into a box during a game of hide-and-seek. The Devourer flicked through her memories.

He is old and small inside. You see much better. I need you, Isis.

Philip mumbled along with the words, only becoming clear as he said, "I need you, Isis."

"What?" snapped Cally, moving in front of Isis. "You're not coming near my daughter!"

Philip took a step, jerky and awkward. "I'm so tired of it, and you're a terrible mother." He took another step. "I've seen Isis's social services file. She'll be taken into care, and then she'll be all alone. Except for—"

"No!" cried Isis.

"What are you talking about?" said Cally. "Isis isn't going into care! And how did you even see her file? Unless..." She flung her hand out, slapping Philip across his cheek. "Are you in one of those *rings*?"

"Mummy do it!" cried Angel, jumping up and down excitedly.

"Leave my daughter alone," snarled Cally. She turned to Gray and Isis. "We're going back to the others now. And then we're going home."

Behind them, Philip turned his head, blinking and dazed. "Calista?" he croaked.

Cally glanced back, and his hand was a blur as he punched her. Her head flew backwards, and she fell into the wheat without a murmur.

"Mummy!" screamed Angel.

"Come on!" shouted Gray, pulling Isis, trying to get her moving.

Isis.

She remembered the word, even as Philip Syndal spoke. "Isis," he said.

There wasn't time to run. The long, oily dark tentacle pulled out of Philip's skull, wavering in the air and seeming to sniff, then it shot over to Isis and plunged down into her head. Pouring in its darkness, washing all her thoughts away.

Chapter Thirty-one

Gray

She didn't scream or anything. She just made this sound. "Uh." Like all the breath had got pushed out of her. I mean, it just poured in. Like a freezing sea, down through her head, rushing inside her, on and on. There was no way it could do that, no way it could fit! But it did.

I shouted out, let go of her hand and stumbled backwards. I couldn't help it! If you'd seen all that stuff, a thousand eyes and mouths pouring into someone, you would've too.

Of course, as soon as I let go I couldn't see any more. It was a relief actually – in that second I didn't even *want* to see. Now Isis just looked ordinary, like she was daydreaming or something, and the light in the sky was just light again. Beautiful and swirling, like the other ones I'd seen with Dad.

I'd been excited back then, thinking aliens were trying to talk to us. Now I was just scared. And the light wasn't the same as before, either. There were black specks floating on it, drifting and joining together, like oil slicks.

Even if I couldn't see it, the ghost-eater was still there. I could feel the cold of it, and the light in the sky wasn't growing, like the others had, it was fading.

On the ground, Cally groaned. She was flat out, blood trickling from her nose. Philip Syndal looked dazed or whatever, staring from Cally to his hand and the blood on his knuckles.

"I'm sorry," he said to her. "It wasn't me." Then he started this snuffling and giggling, like he couldn't stop himself. He looked at Isis for ages, his eyes so wide you could see the whites all the way round.

"I waited such a long time for someone else to come along," he said to her. "It's yours now." He started giggling again.

I put my hand out to Isis, not quite touching.

"Isis?"

Nothing.

Something cold touched my other hand. This time I knew it was little fingers grabbing onto me. I swallowed down this horrible, shivery feeling, like all I wanted was to run away, and I put my hand on Isis's. Fingertip to fingertip, that's all.

She was the eye of a storm! Darkness was boiling up through her eyes, wriggling out of her like a swamp climbing into the sky, like it was made out of maggots. Teeth and mouths were everywhere, you could hear them chewing. I had to make myself hold on, because I nearly threw up all over myself.

Overhead, the trees of light were charring and turning rotten, their silver leaves crumbling into ash.

"Fight it!" I yelled at Isis, but she didn't move.

Angel was tugging on her clothes, crying out, "Come back, Isis, pease! Pease!"

I took proper hold of Isis's hand. Shaking it and trying to wake her up.

Philip Syndal stopped giggling. "Leave the girl alone."

"Shut up!" I shouted at him. "Go away or I'll *kill* you!" And I wanted to, I hated him so much.

I squeezed Isis's hand, talking to her. But there was nothing in her, not even a hint. And the thing, the Devourer, all the murk and slime, it just kept on swelling. Dripping up into the sky, oozing across the field, so all you could see was squirming blue-black muck and eyes drifting everywhere. And mouths.

It pulsed, you know? Like a heart. But it was colder than a freezer, and getting darker too. Now it was really ripping the golden leaves from the sky, tentacles whipping all over, never missing a single one.

"Wake up!" I screamed at Isis.

"I don't know who you are," said Philip Syndal, "but you're really very annoying."

I should've run then, because it was obvious he was mad, but I couldn't just leave her. A second later his hands were around my neck, squeezing. I couldn't breathe, couldn't even gasp a word. And it really hurt. I was scrabbling at his fat fingers, trying to pull them off my throat. He was so strong though. Crazy-strong.

I thought I heard Mum calling my name, maybe I imagined it. I couldn't have answered anyway.

Philip Syndal kept on throttling me. My head was bursting, my feet started twitching. I could see Angel and the Devourer too, even though I wasn't holding onto Isis any more. Not so clearly, but they were definitely there.

It never happened like that any other time, I think it was… because I was nearly dead.

"After you die," Philip growled, "it will eat you."

Angel was hitting him with her tiny, not-really-there hands. "Let Gray go!" she cried. "You stink! You horrid!"

It didn't make any difference, except Isis turned to look at her. Eyes as black as Philip's had been, looking at Angel like she didn't even know her.

"The bargain is ended," she said.

Angel screamed as a slug-squirl snapped out and grabbed her. She was gone, into one of its mouths. As quick as that.

I would've screamed too if I could've. I knew no one was going to help me, not in time, and I could feel myself going. The world was turning dim, and the Devourer was getting clearer. This energy came to me then. Out of fear, you know? I started really struggling, kicking at Philip Syndal, trying to get free. He grunted, glaring at me eye to eye, but he didn't let go. Then Isis… I don't know, she shouted or something, and Philip jumped in surprise. His hands slackened on my neck, just for a millisecond.

I threw myself backwards, using all my weight. My neck scraped out through his fingers and I flung myself as far away from him as I could get, which wasn't far. I had the worst sore throat ever, but I could breathe! Gargling and making these really weird noises, actually. All wobbly and weird too – I could hardly stand, let alone run. I only managed to get a few steps before Syndal grabbed me again. I made this raspy shrieking noise, as I tried to scrabble away from him.

"Won't you just die?" he hissed, grabbing me.

I had to do something, so I head butted him.

CRACK. It hurt like *anything*, like getting a hammer put through your skull. I saw stars and everything. But Philip made this 'oof' noise and fell backwards. I stared down at him, not quite believing it for a minute. I'd knocked him out!

I staggered in a little circle, trying not to fall over too.

"Isis!" I croaked. "Isis!"

It was totally dark by then. Clouds had moved into the sky and there was nothing to see by. I couldn't see her anywhere. It was like she'd vanished into nothing, into the night.

Philip Syndal...

I checked our file on him when he first got involved, but I thought the same as everyone else, that his worst crime was being a conman. But after what he did to Isis, I think I'll give him as my reason for coming here. He was brought to this hospital too, so it fits, and a transfer to one of our facilities will be easy to arrange.

My colleagues will want to investigate how he kept something so large inside his head. He'll probably be with them for a long time.

Chapter Thirty-two

Isis

"Angel!"

She ran, pushing her way through the plants, her hands brushing the feather-heads of wheat, her feet catching on the rough soil. Clouds blew in across the sky, charcoal-smudging the night.

Where was Angel? Where *was* she? Angel had been trying to make Philip let go of Gray, she remembered that. And she'd just stood and watched. An empty shell, filled with bad dreams and hunger.

The bargain is over.

She'd heard the words in her mind, and spoken them out of her mouth.

Then a writhing coil of darkness, coming out of nowhere,

wrapping around Angel and lifting her screaming. It had shocked Isis out of her trance and started her fighting again, but too late. Angel was gone before Isis had even moved. She couldn't bear to remember the rest.

It wasn't true, it couldn't be! This had to be one of the Devourer's mind games.

"Angel!" Isis shouted for her moonlight-sister, running further into the crop. Swathes of cold darkness travelled with her, clinging to her mind, as claws still clung to the sky and the last particles of light. Shadows bulged and washed around Isis, unconcerned by her distress.

She stopped running.

"Angel!" she sobbed. She felt turned inside out. She understood at last, what Cally had gone through all these years. Grief, with nothing to ease the pain.

And still the creature kept its hold. In her mind, relentlessly, every meal she'd ever eaten was being played back with gloating satisfaction. Chips, sausages, fish fingers, ice cream, toast, porridge, chicken curry, spaghetti bolognese, apple juice, Easter eggs, birthday cake... on and on, every mouthful as if she were eating it all at once, gorging herself, shoving food in by the handful, not caring as it slid back out of her mouth through her fingers.

She retched, but there was nothing real inside her.

"Gray?" she called weakly. Come and save me.

The Devourer gave her an image of him: dangling from Philip Syndal's hands, head lolling and body limp.

He is part of the feast.

"No!" she sobbed, trying to shake the Devourer out of her mind. But her head weighed a hundred tonnes, and her skull was being pushed outwards, the bones cracking and splitting apart with the pressure of the creature inside.

"Get out!" she screamed, clawing at her hair. She ran a few paces, pushing at the creature with her thoughts, managing to squeeze a tiny space for herself in her mind. Still it bubbled around, like cold lava, poking and trying to get back in.

She remembered Philip Syndal crying.

"Cally?" she called. "Gil?" But in the inky blackness of the field, she could only see the vaguest shapes of anything. How could anyone help her anyway? She'd been lost from the moment she'd blinked at Cally's seance.

Tears trickled down her cheeks. She hadn't done anything! She'd just watched it take Angel!

She turned back to face the sags and folds of the ghost-eater.

"You can save us!" That was a true memory. Mandeville had said that.

But how?

And she remembered Angel, just before she was taken. *"You bite it!"*

Isis looked down at her hands, barely visible in the dark. At her fingers, topped with short, bitten nails. She turned her hands over, peering at the padded flats of her palms, concentrating on every crease and line, every hair and freckle.

No.

She imagined all her blood, all the heat of her body, pumping into her fingertips. Just as she did when she needed to hold Angel, or drive back the ghosts who mobbed her at Cally's performances. The way she'd pushed away the ghost with the sliced-open throat.

No.

The vast, enveloping bulk of the monster loomed around her, inside and outside her mind.

No.

Its eyes were pinpricks in its slick and bloated flesh. It rippled with strange reflections of the night-time clouds, like a threatening storm.

"I won't let you take me over," Isis whispered to it, her voice shaking.

Do not do this.

"I never made any bargain!" she shouted.

She plunged her hands into the creature's body, forcing them into its flesh. A breathtaking, staggering cold washed over her, pushing the air out of her lungs. Like walking into a snowdrift, or diving into an icy lake. Her breath turned to ice-crystals, frost crackled inside her nose. Shaking with uncontrollable shivers, thinking only about her hands, she managed to grip hold of the creature's formless skin.

"I can fight you!"

She ripped her hands apart, tearing open a hole, looking through into charcoal-soft darkness, flashing with distant glimmers. She cried out in triumph. She'd hurt it!

And then, pain.

Cally slapping her cheek. Her dad pouring scalding tea onto her arm. Falling down a flight of stone steps, slicing her skin with a knife, wasps stabbing stings into her face. Real memories layered with false ones, each vivid and searing. She was hit by a car, her hand blistered in a fire. She was paralysed, panting with pain.

I can fight you back.

Her leg broke, and she screamed in agony. She was dying from the pain, it was ripping her to pieces...

... and everything was quiet. She was standing in dappled shade by a roadside, a bird singing in a nearby tree.

It was that road.

Angel was lying on the warm tarmac, her legs grazed and dirty, her dress torn and bloody. Her head was twisted the wrong way, her chest lifting and falling its last tiny movements. She turned her head on a broken neck and said, *"I still here..."*

Isis gasped back into torture. Her fingernails were tearing away, her scorching skin gave off a stench like bacon.

But she'd seen Angel! She was caught, somewhere deep inside the flesh of the Devourer, using its link with Isis's memories to speak. How long could Angel last in there? How long before it melted her into nothing?

Isis clenched her blistered hands into fists and took a breath. Shaking, shivering, she pulled herself up and punched straight into the creature. Its shriek echoed soundlessly above the field, and two circles were stamped in its flesh.

Stop.

"No!"

Her fingers crumbled into dust, her arms ending in the white of protruding bone. She screamed, staggering backwards, trying to see past this vision of powdered bone and reveal her hands. But she couldn't.

I was stronger than the foolish ghost who found me, stronger than the lonely boy, I am stronger than you.

Her teeth started chattering. Her body was going into shock, instinctively trying to shut itself off from the horror at the end of her arms.

She heard a distant thudding: feet running over dry earth, the rustling of wheat stems.

"Isis!"

"Gray?"

And there he was. Face in front of hers, a cut on his forehead dribbling blood down between his eyes, with a bruise like an egg puffing up around it. She wanted to laugh, or maybe cry.

"Isis, are you… you again?" he asked nervously. She nodded, and he grinned with relief.

"I knocked Philip Syndal *out!*" he said. "And your mum's okay, she's looking for you. Everyone is, I think. But they've gone the wrong way – I heard them shouting our names right at the other end of the field. Come on. I think I can find the way back... Are you all right?"

She couldn't answer, unable to take her eyes off the bloody stumps where her hands had been.

It was just an illusion. It felt more real than she could bear.

"Come on," said Gray, reaching out to take her hand. The Devourer would only let her see Gray's fingers curl around the broken bone of her arm. She shrieked, wrenching away from him. He jumped back.

"What is it? What's the matter?"

"It's got me," she cried. "It took Angel."

"I saw," he said. "I think I was nearly..." He paused. "Now I'm okay, I can't see any of it."

The Devourer rippled around them, smothering the countryside, only visible to Isis. Gray looked up at the sky.

"The light should've come back by now. The other times there was a massive explosion of light, then it went off into space."

"The Devourer swallowed everything," said Isis.

Gray stared up at the night. "Is it... big?" he whispered. "It's so cold everywhere, I wasn't sure..."

"It's all around us."

He turned back. "You're okay though?"

She shook her head, holding up her bone-stump hands. He looked down at them, frowning.

"Angel's survived inside it, I know she has," said Isis. "And I think I can hurt it. I can use…"

BE QUIET!

The words were shouted at her by every teacher she'd ever had. Her lips glued themselves shut, stinging and tingling. She had to force them open again.

"I can free her," she mumbled.

"Come on then!" said Gray. "How?"

She nodded at where her hands used to be. The Devourer pressed in closer, working its tendrils up her legs, binding her with twines of what felt like freezing seaweed.

"My hands," she said. "I can push through ghosts, make holes in them. I already made a hole in the Devourer's side. If I widen it, I could reach through to Angel."

Gray's eyebrows shot up. "Where did you learn to do that?"

Isis didn't answer, because her arms were crumbling further. Now there was nothing past her elbow, only the bony joints, dangling with threads of dry flesh.

no hands no hands no hands no hands

"Go on then," said Gray.

She tried to see past the ghost-eater's illusion. But she felt nothing, she couldn't even remember what her fingers looked like. There was only an aching numbness where her forearms had been.

"I can't!" she cried. "It won't let me see my hands."

She held up her arms, and he squinted at them.

"Like there's nothing there?" he asked, not quite believing.

"I can only see bones," she whispered, trying to stop herself wobbling into tears.

Gray pressed a gentle finger onto what looked like a patch of air. "They're still there, you know. *I* can see them."

He looked at her with a smile. After a moment to understand, she was smiling back.

"Over there!" she said, pointing with nubs of bone.

I'll hurt you.

"It won't be real!" she snapped, holding out her arms.

"What won't?" asked Gray.

"It doesn't matter."

Gray nervously took hold of the space beyond her stumps, where she knew her hands should be. A slight frown crinkled his brow.

I'll HURT you.

Instantly, her arms were agony, pure fire burning up her arms. She yelped in pain, and Gray's hands flew off.

"What? What's the matter?"

"Nothing," she said, gritting her teeth. "It's not real." She lifted up her stumps, so Gray could take hold of hands she couldn't see. He nodded, getting a careful, uncertain grip. To her eyes he seemed to be holding nothing but air, and yet he pulled her forwards a couple of steps.

"Where am I going?" he asked. "Where is it?"

The Devourer surrounded them in slimy piles, darkly glistening except where Isis had torn a hole in its skin. Around the wound its flesh was shivering in tiny waves, trying to heal itself.

"There," she said, directing him. Gray moved his hands and hers, pushing them into something he couldn't see. Isis tried to focus on her invisible fingers and they waded into the vast, blue-black body wallowing around them.

"It's f-freezing," gasped Gray, instantly shivering, his breath suddenly steaming.

"We're inside it now," said Isis. He nodded, looking as scared as she felt. "Move my hands a little to the right. There."

He push/pulled her nothing hands straight into the gash in the Devourer. Memories flew into Isis's mind, and in every one of them Cally was screaming, begging her to stop.

"This is crazy!" said Gray, with a high-pitched laugh. "All I can see is me holding your hands in the air."

"Well it's here," Isis whispered.

"I know."

The rip in the Devourer was widening around their arms. She was shoulder deep now, tearing through the slug-coloured jelly. Inside its body small flashes glittered distantly, like fish in dark water.

"Do you want to k-keep going?" asked Gray, his teeth starting to chatter. Isis nodded.

I AM STRONGER.

She screwed her eyes shut against its shouted thoughts. Her eyelashes froze together, and she had to wrench her eyelids apart to open them.

"We need to make it wider!" she said.

Gray moved his hands away from each other. The rip opened further, the grey-black ooze peeling back in curls.

"Angel!" she shouted into the darkness.

"Can you see her?" Gray asked. She shook her head.

"Angel!" she called again.

"I still here." A tiny voice, impossibly distant.

"Angel!" Isis cried, tears freezing onto her cheeks. Gray's face split into a grin.

A tiny hand, candle-bright, reached towards her out of nothing.

Do NOT touch her!

Cally, her dad, Grandma Janet all screeched in Isis's memory. The Devourer rolled its huge body, trying to crush her, snapping at her with sudden teeth-filled mouths. Tentacles whipped from nowhere, poking like fingers into her head, searching for a way back into her mind.

But in the glittering dark, she could see Angel's face, as thin and clear as glass.

"She's there!" Isis shouted. Gray blind-fumbled their hands towards Angel's tiny fingers. "There, there!"

"Isis!" cried Angel. "I here!"

They all touched. Isis, Angel, Gray.

"Oh…" breathed Gray, wide-eye staring at the flesh-walls surrounding them.

And Isis had her hands back, holding tightly to Angel, working to pull her out through the gap they'd torn in the Devourer. Except Angel wasn't coming free, she was only stretching. And this time it wasn't just her feet that were caught inside the monster.

"Come *on*," grunted Isis, heaving with her whole weight.

A flickering, dancing light whizzed past them.

"What was that?" said Gray.

Isis shook her head, it didn't matter. "Help me!" she snapped at him, as the oily layers sucked around Angel, drawing her back into the slithering dark.

Another light popped out past them, then another. In the brief moments of brightness, Isis noticed the blue of her own fingernails, the bloodless white of her arms. Ice was glittering on Gray's hair and eyebrows.

"Leaves!" he cried. "They look like leaves!"

My feast.

The words dropped as stones into Isis's memory.

"My feast," she said. The tentacles had found their way in.

She turned to Gray. "I can't hold it off…" Her words began to slur as dark sludge flowed across her mind. With every breath she was losing herself, her fingers slackening, letting go of Angel's.

Gripping tightly, Gray held Isis's hands over Angel's, keeping them all together. "Tell me what to do, Isis. I don't know what to do!"

She watched him blankly. Angel started sinking back into the murk.

"It biting me!" screamed the little ghost. Her cry splintered through the sludge. Isis gasped, almost freezing her lungs, and yanked hard at Angel.

Angel was out a little further, but she was turning thin and glassy, disappearing in front of them.

I won't give up my feast.

"What can we do?" Gray asked Isis. But it was Angel, insubstantial as spider silk, who answered by opening her arms, still holding hands with Isis and Gray.

"Let them all out," she said.

Angel had pulled their linked arms into a wide circle, and wherever they touched the Devourer, its flesh scuttled back, as if stung. A huge hole was forming in its flank, and a light whooshed out, then another. Swirling past, blindingly bright. Some looked like leaves, flying straight up into the night. Others were more human in form, phantoms and spectres fleeing out into the fields.

Nonononononononononononononono

The ghost-eater screamed in Isis's mind. Unbearable, relentless.

But she kept her place, holding hands with Angel and

Gray, as the trickle of light turned into a torrent. She couldn't see Gray through the glare. Her hair was floating and her clothes were flapping in the frozen wind made by the golden leaves and other ghostly forms pouring out through their arms. For a moment Isis saw a mouldy plume of green dust, but it was instantly carried away by the light surging all around them, blazing upwards. Her arms ached with the strain of holding onto the others, and she felt Gray's fingers start to slip out of hers.

"Don't let go!" she screamed. His answer was a shout as his fingers left hers, and he was thrown out of the blinding river of light. Isis waved her hand in the air, trying to reach him, but it was Angel's fingers she caught. Gripping onto her tightly, holding them together as phantoms shot past their faces. Lights, leaves and the bewildering shimmer of a ghost-forest poured out between them. An impossible waterfall raged up into the sky. At its top, trees blossomed and filled the air with gold.

Let go! Run away!

The Devourer shrieked at Isis, tearing through her memories like it was ripping pages from a book. But it made no difference, she was too numb to let go. She'd spent too long surrounded by the frozen body of the

379

Devourer. Her arms were turning from white to pale blue, her heart failing as the blood cooled in her veins. She held onto Angel as ghosts of all kinds poured out of the Devourer, almost tearing it to shreds. Its billowing body shrivelled like plastic burning in a fire, falling off Isis to lie at her feet, waving feeble tendrils.

And now there was just Isis, holding hands with Angel.

Above them, light blazed in the night sky. A huge sphere, a new sun.

Isis felt her heart beat, but only once.

"Do you remember?" she whispered, her ice-crusted lips stiffening into silence.

Do you remember how we held hands like this, back when you were alive? How we spun ourselves into dizzy, laughing circles?

The little ghost nodded, her eyes wide. "Stay, Isis!" she pleaded. "Stay."

And she wanted to answer, but the ice was too thick on her face. Dimly, she noticed the bright wheat falling into circles, and shapes of people in the field. Then her eyes froze over, dazzling the world into a kaleidoscope of stars.

Her heart stopped.

"Isis!" Gray was calling her name from somewhere,

but she didn't answer. She was only a leaf rustling in the forest, only the speck of a bird circling into a wide and empty sky.

Chapter Thirty-three

Gray

It was like an electric shock or something. When all the light blasted out of the ghost-eater, I got thrown clean off. I landed with a thump, somewhere down in the wheat. I think I was knocked out for a few seconds. And I'd let go of Isis, so I couldn't see the Devourer or Angel, or anything.

Just Isis, lighting up the field. Light pouring out between her hands, like she was made of it.

I tried to stand up, but I was shivering so hard I could hardly move. My legs and arms were all rubbery and useless with it.

"Isis!" I shouted at her, but she didn't notice, didn't move. I heaved at myself, and stumbled to her on dead legs. She was shimmering, sparkling, like she was made of glass or something. But it wasn't glass, it was ice, covering her from head to foot. Her hair glittered; every part of her shone back the light still rushing out of her. She was dazzling. She was a winter fountain.

"Isis?" I could feel the cold off her, shaking me into shivers. "Are you all right?"

Under the ice, her skin was starting to crack, like she was drying out or something.

"Isis?" I reached out, touching her hand.

She was still holding onto Angel, so my fingers caught both of theirs. And I could see then.

The light pouring out through their hands was a golden tree, as tall as the sky. Like Stu said, the ghost of any species is millions of lives over millions of years, and this one was free again, going up and up into the night, wider than the world. Gathering up the stars.

At their feet, the Devourer looked all shrivelled and tiny, not scary any more. A blue-black sag with wings, flopping about on the ground.

I kicked at it, and it scuffled away. Flapping a little, skidding above the plants towards Philip Syndal, who was just standing up out of the crop, hand to his head. He screamed when he saw it, and started running. It shot right into him, and he fell down. I didn't see him after that.

"Stay!" Angel cried. I thought she meant me.

Then I looked back and Angel was gone, the shining tree was gone.

There was just me and Isis in the field, with the rustle and crack of the wheat, and the sighing of the wind. And a massive, boiling sphere of light, right over our heads, pulsing white-hot, and each pulse getting a bit bigger.

"Oh no," I whispered. I'd never been anywhere near as close as this before. I didn't even know what would happen.

"We've got to get out!" I shouted at Isis. She didn't move, so I grabbed her under the arms, trying to drag her backwards. It was really hard, you know? My arms and legs were hardly working, and she was solid and heavy, like a lump of stone.

"Please! Can't you just try and walk?"

BOOM!

I was flattened by light, caught in waves of it. I crawled on, scrabbling and trying to hold onto Isis, trying to get us both out of there. I didn't know which way to go, I didn't know which way was up.

"Gray! Oh my God, Gray!"

Someone grabbed me. Mum was hauling me out

of there. Saving my life, probably.

But I screamed, fighting her, trying to keep hold of Isis. Mum wouldn't let go, wouldn't stop pulling me out. Because she couldn't see Isis in all the glare. And she didn't know Isis was so slick with ice, that she just slipped through my hands.

You wanted to know what seeing a UFO had to do with Isis dying? Well it's this. I left her behind in all that. I left her behind, and she died.

That's all there is, really. The burning ball of light did what the others had, the times before. Unravelled into a blinding line across the night, and flew off to the stars. Not UFOs heading back to their mother ship, like Dad said, but the biggest ghosts in the world. Maybe if I'd been with Isis I might've seen where it was going, what it was doing. But I wasn't.

It went with her, that whole way of seeing.

Mum got me to where Dad was, and when it was safe he ran out into the field and started searching for everyone who'd got caught out there. He found Cally first, half-cooked with sunburn, then Philip, lying in the middle of all the smashed-down crop circles, his clothes shrivelled off and burned.

Then he found Isis.

Cally started sobbing and screaming. Mum wouldn't let me go near. She held me back, squeezing really tight and patting a hanky at the blood on my face.

"Oh my God, Gray," she said, loads of times.

Dad came running back, grabbed his mobile phone and jabbed in three numbers.

"Ambulance!" he shouted. "We've got a man with major burns, and a girl with…" He looked at me then, and he was crying. "She's been frozen, I think. She's not breathing."

It seemed like hours until the ambulances turned up, and the police after. There was even a helicopter, not that it made any difference. Mum shouted at people until they got me in one of the ambulances and brought us to this hospital, and then you came and said I needed some tests, and you took me away from the treatment room…

What happened then? Where am I anyway?

It's all right, Gray, just relax.

Thank you for telling me. I had to know. I never stopped caring, even though I left.

I'm cold. It's really cold in here.

You're probably a little tired, that's all. I've unlocked the door, and in a moment I'm going to count down from ten, bringing you out of your hypnotic trance. By the time I get to one, you will be wide awake and feeling fine.

My hand's freezing.

Your mother and father are waiting for you downstairs, rather worried at your absence, I'd imagine. When you find them, you'll tell them you got lost. You'll have a vivid memory of wandering the corridors of the hospital, and not being able to find your way back after a blood sample was taken from you by one of the nurses. You'll remember nothing about me, or this little conversation we've had.

I'm going to start counting now. Ten... Nine... Eight... Seven... Six... Five...

Angel?

Four... Three... Two... One...

Angel!

Gray! Stop! Where are you running off to?

Chapter Thirty-four

Isis

She was a ghost, travelling with ghosts. One ghost, formed of numberless smaller ones. A golden chain of lives, unravelling behind them.

My life was a million years, it said.

Breathe.

The atmosphere rushed past, thinning and weakening, gravity losing its grip.

You got to breathe.

They passed beep-whispering satellites, drifting out above the blue curve of the world.

Isis, pease stay.

Clinging to the ghost's tail, she saw the others. A delicate, thin-beaked bird, silently flying past, bigger than a jumbo jet.

A butterfly flapping slowly, covering the sun like an eclipse. A long-legged cat made of the purest light, running across the top of the sky. The more she looked, the more she saw them: the ghosts of extinct species. Animals and birds, insects and plants, fish and strangely shaped sea creatures. Circling the planet, haunting humankind…

Don't go with them.

"Am I cold?" she asked. "Should I be this cold?"

She gasped. A wrenching, painful, pulling-in of air. Hearing her own strangled gargle as the air rushed down her raw, sore throat, and into her lungs. The breath turned into a cough, which hurt even more. She breathed in again, having to think about it.

Somewhere nearby, out beyond her eyelids, a man cried out. Something metal tinkled onto the floor.

She tried to move her hand, but it felt leaden and numb. Cold. Her arms, her legs, her body, all cold. She was lying on something hard, as cool as stone.

There were clankings, and the man shouted, "I need a crash team in the mortuary, right now!"

A blanket was laid over her, not nearly thick enough to make her warm.

"We're going to get sued for this one!" he muttered.

She thought for a long time, until she remembered how to open her eyes.

She was lying flat, on a table. Strip lights lined the ceiling, and a brown-eyed man in green overalls was frowning down at her.

"Do you know where you are?" he asked.

No, she wanted to say. But she couldn't speak, her mouth didn't seem to have any spit in it. She tried to shake her head, managing to tip it on one side.

And she saw a little girl next to the table, holding onto her hand with plump little fingers. She had curly hair in a short bob, and she was wearing a pink dress with flounces. Her dimples showed as she smiled at Isis, the shelves on the wall behind clearly visible through her.

"I do it!" said Angel proudly. "You tried to go with them, but I maked you stay."

Isis tried to remember how to smile.

"I going to get him too," said Angel, letting go of Isis's still-numb hand and running across the room. She waved goodbye with both arms, then vanished into a wall.

Across the room, the door slammed open and a tall, dark-haired woman stormed in, wearing a white coat and an air of authority. She stopped when she got to Isis, her eyes widening. Then she turned to the man.

"When did this happen?" she snapped.

"Just as I was about to start the autops—" He stopped, wincing. "I don't know how—"

"Misdiagnosis!" said the woman briskly, taking hold of Isis's wrist, feeling for her pulse. "A paramedic getting it wrong again, or some junior doctor upstairs." She smiled down at Isis, her face suddenly warming. "Well, you're clearly not dead."

"Muh…" said Isis, her tongue like leather.

"Shh…" said the woman, "it's going to be fine."

The door crashed again, and more people came rushing in, wearing green overalls and white coats. They filled the room with noise and activity, and Isis with injections and drips. They wrapped her up, putting an oxygen mask over her face.

"Muh um," she said into the plastic.

At last, the door opened.

Cally's face was streaked red with burns, her eyes purple and blotched from crying. A nurse was leading her, almost holding her up.

"This has never happened before…" the nurse was saying, while Cally ignored her.

"Isis?" she whispered. Staring. Motionless in disbelief. Only for a heartbeat, then her arms were tight around Isis, hugging her through the crinkling space-blankets, tangling them both in the trailing drip-lines. "I thought I'd lost you," she whispered, kissing Isis's hair.

Cally pulled back a little, putting her palms on Isis's cheeks, gazing at her.

"I'm so sorry," she whispered, a tear running down the side of her nose and landing warm on Isis's cheek. "For all the times I let you down."

Isis tried to shake her head, but she couldn't with the mask strapped to her face. She lifted up her arm, pulled the mask off.

"Mum," she said.

Isis turned her head, and saw her little ghost-sister run back in through the door, pulling Gray behind her. He stumbled to a halt, shocked-looking. Isis held out her hand, and Angel shot through one of the nurses, making the woman shiver.

"I do it," Angel said again, proud of herself.

Isis looked up at Cally.

"I've got to tell you…" she whispered. "I should've before, but I never knew how."

Cally smiled through her tears, smoothing a hair away from Isis's face. "Whatever it is, it doesn't matter."

"Yes," said Isis, "it does." And she smiled back, a smile that started at her mouth and reached all the way to the stars.

"Look."

She took Angel's cold little hand, and placed it in Cally's warm one. Then she put her own hand on top, and held them tight.

Acknowledgements

A book results from the efforts of many people, well beyond the author, and I owe a great debt to all those who have pushed this one along. I'd like to thank my agent Penny Holroyde for her hard work, support and many words of sense. I am also incredibly grateful to the people who gave comments on early drafts: Pat Walsh, Susan Goundry-Kruse and especially Graham Lusby, who is always my first port of call in a plotting storm. Gray is for you, Graham.

Next, thank you to everyone at Templar for turning a pile of paper into a book. Especially Helen Boyle, who saw something in it and the designer and illustrator who have made it look so wonderful. And for making the final writing stages so pain-free, thank you to my editors: Emma Goldhawk for her help, advice and hard work; Catherine Coe for turning around my terrible grammar; and Sara Starbuck, for her warmth, wit and invaluable insights.

Finally, Matt and Arlo, you have my gratitude and love, always. Without you, it would be nothing.

About the author

Emily Diamand was born in London. She would have been a streetwise city kid, but when she was two her parents moved to rural Oxfordshire, surrounding her with fields, footpaths and the kind of things they thought would be wonderful for children to grow up with. She never got to be streetwise, but her parents were right about the fields and footpaths.

Emily was the booky type at school, but what she really wanted to do was save the planet. So she filled up her parents' garden with ponds, chucked wildflower seeds about and worried about the rainforests. And then she went off to study environmental science at university.

After that, Emily did lots of things. She got paid to ask people in forests if they like trees, had a go at road protesting and worked on organic farms. For nearly eight years, she worked for Friends of the Earth.

Then she wrote a book, *Flood Child*. It won the Times/Chicken House award in 2009 and Emily went on to write a sequel, *Flood and Fire*.

Emily now lives in Yorkshire with her husband and son.

www.emilydiamand.com